A Secret Revealed
Kit McKenna

McKenna Publishing, LLC

Other Books By Kit McKenna

THE OKLAHOMA SKIES SERIES

All Sorrows Are Less

https://mybook.to/AllSorrowsKitMcKenna

Paint the Earth Red

https://mybook.to/PaintEarthKitMcKenna

The Heart That Returns

https://mybook.to/HeartReturnsKitMcKenna

Perfect As You Are

https://mybook.to/PerfectKitMcKenna

The Art of Passion

https://mybook.to/ArtPassionKitMcKenna

A Matter of Trust

https://mybook.to/MatterTrustKitMcKenna

Get a FREE copy of the Valentine Short Mr. Wrong door

https://dl.bookfunnel.com/myptwbvjh0

THE BELLADONNA SOCIETY SERIES

A Pointed End

https://mybook.to/PointedKitMcKenna

A Murderous Intent

https://mybook.to/MurderousKitMcKenna

A Secret Revealed

https://mybook.to/RevealedKitMcKenna

A Devil's Snare

https://mybook.to/SnareKitMcKenna

A Predator's Threat

https://mybook.to/ThreatKitMcKenna

THE MORRIGAN MAFIA SERIES

Crossed

https://mybook.to/CrossedMcKenna

Coup

https://mybook.to/CoupKitMcKenna

Crashed

https://mybook.to/CrashedKitMcKenna

Prologue

Sometimes people don't know what's best for them. He thinks he's fine on his own, but that's simply not true. He needs me.

I'm the only one who understands him. Heaven knows his family doesn't. They act like he's invisible most of the time. He's never invisible to me, though. I see him all the way to his core.

Besides seeing him, I'm the only one who knows everything about him. There are things which he keeps hidden from everyone, but I found out. He doesn't know that I know, and I've been loyal to the bone, keeping his secrets.

I don't need his thanks, though. It's what you do for someone else when you love them and I've loved him from the moment we first met. That day was one of the best of my life and today will be another one to add to the vault of my heart. He's perfect for me and I am for him, too.

So, what do you do when someone you love simply can't see the truth? There has to be a way to shine a light on it so bright that they can't deny it any longer. That's my plan for tonight.

I've made his favorite meal. His favorite wine has been purchased. Even the dessert is something he will enjoy even though he doesn't often indulge.

Once his belly is full and his senses titillated, I'll take off these casual clothes to reveal the sexy new outfit purchased just for the occasion. I intend to make this a night to remember.

He'll be here any minute, so I quickly go over everything to ensure it's in place. Once I've run my checks for the millionth time, I relax by fractions. Now it's just a matter of carrying out my plan.

The doorbell rings, making me jump. I smooth my hands down the thighs of my pants, trying to make them less sweaty. It's only twenty degrees outside, so I'm not warm, but my nerves are off the charts.

Best not to keep him waiting. "Showtime," I say to no one and head toward the door.

"Hi!" I say when I open the door. "Come in out of the cold."

I tamp down my excitement because I want him to think this is a night just like any other when we get together. He thinks we're just two friends having a pleasant dinner together and probably doesn't even realize the significance of the date. That's okay. By the time tonight is over, he's going to know. He'll see me in a different light. I'm sure of it.

"Something smells good, he says."

"Thanks."

He hangs his coat in the closet by the front door, then comes into the kitchen. I pull the dish out of the oven. "Will you put some of those potatoes on the plates I have set out, please?"

I saved the task for him because I know how much he likes to cook and help in the kitchen. When I open the lid to the dutch oven, he inhales the aroma.

"Wow," he says. "When did you learn to make that?"

"I took one of those cooking classes at that fancy kitchen supply store over in Classen Curve. This is my first time trying it on my own. I just hope it tastes as good as it smells."

I know it does. This is actually my eleventh or twelfth time trying it on my own since I took the class, because I wanted it to be perfect.

Like a professional chef plating in a restaurant, I carefully arrange perfectly cooked carrots on top of the potatoes then put the meat on top. Each plate gets a drizzle of the juices from the pan and they're ready to go.

We carry out meals to the table where I've had the bottle of wine open to breathe. He spots it and says, "I love this wine. Thanks for getting it."

"Do you?" I ask innocently. "Maybe that's why it seemed familiar. I knew something red would be better with the beef and you know how I mostly drink white. When I was roaming through the store, I saw this one and decided to get it."

During the meal, we keep the conversation light. He talks about his job; I talk about mine. He asks about my sister, but

I don't ask about his family. That's a surefire way to darken his mood.

I keep refilling his glass and he keeps drinking it down. Soon, he's very loose, more relaxed than I've ever seen him. That's exactly how I want him.

I need to overcome that overactive brain of his so that he's able to let his body and baser needs take over. He doesn't date. I'm his go-to person when he needs someone on his arm. He also doesn't do casual sex, so that cock of his is probably dying for some attention and I intend to provide it.

Just once is all it will take. If I can get him to lower his walls long enough to make love with me, I know he'll see the big picture. He'll see how perfect we are together because I know our bodies will fit perfectly together, too.

The meal is finished, and he's incredibly relaxed and happy when we move to the sofa. It's an unusual state of being for him and it makes him more handsome than ever. He almost collapses onto the couch.

"That was so good," he says, drawing it out a little as if he's having difficulty connecting his thoughts. "Thanks for making it."

"You're welcome."

"I think I might be a little drunk, so I might need to sleep on your couch."

"That's fine, but I have a spare bedroom you can sleep in instead of roughing it on the couch," I say, moving closer to him.

A hand flops out and pats my knee. "You're such a good friend," he slurs.

I talk at him for a few minutes, letting the alcohol marinate those brain cells and put them to sleep. Timing is everything, but I think it's time to move him while he can still help.

Rising from the sofa, I take his hand in mine and pull. "Come on, let's get you to your bedroom."

I don't maneuver him to the spare bedroom, though. We're going to my room. He falls back onto the bed like a redwood being felled and I busy myself with getting him out of his shoes.

Next, I unzip his jeans and pull them down and off. When I pull down his boxer briefs and take his shaft in my hand, I'm happy to see that he's not too drunk to get it up. He hardens quickly, and a moan oozes from his mouth when I run my tongue around the head of his cock.

Just as I had hoped, his natural instincts take over. His fingers tangle in my hair as I pump his dick in and out of my mouth, working him with my tongue, lips, and hands. I don't let it go on too long, though.

My pussy is dripping wet and aching with need, and I want him inside of me. He's not the only one that's been without sex for a while.

When I can stand it no longer, I stand and undress quickly. The sight of me in my lingerie is lost to his inebriated vision, but that's okay. I know I look good and if he could see me, he'd be impressed.

Once I'm undressed, I climb on top of him and slide his long, thick cock into my hungry cunt. Just as I thought, we fit together perfectly. My hips begin to move, undulating to stroke his cock in and out of me.

Much too quickly, he comes inside of me. That's what happens with too much booze. But I don't stop riding him. I reach down and rub my clitoris with one hand and with the other, I pull his hand up to my breast, helping him to squeeze and mold it.

I find my release soon after and come all over his softening cock inside me. Once I've cleaned both of us up, I shove and pull him into a better sleeping position, then crawl in beside him. We'll wake up in each other's arms and he'll know.

Before sleep can sneak in to steal me away, I stretch up to kiss him and breathe "I love you" against his lips. This is the start of our future together, and it's going to be perfect.

Chapter 1

Demeter

I'm relaxed, controlling my breathing, focused on the man in front of me as I circle him. My eyes watch closely for the slightest hint of his intended actions. He wants to hurt me, and I know it, but I'm going to do everything I can to keep him from it.

He lunges and jabs at my face. I block, shift, and throw out a kick, making contact with his thigh. He is twice my size, and my legs are stronger than my arms, so kicking will do more damage than I could ever do with a punch. I snap the striking foot back, plant it, spin and hit him in the gut with my other foot.

He lets out an *oof,* growls, and tries to grab me. If he gets me on the ground, it's over. I shuffle back, but I'm not fast enough. He whips out a foot lightning quick and catches me behind one ankle. I go down and try to turn it into a roll so that I can gain my feet again, but just as I get my feet under me, he's on top of me.

My adrenaline kicks in and I try to shove down the rising panic. We grapple. I'm hitting him in the side, but his size is an advantage that I'm unable to overcome. He's got me pinned and with his strength, he easily maneuvers me where he wants me.

Both legs come around my waist as he puts my head in a neck lock. With a little pressure, he'll render me unconscious. With a lot of pressure, he could break my neck.

"Break!" Gunnar shouts.

Victor lets me go and I gasp for breath, scrambling to my feet. It still pisses me off I can't manage to beat him. I have bested every other man in class, but not Victor.

Well, I can't best Gunnar either, but that's to be expected since he's the owner and lead instructor for the school. You kind of want that guy to be unbeatable, right?

"That one was pretty good, Hobbit," Victor says with an affectionate cuff on the arm. "You're still letting your panic get the best of you."

I shake my head. "Only with you and Gunnar. I don't know why, but with everyone else, I can successfully push it down, but with you two, it gets out of control. It's like it's primal and I can't figure out why. You would think that with the attack having been so long ago, I would have mastered rechannelling the repercussions by now, particularly since it's just sparring. I know that it's not truly dangerous, but my amygdala takes over."

Victor is a big guy and solid muscle. He is also former military, which you can only tell from his bearing and demeanor these days. Nowadays, he looks like he could have been Ragnar Lothbrok's twin from that television show.

His dirty blond hair is short on the sides and very long on top. He has a beard long enough to be braided, which he does from time to time, including silver barrel beads and occasionally beads that are meant to look like bits of bone. I wouldn't be surprised if they really were bones he carved holes in.

Full sleeve tattoos on both arms only make him look more intimidating. In all honesty, though, he's really just a big teddy bear. But trust me when I say that I would not want to be the object of his ire if the fight was real.

"Wow, you really sound like a psychologist," Victor says with a mocking voice.

"Well, duh." I reply with a chuckle and a roll of my eyes.

He laughs because he knows what I do for a living. I take my leave of him, walking off the adrenaline let down. Students are filtering into the building since it's getting close to time for class to start.

I come early whenever Victor is available to spar in order to get in the additional practice. With Victor, I can go all out with little fear of hurting him, whereas in regular class sparring, we're expected to be a bit more controlled.

I am stretching in the corner when a familiar pair of sneakers comes into view. I look up to see my friend, Gabriella Carmichael. "Hey Ella!" I say, grinning up at her.

She takes up a position next to me and starts doing stretches to warm her muscles. "Hey! So, did you do it today?"

"Nope," I say, deepening my bend and putting my head down. My ponytail flops over and touches the floor. "He kicked my ass, as usual. I was doing pretty good until he got me off my feet, then the giant gorilla twisted me around into a neck lock. One of these days, though, I'll do it."

She chuckles. "One of these days, pow! Right to the moon!"

I laugh at the vintage television reference. "Exactly!"

An alarm sounds. It isn't loud, just a single ping, but everyone falls quickly into rank-and-file positions.

After class, I'm gathering up my things. I get the feeling that Gabriella wants to talk, but I won't push her. She was attacked a few weeks ago, and I made her an offer of being available to listen as a friend when she's ready to talk about it since I'd been through something similar. My psychology degree will only help.

When I first started at OU, an ex-boyfriend and a disgruntled co-worker convinced three other men to kidnap me, intending to gang rape me. If it hadn't been for my boss seeing the men take me, I would have been much more than just beaten from head to toe.

He followed the car into which I was thrown and called the police, who arrived just as the first man was about to rape me. I was rescued. Gabriella was, too, but like me, she wasn't completely unscathed.

Despite the fact that the absolute worst didn't happen, it is still a long process to recover from the impact. There are times, mostly when I'm over stressed, that I still feel a panic attack starting to wriggle under my skin and I have to use the coping skills I've learned.

The attack was over ten years ago. That just goes to show that trauma burrows deep and can manifest when you least expect it.

I know what it's like to try to find your way through the aftermath. The telltale signs are written all over Gabriella from the dark circles under her eyes, caused by the lack of sleep to the way she is constantly monitoring everything around her.

Nightmares and panic attacks are desolating and when they happen, when you're in the midst of it, your mind and body have no way to know that you're not really being attacked again.

"Um, Demi?" Gabriella finally says.

"Yeah, Ella?"

"I was wondering if maybe we could meet and talk before dinner tomorrow night?"

"Sure. Do you want to meet at the Society or somewhere else?" I ask nonchalantly to reinforce that her desire to talk is no big deal as far as I'm concerned.

"My studio isn't far away from the Society, so maybe there? Just in case I go a little bonkers, I'd rather not do that in public."

"I understand. Just shoot me the address of your studio and I can be there at say, sixish? Will an hour be enough, do you think?"

"Yes," Ella says, obviously relieved. "I think that will be fine."

"All right then, I'll see you tomorrow at six," I say, hooking a thumb at the door. "I've gotta run. Henry will be wanting a story recap before bed."

"That's important stuff right there. Go, spend some time with your boy. I'll see you tomorrow."

I make sure I have everything before I head outside to my car and home. Ten years ago, or not, my sense of hyper-alertness is something I don't think I'll ever let go of, especially in parking lots.

I know that Gunnar or Victor would come running to my rescue, but they'd have to notice. When I was taken all those years ago, I was standing at a bus stop across the street from several restaurants with a steady flow of customers coming and going.

It's possible that someone saw and called the police, but no one came to the aid of a petite woman being chased down by four men while the driver waited in the car.

Chapter 2
Demeter

"Thanks so much for coming," Gabriella says when she lets me into her studio the next day. The faint smells of turpentine and paint leak into the office area from her workspace. It's not overly pungent, but it's enough that it stings my sinuses, so I start breathing through my mouth instead of my nose.

Ella is an amazingly talented woman. She works with her fiancé, Morgan, in his family's construction business, where she runs the design arm of the company. She's also a fantastic artist. She refinishes furniture as a hobby and when she officially moved in with him, he got this studio for her to do her hobbies until they can build a house on some open land his family owns.

She's clearly pensive. Dressed casually in jeans and a filmy red-orange blouse, her demeanor is anything but casual and relaxed. She looks wound up, and it makes me wonder how long she has been sitting here waiting for me.

"Hi! I love that color on you. It really pops with your skin tone." I look around at the room. "So, this is the studio. What are you working on?"

I want her to relax, so I jump in and ask her about a more comfortable topic without giving her a chance to think too much. This will hopefully get her talking instead of stewing on whatever she has running around in her mind like a hamster on a wheel.

"Oh," she says, looking down at herself as if surprised she has clothes on. "Thank you."

"You okay?" I ask.

"Yeah, just tense today."

"Well, as my college roommate would say, you appear to be wound up tighter than my grandma's girdle at a church potluck."

She laughs as I hoped she would, then takes a deep breath and lets it out. "Sorry. I didn't get much sleep last night and I think I'm driving Morgan crazy with all this..." She waves a hand up and down at herself. "This."

"I'm sure that's not true. Why don't you show me what you're working on? Then we'll talk."

"Oh, okay."

She goes to a door across the room and opens it, the smell of turpentine and paint growing stronger. As she talks about each piece and her plans for them, her shoulders come down from around her ears, her breathing deepens, and the frenetic look in her eyes lessens. When she's relaxed, she starts in on what she really wants to talk about.

"I just don't know how to get over it," she breathes.

"Ella," I say, keeping my voice conciliatory, "it's been what? Two and a half weeks since you were attacked? You're probably still experiencing some aftereffects of dumping the benzo out of your system. It's going to take time."

Gabriella was attacked in her home by a serial killer that had been hoping to make her victim number eight. The man drugged her and was playing out his psychopathy of dressing women like they were out on a date when Morgan, Ella's fiancé, showed up with his brother. They were able to catch the intruder and hold him until the police arrived.

I'm just glad she was saved from the additional trauma of a trial when the man died in a car accident soon after getting out on bail. He had a tracker on Ella's phone and had followed her halfway across the state where she was on a weekend getaway with Morgan.

The court system isn't particularly kind to women who are victims of assault, especially when there's a sexual component. It seems every defense attorney's favorite tactic is to put the victim on trial and make her at least culpable, if not completely at fault for being assaulted.

"I'm already sick of it!" she exclaims, throwing her hands up in the air. "I have been strong and independent for thirty-four years and now I can't even make it through twenty-four hours without having a nightmare or panic attack and ending up a sobbing mess or trying to hide under the bed to escape a non-existent attacker. Poor Morgan is exhausted, and I'm exhausted, and I don't know how long he's going to be able to stand it."

"Believe me, I understand. I can give you some exercises to help you redirect your thinking when you feel a panic attack coming on. There are also breathing exercises you can do when you feel yourself starting to hyperventilate. Learning coping methods for the panic attacks will also help ease the nightmares as your brain starts to find new neural pathways when you're triggered."

"I thought I was getting better, but then the news broke with everything they found at his house. His poor wife and what he put her through is all I can think about. Can you believe he used to keep her locked up in a box that he would shove under the bed for days at a time? How insane is that?"

I decide to let her in on, not exactly a secret, but something that isn't widely broadcast. "Few people know this," I say as I walk through the area, taking in the artistry of her work, "but I knew Andrew. I actually went out with him a couple of times."

Andrew Felton is the man who murdered several women in the metro before he died while still pursuing Gabriella. When I knew him, there was nothing to let me know that level of hatred toward women was lurking under the surface.

"What?" Gabriella gasps.

I nod. "Yep. I first met him when I was on my very first date with Jeremiah at the masquerade gala they hold at the Skirvin every year. Then Jeremiah and I broke up for a time and Andrew and I crossed paths again. He asked me out, and I went. He thought that Jeremiah and I were in a financial arrangement because we were from such different economic backgrounds, and he was ten years older than I."

I stop at a chest with a color palette on top. "Is this the palette you're going to use on this piece?"

She's confused at my question, but catches up. "Oh, yes."

I return to my story. "The second time Andrew and I went out, he took me to a BDSM club to introduce me to some of his proclivities, mostly related to bondage and punishment, but after being attacked, I couldn't submit to being restrained. We ended up at his house, had sex, consensual," I say, looking at her with a nod of my head, "and went our separate ways. I saw him a while later and the woman he was with is the one he married."

"Wow," she says flatly.

"I know. I dodged a bullet with that one."

That trip to the club was an eye-opener for me. The philosophies of BDSM were fascinating to me, and I loved how they focused on communication and mutual agreement. It was so intriguing that I took a job working there for a while.

I incorporate those philosophies in my practice all the time to help couples work through their marital and sexual issues. Later, I began to believe that Andrew used the idea of BDSM as a crutch for indulging in his darker fantasies and he devolved from there, but what he did was against everything that the BDSM community believes in.

"Wow," she says again.

I give her time to absorb the information. She is settling and relaxing, so I smile and get down to work.

"Now, why don't we talk about some of those techniques I mentioned?"

For the next thirty minutes, we discuss methods for reprogramming her brain and redirecting her emotions when she feels the first hints of panic creeping in. She stops me about ten minutes in to get a notebook so that she can write things down and I start over. When she feels like she has what she needs, we head over to the Society for dinner with Cait and whomever else in our quint decides to show up.

The Belladonna Society is like an old school invitation only gentleman's club with dining and fitness facilities and such, but for women. It's supposedly the most prestigious women's club in the nation, but I find that hard to believe because we are in Oklahoma, after all. When people in the world think of prestigious locations, Oklahoma City, Oklahoma probably isn't one that comes to mind.

I joined for the networking aspect and a hope to form some connections with like-minded women. The club has a very philanthropic community within its ranks, and I want to be a part of that. Ella has said that it's been a real boon to her business.

Besides networking and philanthropy, I thought that if I made some friends, too, that wouldn't be a bad thing. In short order, I have made two very dear friends and learned about some very worthy charities that I've started supporting.

Caitlynn Foster, Ella, and I are leaving the Society after supper. Cait is a socialite who joined for the same reasons I did. If we hadn't met at the Society, we likely would have never become as close as we have. We have very different backgrounds, and our ages span over fifteen years.

It is often just the three of us and just Ella and Cait more often still. I come as often as I can for dinner, but my son Henry is my priority and if he needs me for something, that's where I'll be.

My son is eight years old. If you were to ask him, he'd probably tell you he's a man full grown. However, he's still a boy who is growing up without a father, so I do everything in my power to be there for him as often as possible.

As we're walking through what Cait calls the lounge, an open area with sofas and chairs grouped to promote lingering conversations, I notice the fortune teller machine that sits in the room's corner. "What do you think of that?" I ask, directing a finger that way.

"I made a wish, and it came true," Ella says. "Cait, too."

"What?" I sputter, incredulous.

"It's true. I wished for a man who could love me, even the broken parts. A few days later, I ran into Morgan again after initially meeting him three years ago."

"What was your wish?" I ask Cait.

"Well, I probably shouldn't say," she replies hesitantly.

"Oh, come on, Demi won't say anything," Ella urges.

Cait takes a breath.

"It's not something I'm proud of and I certainly can't make an unequivocable correlation, but I was particularly miffed with my husband and had been thinking that the only way that he would let me go is if he were dead. Sooo…I wished my husband would die. A few weeks later, he attacked me, and I killed him in self-defense. It is not at all what I expected to happen, but my wish came true, nonetheless."

I look at her with wide eyes and drag my friends over so I can get a better look at the machine.

"What do you think?" asks Ella. "Any heart's desire yearning to be realized?"

"I don't know," I say.

Make a wish, the machine says in gilded gold lettering. I don't really have any wishes. I have a really good life, plenty of money, and a career I love. If I had any wishes at all, they would be for Henry.

He is such a special boy and sometimes, while I don't need a man in my life, I think it would be great if he had a strong male role model to whom he could relate more. Don't get me wrong, my parents are close to us and my dad loves Henry wholly and unconditionally. However, he has a bit of a skewed view of the world. If it's not growing in dirt, it doesn't hold his attention long and Dad can be fearful of the big wide world beyond the backyard.

Then there is Jeremiah's father. Robert has a broader view of the world, but it's a very superficial and predatory view. Jeremiah was a lot like Henry, but maybe a bit more gregarious and extroverted. He would have been a great dad for our son.

I speak my thought out loud. "I don't need a husband, but I wish Henry could have a surrogate dad that could understand him."

The machine whirs and clicks and a card pops out. I stare at it for a moment. "I didn't push the button," I say.

"Take it," Cait urges. "Let's see what it says."

A love that is lost is hard to replace, but it is often accomplished if you look under the face.

I read it for the others. "What's that supposed to mean?"

"I have no idea," says Ella.

Cait tucks her arm into mine. "I think it means that there is a change on your horizon."

"Definitely," Ella agrees, taking my other arm.

Chapter 3

Demeter

"Hi Mom," I say as I enter my kitchen, putting my bag and keys on the island. "How'd things go today?"

"Good," Mom replies, not stopping as she wipes down the spotless countertop. "Henry and your father tended the yard, then spent a significant amount of time in the pool."

"With plenty of sunscreen, I hope." Both Jeremiah, Henry's father, and I loved to swim, so I can't be surprised that he takes to water like a fish, too. He was so fascinated by the water in the pools that I started him in swimming lessons before he could even speak or walk.

"Of course, dear."

"I appreciate you guys so much, Mom. I don't know what I'd do without you."

"You'd be just fine, but we're happy we can be close to help you. It is wonderful to be able to be with Henry as he grows up. I just wish your brothers and sister were closer so we could see the rest of our grandchildren every day, too."

"Anytime you want to go see them, you can, you know."

"I know. We'll be going to see Tilly in a few weeks." She looks around and sighs, putting the washcloth away. "Well, you're home now, so I'm going to go across the street. Henry's fed, bathed, and in bed waiting for you."

"Thanks Mom, give Dad a hug and kiss for me when you wake him up to go to bed." Dad always falls asleep in his recliner watching television.

She chuckles and pats me on the arm before she leaves to go home to the guest house across the street from the main house. I was bequeathed the property along with a significant amount of money by a dear friend of mine whose biological children didn't want to have anything to do with him. I send up thanks to him every single day for his generosity.

Bert and I met at a seminar on the psychopathy of serial killers when I was in college. I was attending for my coursework; he was attending because he found it interesting. He asked me to lunch to discuss the topic and there was nothing untoward in the invitation. He simply liked the way my brain worked based on the questions I asked and wanted to talk about it more.

We started having lunch weekly and soon were joined by my roommate and two other friends. When my friends and I were looking for a place for the four of us to live together outside of campus apartments and dorms, the places we found were less than desirable. Bert went with us to one of the potential houses and was so disgusted by the property he invited us to move in with him.

It was an odd prospect, the four coeds moving into a house with a sixty-something man, but it turned out to be one of the best decisions of my life. I gained an amazing and dear friend.

Bert gained four women who became like daughters to him and who were there for him during his last days.

He passed away unexpectedly and during the reading of the will, it was discovered that he'd left me more cash that I'd ever imagined having in my bank account. Included was the house, property, the guest house, and all the contents of both.

I was flabbergasted and oh so grateful. His generosity allowed me to move my parents into the guest house once my father retired from being a groundskeeper from the prep school where he worked so that me and my siblings could get an above average education.

Jeremiah and I had been living here when he was killed. We had planned to marry once Henry was born, but that obviously didn't happen. I don't know how I would have gotten through having Henry and raising him alone without my parents being so close.

I turn off the lights downstairs and go up to my waiting son. "Hey buddy, how was your day?"

He sets aside the book he's reading. "Good. Me and Pops went swimming."

"So I heard."

I cross the room and sit down on the bed next to him. He's only eight, but he is almost as big as I am. I'm glad it looks like he's going to take his size from Jeremiah. Henry's father was tall and solidly built, whereas I am very short and petite except for being overly blessed in the rump area. My height earned me the nickname Hobbit from my former roommates, and it has bled over into other friendships as well.

"Fill me in on what's happening with Benjamin and Janie."

I haven't been able to read to Henry for over a year now. He loves books, just like I always did, and learned to read very early. His reading skills grew at a fast pace and now he reads books meant for children two or three years older.

He quickly grew tired of waiting for me to read to him each night, so he started reading the books on his own. We developed the pattern of him giving me a verbal recap each night about what he's read that day. I miss holding him in my arms and reading to him, but I'm thankful that he at least still allows me to cuddle up with him as he tells me about his stories.

He catches me up on the book, then tells me about all the plants my dad showed him. Dad, the plantophile wants to make sure that Henry knows everything about growing things he possibly can. Henry loves plants because his Pops does.

However, in reality, he is fascinated by many different things and seems to soak up information like a sponge. It's fascinating to see how he gets absorbed in something until he is satisfied that he knows all he is ready to know on a topic, then moves onto something else. We were stuck on dinosaurs for a while; now it's astronomy, but I'm getting the feeling that the stargazing phase is almost over.

Once Henry has me all caught up with appropriate commentary from me, I ask him, "Do you remember meeting my friends Gabriella and Morgan at the farmer's market a few weeks ago?"

"I think so," Henry says. "He was a gigantic man with paintings on his arms, right?"

He draws swirls on his arm with a finger. Paintings on his arms? Oh, he means Morgan's tattoos.

"Yes, that's them. They have invited us over to their house for a party they're having for the 4th of July. There will be fireworks and food and they invite their entire company to come, so there will be lots of other kids. Do you think you'd like to go?"

"What about Nana and Pops?"

"Nana and Pops will be visiting Aunt Tilly and Uncle Drake that weekend."

"Oh."

"We don't have to go if you don't want to, but I think you'll like it. They get the really big fireworks that go up high in the sky."

"Do you want to go?"

I shrug, not wanting to pressure him, but I'm always trying to get him to venture out a little. He's a bit of an introvert and would stay at home all day every day if I let him, but I want him to experience new things, too.

"I think it will be fun," I say.

He thinks for a moment. "Okay, we can go."

"Good. Are you excited to see Grandmother and Grandpa on Saturday?"

It's his turn to shrug. "I guess so."

"I know they're excited to see you."

Jeremiah's parents don't like me much and the feeling is mutual, although I would never tell Henry that. He's perceptive enough that I think he knows, anyway. Henry bears their surname and unless they're doing something I deem unacceptable like badmouthing me to my son, I won't keep their grandson from them.

We just have very different ideas about how to raise children. Their world is one of power and money and they treat their family members like pawns on a chessboard. If I ever get a hint of them doing that to Henry, their visitation privileges will be revoked. I have told them as much and they know I'm serious.

"I know. It's just not very much fun at their house and Grandmother doesn't like it when I start reading when I'm bored. I get bored a lot at their house."

"Well, just remember that we're going to go to the Science Museum on Sunday with Nana and Pops, and we'll get to listen to Pops snore through the show at the planetarium."

That makes him giggle. He snuggles down onto his pillow and I smooth back the hair that likes to flop over his forehead, just like his father's used to. It makes my heart squeeze. "I love you Henry Jeremiah Lawson McLean. Good night and sweet dreams."

"I love you, too, Mom. Night," he says as he sets his book on his nightstand. I turn off the light and bend over to kiss his forehead. I leave the door cracked and go to my room down the hall.

Once I've changed, I climb into bed. I'm not sleepy yet so I pick up my current read off the nightstand. Lately I've been on a romance kick, and I have found an author I really enjoy, so I'm working my way through her entire catalogue.

At least I think the author is a her. The author goes by M.K. Edwards and her identity is apparently quite the mystery with one wild theory being that it's a man although the website shows a woman's picture, and the bio uses the pronoun she.

If it really is a man, he has some in-depth insight into women and sex. That's very different from some male writers who write things such as one who penned the phrase about a woman's breasts being "three and a half milliboobs per handful." I mean, seriously.

I read all kinds of stuff, but for a long time after Jeremiah died, I couldn't read romance books. In fact, it's only been in the last year that I've been able to even contemplate the existence of romance in the world. Oh, I knew it was a reality for others, just not for me.

I don't know that I'm ready to fall in love again or if I ever will be, but I'm at least willing to entertain the concept of people falling in love and living happily ever after again. At least the way M.K. writes it.

She doesn't do the whole barely eighteen helpless damsels in distress trope but writes women who are easily believable in today's world, not helpless, but not perfect either. And the sex, oh my goodness, the sex goes beyond steamy to hot, hot, hot.

There has been more than once when I've had to put down the book and masturbate.

If M.K. is a man, I would love to meet him.

Chapter 4

Demeter

I pull up to the McLean's house to leave Henry with his grandparents. We climb the steps and ring the bell, unsurprised when their maid, a woman whose name they can't keep straight, answers the door. "Hello Angelica," I say.

"Hi Gel!" Henry says, happy to see her. It says something about the McLean household that Henry is happier to see Angelica than his grandparents.

"Good morning, Henry," she says in reply, smiling warmly at my son.

She loves my boy and I know that if anything happens to harm Henry in any way, she will tell me. I know the McLean's pay her well, and it seems that's the main reason she stays, but I, for one, am extremely thankful for her presence.

What does it say about me that every other weekend I leave my son in a place where I have to worry about him being harmed? I don't worry about them harming him physically as much as I worry about his emotional well-being.

However, his father grew up in this house and turned out to be a pretty wonderful human being, so I have to be satisfied by doing everything I can to counteract their influences. They are his grandparents, and it's good for Henry to have ties to his father's family.

I bend down and look him in the eye; it wasn't so long ago that I had to squat down to do it. He's growing so fast and there are days when I wish I could squish him back down into swaddling and hold him in my arms.

"Have a good day with your grandparents. I'll be back to get you in the morning, okay?"

He nods and takes Angelica by the hand.

"I love you Henry Jeremiah Lawson McLean."

"You don't always have to say all my names, Mom," he chides.

"I know, but I enjoy reminding you who you are. All parts of you." I lean in and kiss him on the forehead, smoothing back the hair that fell there.

"Don't forget to come get me in the morning," he says.

"I will never forget to come get you," I assure him, and watch him go into the house while standing on the steps until the door closes behind them.

Since I'm in Nichols Hills, I decide to visit my favorite bookstore in the City because it's nearby. If you live in Oklahoma, the state's capital, Oklahoma City is often referred to as 'the City'. Even if you're in Tulsa, the second largest metropolitan area in the state, if someone mentions 'the City', they're talking about Oklahoma City. Weird, I know.

I have some time to kill, so I meander through the shop. Ah ha! They have an M.K. Edwards book I haven't read, so I get in line to purchase it.

I had hoped to get something for breakfast, as well. Henry eats breakfast with his grandparents on the days he visits, so we don't eat before leaving the house. However, the store's café isn't open for food yet, so I get a coffee to satisfy my growling stomach until I can grab something to eat.

I'm headed out of the shopping center, juggling the coffee, bag with my book, and fishing in my purse for keys. The keys are eluding me, so I put my back to the exit door and push, but when I do, it swings open from someone pulling on the other side. My balance is lost for a moment, but I twist around and manage to stay on my feet.

Everything would have been fine, but the man coming in stretches out his hand and hits the coffee cup, sending lukewarm java all down my front. Thank goodness it wasn't scalding hot.

The coffee spiller just looks at me and blinks with owl eyes. Another man behind him, the one actually opening the door, looks me up and down over the top of his sunglasses.

"Oh my God," says sunglasses. "I'm so sorry, the doors are mirrored on the outside and we didn't see you coming. Please, what can we do to help?"

I look between them. They're obviously brothers and now that I get a good look at them, they could totally pass for being related to my son, brown-black wavy hair, blue eyes, olive skin, and all.

Sunglasses is dressed sharply in a blue button-down shirt, white shorts and loafers. His hair is expertly tousled in an "I just got fucked" look that I'm sure took him hours to get just right.

The coffee spiller is in a polo, khaki shorts and sneakers. His hair is a bit unkempt without the expert styling sunglasses was able to achieve with a lock of his bangs falling across his forehead. If I wasn't so pissed, I'd be tempted to smooth it back like I do with Henry and did with Jeremiah.

"Kellen, get out of the way," sunglasses says, taking charge. "Here, there's a restroom over by the elevators." He starts to put his hand under my elbow.

I jerk my arm away. "I know where the bathroom is and the answer to your question is nothing. There is absolutely nothing you can do to help other than maybe teaching your brother some manners."

"You weren't looking where you were going," the first man, Kellen says, sounding hesitant.

I narrow my eyes at him. I would really like to break out a round house kick across his high cheekbone, but I restrain myself. He's tall, so he'd have to bend down for me to connect, and I don't think he'd be willing to do that. Anyway, the last thing I need is an assault charge, although he started it.

"You are correct. I was trying to find my keys, but that's no excuse for you slapping the coffee out of my hand and causing it to spill all over me."

"But I didn't; I was trying to..."

I don't wait for him to finish. With a muttered *asshole,* I turn on my heel and go toward the restrooms to see if I can clean up a little so that I'm just stained instead of dripping before I race across the street to the mall and buy all new clothes for the day.

It's either that or go all the way back home and I don't want to do that. Nor do I have the time.

I come out of the restroom several minutes later to find sunglasses waiting with a fresh cup of coffee. I raise an eyebrow.

"You'll have to forgive my brother, Kellen. He's a bit socially awkward."

I take the coffee from him. "That's putting it mildly. Thank you for the coffee."

"You're welcome. I hope we haven't ruined your entire day. Here's my card. If you need to replace any part of your outfit or have to have anything professionally cleaned, please send me the bill and I will see that you're reimbursed."

"I appreciate that, and no, you didn't ruin my entire day. I'll just dash across the street and get something else to wear for the day. Now, if you'd made me miss my nail appointment, I might have been a little put out." I look at the card. "Beckett Masters with Masters Construction. Are you Morgan's brothers?"

"Yes, we are. How do you know my ugly older brother?"

"I'm friends with Gabriella." I hold out my hand. "Demeter Lawson."

He holds his hands up, palms out, and takes a step back. "Well, I feel very lucky that I haven't gotten my ass kicked yet for Kellen's mess up. Ella told me all about you and Krav Maga."

I laugh. "A big guy like you is afraid of little old me. Now that's funny."

He's obviously athletic, solidly built, with a purposeful stance. Based on his broad body, I'd peg him as a wrestler or something like that. The man looks as if he would know how to grapple.

"I'm a lover, not a fighter," Beckett says. "You'd knock me out in the first round."

"Well Beckett, it's nice to meet you, but I'd better get moving if I'm going to get re-outfitted and still get to my appointment on time. Where's your brother so I can stay away from him?"

"He's in the art gallery waiting for me, so you're safe. I mean it, send me the bill."

I wave a hand and take off, hurrying for the exit. When I pass by, I glimpse Kellen in the gallery. He's watching for Beckett and doesn't notice me at first. Once he does, I look to the exit. I can feel his eyes on me until I go out into the bright day.

I have half a mind to raise my middle finger in salute, but I refrain.

Shopping has never been something I particularly enjoyed, but this time I'm going to set a record for speed. I race into the department store's petite section and tell the saleswoman exactly what I need and why. She takes one look at me and goes off like a shot and brings everything to me in a dressing room.

She rings me up, and we stuff my soiled clothes into a shopping bag. I thank her profusely, then race out the door, barely making it to my appointment on time. I'm so flustered by the time I get there that I ask for the pedicure first just so I can sit and relax.

I take out my phone and text Ella.

Me: *Met your future bros in law. Beckett's cute, but Kellen's an asshole.*

Ella: *Kellen is a bit odd, but he's growing on me. Think he's misunderstood. Beck is cute and knows it. Luv him dearly, but he's a player with a capital P.*

Well, damn. The first interesting man I meet in a long time, and he's definitely not the kind of man I want in my life. I remind myself that I don't need a man, sit back in the chair and let the technician work her magic. By the time I leave, all ten nails are buffed and polished and I'm ready to face the rest of my day, but first, I still need something to eat.

Chapter 5

Kellen

When Beckett comes back, his smile is broad. It's what Morgan calls his shit-eating grin. I wonder if he got the woman's phone number. He always gets their numbers.

"Is she okay?" I ask him.

"She's fine. You'll never guess who she is." He doesn't wait for me to guess. He never does. "She's Ella's friend Demeter Lawson. You know, the ass kicking psychologist."

"I've heard Gabriella mention her. She's helping with the panic attacks," I say. "Demeter is the Greek goddess of the harvest, of plants, and fertility."

Beckett looks at me sideways. "Your brain holds onto some of the oddest things."

I shrug. He's right, but I have no way of controlling it.

"Why did you hit her cup like that?" Beckett asks.

"I didn't mean to. I was trying to take her by the arm to keep her from falling."

"That makes sense. Why didn't you apologize?"

"I wanted to. She was just so angry, and an apology seemed to be insufficient."

"Little brother, you have a lot to learn about women."

I can't argue with that and don't even attempt to. Beckett's attention is already drawn to the painting we came here to see. I don't know why he dragged me along with him.

I would have much rather stayed at home. There are innumerable things I need to do and running around with him on errands is a waste of time as far as I'm concerned. However, I know Mom worries about me if I don't let one of them drag me around town at least once a week, so I go to keep her happy.

"What do you think?" Beckett asks.

"It's abstract," I reply.

"Yes, it is. I met the artist once. She's a lovely girl, married to Preston Kearney."

"It will go with the colors in your living room nicely."

"Yes it will," he says. "I'll take it."

"You could have just borrowed my SUV," I say. The painting would never have fit in his sports car.

He puts an arm around my neck. "I wanted you to come with me, Kel. I'm hungry. Let's go find brunch somewhere. I'm thinking Latin. How does that sound?"

"It sounds fine," I tell him because I know where he intends to go and it's one of my favorite places, so I'm happy to concede.

It takes forever to get the painting wrapped up and travel worthy, so by the time we get to the restaurant, it's crowded. We're waiting for a table when the door opens behind us. "Well, isn't this a pleasant surprise?" Beckett says, looking over my shoulder. "I like the new dress, Demeter. Cute toes, too."

I turn and see Demeter Lawson. She looks as if she wants to bolt back out the door and go elsewhere. Beckett grabs her hand before she can. Maybe he read the same thing in her eyes.

"Please, let us buy you brunch as an apology," I manage to say, surprising Beckett and myself. I decide to keep moving my mouth and see if something else clever comes out. "I really am sorry about what happened. I was trying to take you by the arm to keep you from falling, but hit your cup by mistake."

Wow. That was pretty good.

She looks at me with narrowed icy blue-gray eyes but eventually says, "Well, I'm starving, and I think if I have to go find something else to eat, I'm going to faint, so yes, I'll be happy to let you treat me to brunch."

With ease, we change our request from a table for two to a table for three and, in short order, are being shown through the restaurant. We let Demeter take the lead and I want to put my hand on the small of her back to guide her as I've seen my brothers do, but there's not room for us to do anything but walk single file. That also seems like something more intimate than she'd be open to, so I content myself with studying her backside.

She's tiny, maybe five feet tall. Her hair is very curly and a blond so light it looks almost white. I'm mesmerized by her bouncing ponytail hanging down to the middle of her back. I want to reach out and touch it to see if it's as soft as it seems it might be, but I don't dare.

She sits and I push her chair in, drawing on the manners our mother taught us. I'm about to take my seat when I see Beckett watching me, a small smile on his face. He sits and leans back in his chair as if he's on his sofa at home.

"So, what's good here?" Demeter asks.

"You've never been here?" I ask.

"No, I've heard it's good, though."

"It is," I confirm. "I eat here all the time, so if you have any questions, let me know."

She looks at the menu for long minutes then sets it aside, having made up her mind.

"What did you decide on?" I ask.

"Machaca," she says.

"That's a good one."

"I'm having Huevos Rancheros," Beckett says. He's always confident to voice his opinion in any situation. He just assumes that everyone wants to know.

"Ooh, I thought about that, but the other one won out," Demeter says.

"Well, you can taste mine to see what you're missing out on," Beckett says. "What are you having, Kel?"

"The Izabal," I answer. "I usually get it or what Demeter's having. You can taste mine, too, but really, it's all good. I've never had anything here I didn't like."

The server chooses that moment to stop and take our orders while leaving water glasses on the table.

"Please, call me Demi."

"Did you know Demeter is a goddess?" Beckett asks.

She smiles as she arranges her napkin on her lap. "Yes, actually, I do. My Dad has a thing for plants."

"I didn't know, but Kellen did," Beckett says. "Harvest, plants, and fertility."

"Yep," she says with a chuckle, "just don't expect me to grow anything. That gene skipped me, but I think as much time as my son spends with my dad, he'll have the same hyperactive green thumb."

"You have a son? Are you married?" Beckett asks.

I'm glad he does because when she said son, I felt tongue tied again.

She shakes her head. "No, his father passed away when I was pregnant with Henry."

"I'm sorry to hear that," I tell her. I am, too. It's unimaginable how hard it must have been for her.

The table goes quiet, and I see her paying acute attention to the tabletop. I look over at Beckett, but he seems at a loss for words, too. He's all about jokes and having fun, but he doesn't do so well with the serious stuff. Thankfully, our food comes and breaks the somber turn the conversation has taken.

Demi takes a small bite from both of our plates and seems to like everything. I don't know why, but it makes me happy. The rest of the conversation is lighter, and that makes me happy, too, because it seems to make Demi happy.

I'm surprised when Beckett doesn't try to take the ticket from me and lets me pay. I would have thought he would try so that he could be the hero. We walk Demi out and say our goodbyes.

When we're back in my car, he says, "So, that's Ella's friend Demeter."

"Demi," I say.

"Demi," he agrees.

"She's nice."

"Pretty, too."

I don't say anything. If he thinks she's pretty, that might mean that he wants to date her. Beckett can get anyone he wants. He and Morgan both.

If one of them is interested in a woman, I don't stand a chance. They're both bright and shiny with big personalities and I learned a long time ago that I can't compete with them, so I stopped trying.

"She's not my type, though," Beckett says.

"I thought breathing was your type."

"Ooh, good one, little brother!" He gives me a playful punch on the arm. I didn't mean it as a joke or an insult. I was only speaking the truth from my point of view.

He goes on. "And yeah, you're right, I'm usually not too picky as long as they're nice to look at, but moms...Moms are a big no for me unless their kids are grown and on their own. Too much that can go wrong otherwise. Moms put their kids first and I enjoy being numero uno as long as I'm in their life."

Good. It's completely irrational, but the thought of him staying away from Demi makes me happy, too.

Chapter 6

Kellen

I enter my parent's house on Sunday, early for lunch. I'm a little irritated because this is the second day that I'm being pulled away from the things I need to do. However, I can't get too upset about yesterday because I met Demi.

I'm glad we ran into her at brunch so I could apologize for messing up. She was rightfully upset with me; I could have ruined her whole day with my ineptness.

After I apologized, she seemed more accepting and was nice. She also seems very smart. I wonder if Beckett is right about her being a martial artist who could 'kick my ass' as he says.

I really enjoyed talking with her and found her quite intriguing. Thoughts of her have been racing around my mind since we said goodbye after brunch.

Her lips come to mind most often. I would watch her talk and would get so absorbed in the way her lips moved I would lose track of the conversation.

I would have preferred to stay at home today, but they want to talk about the stuff we're doing for the 4th of July out at the farm. They'll want to spend a lot of money, so I will have to rein them in.

If we let Beckett have his way with everything, we'd go broke in a month. It's a good thing he brings in the money instead of spending it every day.

"Hi Mom," I say as I enter the kitchen, where Mom and Gabriella are preparing lunch. Mom's face is flushed, but she looks overjoyed to be having the whole family over for a meal. I kiss her on the cheek, then turn to my future sister-in-law. "Good morning, Gabriella."

She looks at me for a moment, then says, "Hello Kellen. How are you today?"

"Good. Thank you for asking. How are you?"

She smiles at me and says, "I am great."

I really like Gabriella. She's well-matched to Morgan. He likes to act like a big tough guy all the time, and everyone in the company, really everyone that meets him, is scared to death of him, but since he has been dating her, he's much more laid back and relaxed.

She has proven to be a tremendous asset to our family's company since we bought her out and she came to work with us. I think she's fitting in very well with our family, too.

I snitch a carrot from where Mom's chopping them. She gives me a good-natured swat with a dishtowel and tells me to go find my father in the den where he's probably watching golf or something equally boring. She always thinks he's watching golf, but he rarely is.

I find Morgan and Dad in the den and today it's baseball on the television instead of golf. Either way, she's right about it being boring. It's on, but neither of them is watching it.

They're talking business, as usual. Dad trusts Morgan to handle everything at the company. My input is rarely required unless there is a budgeting question, so I only listen with half an ear and take out my phone.

I had an idea on the way over and I don't want to lose it, so I start typing into my note taking app. If I don't write ideas down when they come, they're likely to fall out of my brain, so I keep notepads all over my house in case I don't have my phone to hand.

I'm almost finished when I hear Morgan say, "Kellen?"

I look up to see him and Dad staring at me. "Sorry, what?"

"We were just talking about the possibility of expanding our refit arm. The margins are actually better on remodels than on new construction and we're starting to get a lot of requests now that we've brought Ella over," Morgan says. "What are your thoughts about that?"

Gabriella had her own design build business, and that's how she met Morgan. She is the best designer I've ever seen, but she didn't like the construction side of things and after hearing some stories about how contractors treated her, I can't blame her.

Morgan convinced her to let us buy her out and for her to come run our design department while allowing Masters

Construction to do all the builds. It was a win-win for both companies.

I hold up a finger and finish the thought on my phone, then enter the conversation.

"I think it is more than doable. As you said, we have a demand, and it would be easy enough to meet it provided we are able to reallocate some of our human capital assets from new construction to remodels. It could possibly require an increase in headcount if the demand grows significantly, though, and recruiting takes time. However, with the greater margins, we can pay more for more highly skilled assets that would be particularly useful in remodels and that would be an inducement for recruiting. It seems that the types of remodels that we're getting requests for require more than just our usual framing and dry walling types."

"True," Morgan says. "I like that idea. We can market ourselves as experts. A lot of the clients are located in upscale areas that have a lot of specialized architecture, like Craftsman and Spanish Revival. Specialized architecture often requires specialized skills to retain the characteristics of the style of the home instead of dumbing them down, so to speak."

"Correct," Dad says. "I like it."

I start to focus on my phone again, but pause to add another thought.

"We might also need to add a person to the design team if you want to keep Gabriella free enough to focus on the specialized clients. She has the strongest capability for that, so taking the more mundane, nondescript projects off her plate would likely be helpful," I say.

Morgan nods. "Yeah. Gabriella is able to churn drawings out faster by hand than the others can do by computer, but I can tell she doesn't enjoy the new stuff as much. She says there's no soul, no artistry in them. She cut her teeth watching Bob Vila and Steve Thomas, so I shouldn't be surprised."

"Surprise? What surprise?" asks Beckett, coming into the room. "I love surprises."

"Gabriella," Morgan replies.

"Dude, she's your surprise," Beckett says. "She's off limits to be anyone else's surprise."

"She's a surprise for the entire company," I throw in.

Beckett looks at me. "That's for sure. I can't keep up with all the requests we're getting for her work. Do you think we can clone her?"

"No!" Morgan says with a shake of his head. "One of her is plenty; there's no way I could keep up with two of her."

"Two of who her?" Gabriella asks, coming into the room.

"Two of you," Morgan answers, trying to pull her down onto his lap.

"Nope, you've got to come this way," she says, resisting his pull. "Lunch is ready."

We're all sitting at the table when Gabriella brings up the meeting with Demi. Beckett, of course, has to tell the entire story, and he does it in such a way that casts me in the worst light possible. I don't respond, focusing on my plate instead, but I can feel heat prickling at my collar. Sometimes I wish I was the only child it felt like I was growing up.

"I think our boy, Kellen, has a bit of a crush on the good doctor," Beckett says.

I stay quiet. He can be such an asshole and I've found he works through it more quickly if I just don't engage. Mom is always pushing them to include me, but a lot of the time I wish they'd just leave me alone like they did when I was a kid.

Everyone goes quiet. I figure they're waiting for me to respond, but when I dare to glance up, it's not just Mom glaring at Beckett, it's Gabriella, too. "What?" Beckett asks, mystified by their looks.

"Beckett," Gabriella says, "I love you to death, but sometimes you cross the line into assholedom."

Beckett laughs. "Assholedom? Is that a real place?"

She raises an eyebrow at him. "You should know, you're the one who likes to spend time there."

He puts a hand over his heart. "Ouch! You wound me! Kel, I'm sorry, I'm just playing man."

"She told me to put her and Henry down as attending the 4th of July party," Gabriella says to the table.

"Henry?" Mom asks.

"Her son," Gabriella answers. "He's eight, but will be nine this fall. I'm not sure of the month, though."

"Is she married?" Mom asks.

Gabriella shakes her head. "No, it's really kind of sad; Henry's father was killed when she was pregnant with the boy."

That pulls on Mom's heartstrings hard. "Oh no! That poor girl."

"It was hard for her," Gabriella says. "I didn't know her then, but she's talked about it a bit. She's great now, though."

She goes on to talk about Demi and I listen to every word. I was already impressed with Dr. Lawson, but now even more so. I make a mental note to look her up online and see what else I can find out about her.

We go on to discuss the party and all the plans. Beckett and Morgan want to spend a boatload of money on fireworks. Mom and Gabriella are all about the catering. Dad doesn't care as long as Mom is happy, and I just write the checks.

Often, I think about quitting the company. I don't need to work there. There is enough money in my accounts from savings and investments that I could easily quit, buy a van, and bum around the coast surfing for the rest of my life if I wanted to. However, I don't know how to surf, so that could be a problem.

Just when I about have myself convinced to turn in my notice and buy a van to live in, I realize that if I left, it wouldn't be Masters Construction anymore. They'd have to hire someone new, and it would be Masters and some other rando because Kellan abandoned us Construction. But that's just me. Morgan and Beckett probably wouldn't even notice a bump in the road.

Lunch is over and the family likes to gather in the living room to chat. They all get settled in, so I go down the hall to my old bedroom. I usually disappear for a while, then make an excuse and leave.

I'm sitting on my bed, making notes on my phone, when there's a knock on the door. Before I get a chance to answer, Gabriella quietly opens the door and sticks her head in.

"Yeah? What is it?" I look up and ask.

"I thought I'd find you hiding out somewhere."

I frown. "What do you mean? I was just..." What was I just doing? What excuse could I possibly make to be sitting in my childhood bedroom while on my phone?

She sits on the bed next to me. She doesn't say anything; she just sits there. Sits here in my room with me.

"Gabriella? Why are you in here?" I ask.

"Well, I know what it's like."

"You know what what is like?"

"Feeling like the odd one out. Only in my family, it wasn't just a feeling. I wasn't really considered to be part of the family, just a girl who happened to live in the same house and have the same parents, but totally separate."

My brows draw together. "I'm sorry."

She puts her arm in mine. "The big difference is that for you, it's just a feeling. Your family loves you. Truly they do. Your parents adore you."

I start to speak, but she plows on. "I know Beckett can be an asshole, but that's just his personality, big and brash, and obnoxious. He's an asshole to you, but he loves you, too. He's an asshole to me, but I don't let him get away with it. He's not an asshole to Morgan because Morgan would beat the crap out of him. Morgan loves you. He talks all the time about how he doesn't know what he'd do without you at the company. Because he knows you're there, he knows he doesn't have to worry about a lot of stuff that he'd have to if you weren't."

Out of everything she said, the only part I think is really true is that my parents adore me. Well, Mom does, anyway. Dad doesn't acknowledge my presence most of the time, especially if Mom or Morgan are in the room.

So, hiding out is done; time to make an excuse, go home, and get some work done.

With a sigh, I stand, extricating my arm from hers, and leave the room. In the living room, I cross to Mom, bend down, and kiss her on the cheek. "I've got to go. Love you."

She puts her hand on my arm. "Kellen, please stay."

I shake my head. "I have some things I need to get done today. I'll see you at the party. Morgan, just make sure I get the invoices and I'll get them paid," I say without looking at him.

Then I leave. I get in my car and go home to my empty house.

Chapter 7

Demeter

"Can I take a book?" Henry asks me. "Just in case I get bored."

"Sure. I don't think you'll need it, but you can take one. You can just stick it in the tote with the other things we're taking."

"Thanks, Mom."

"You're welcome."

I check myself in the mirror one more time. It has been a while since I've been to this kind of social event, and I'm surprised that I feel a little nervous. I go through the tote to be sure I have everything, especially the sunscreen and bug spray. We'll be outside quite a bit, even with the tents that will be set up.

Once the sun goes down, it will be mosquito city. I also got some small fireworks, worms, and sparklers, mostly for Henry, in case they don't have anything for the smaller children. I have enough that he can share, as well.

"All right, let's get going," I call to Henry.

He comes racing down the stairs and drops a book into my bag, then keeps going out the garage door. I'm glad he seems excited. I wondered if he would try to back out at the last minute, but he seems gung-ho.

He sometimes has a hard time with new social situations, and I hope this goes well today. I won't push him when he's uncomfortable, but I want him to know that it's okay to be who he is with other people and still have fun. I want him to know that he doesn't have to be exactly like everyone else to be okay. There's no such thing as only one kind of normal.

When we pull into the address Ella gave me, I'm surprised by the number of cars being parked. She said it was something they did for the entire company, but I guess I didn't expect there to be quite so many employees. I follow the guys waving me in and park where they point.

"Ready, buddy?"

"Yep!" Henry says, already unbuckling from his booster seat.

He scrambles out of the car and waits until I gather our things, and takes me by the hand as we head toward the largest of the tents. The whole scene is amazing. I expected there to be food and fireworks, but there is stuff everywhere, bouncy houses for the kids, carnival-type games, even a DJ playing music. This looks fun! It almost makes me want to go to work for Masters Construction.

"Mom! Can I go bounce?"

"Sure, buddy." I start to say more about taking turns and being patient, but he's let go of my hand and is off like a lightning bolt.

I don't see anyone I recognize. However, considering I only know Ella and the brothers Masters and they are four people among what appears to be over a hundred, it's not surprising.

I step under the big tent to find rows of tables with chairs and a long row of tables with food being set up by the caterers. There's also a table with finger foods for those who need a snack to tide them over before the meal.

Then I see the best thing, ever, a bar set up in one corner. Standing in front of the bar are two of the people I know, and it doesn't surprise me that Morgan and Beckett would be hanging out at the bar. I head their way.

"Hey fellas," I say.

Beckett turns toward me. "Demi! Glad you could make it. Need a drink?"

"Something cold and fruity would be nice, but a virgin, please. I have a kid to keep track of."

"It doesn't look like there's a kid with you," Beckett observes.

With an exaggerated look of sorrow, I say, "Alas, he has succumbed to the lure of the bouncy house."

"Hi Demi. Not sure if you remember me," Morgan says.

"Of course, I do; I met you with Ella at the farmer's market at the beginning of the summer. Speaking of Ella, any idea where she might be?" I ask.

"HQ," Morgan says, pointing a finger toward the area behind the main event setup. "There's a small house that's original to the property just behind here. She's in there with Mom, coordinating all the minions."

I laugh and hover a hand in the air. "Thanks. Oh, if someone brings you a little boy about yea high that looks like he could belong to your family genetically, that's Henry. I'm going to go tell him that if he can't find me, he should ask for one of the Mr. Masters or Gabriella."

"Sure, that works," Morgan says.

I take my drink and head toward the bouncy house, glimpsing the structure Morgan mentioned. I find Henry, already getting sweaty from exertion, waiting outside for another turn with several other children. It looks like he's having fun and I'm glad for that.

I tell him where I'm headed and pass along the message of whom to ask for if he needs me. He nods at me and takes a sip of my drink, but is intently focused on the movement of the line in front of him. I'm glad I slathered him up with sunscreen before we left because he would probably be mortified if I were to do it now. I leave him to play and go in search of HQ.

The small house is sheltered by a grove of trees, and out front is a bench in the shade. Perched on the bench, reading a book, is Kellen Masters. I make a detour, thinking about the things Ella told me at the Society dinner last night. She told me about what happened at their family lunch last Sunday and how she can see things in Kellen to which she relates because of her upbringing. It's made me curious.

He watches me as I approach. I sit down next to him on the bench. As I do, he sets the book aside. "Hello Kellen."

"Hi Demi, I'm glad you could come. Did your son come with you?"

I smile. "Yes. The bouncy house has claimed him."

He chuckles. It's sort of a rusty sound, like he doesn't do it very often. "It is popular. You look very pretty."

I look over at him to see him watching me. I smile. "Thank you, Kellen. Are you having fun?"

He shrugs. "I have to be here so I can pay for things."

"There's surely more to it than that, but I'm glad you're here. I enjoy seeing friendly faces among the crowd of people I don't know."

I sit there beside him in the shade for a while. With a nod at the book, I say, "Henry does that, too."

"Does what?"

"Reads. He mostly does it when he gets bored, but if he feels uncomfortable or overwhelmed in a situation, he'll do it then, too."

A look crosses his face too quickly for me to decipher. "He reads that much? I thought he was only eight."

"He is. He'll be nine in a couple of months, but he's a voracious reader. He reads a couple levels higher than his age."

"Impressive."

"Speak of the devil." I see my boy in his striped shirt heading our way. One of his shoelaces has come undone and is dragging in the dirt. When he draws near, I call, "Already done bouncing, buddy?"

He shrugs. "Yeah, the line was too long. It was taking forever between turns and the turns were only like a minute long. May I have another drink, please?"

"First, let me introduce you to my friend. Henry, this is Kellen. Kellen, this is my son, Henry." Henry surprises Kellen as he does most adults by putting out his hand.

"It is a pleasure to meet you," my boy says.

Kellen smiles broadly, and it transforms his face. He seems so much softer and approachable when he smiles like that. He shakes my son's hand and says, "It's nice to meet you, too, Henry."

I lean down and touch Henry's calf. He automatically puts a hand on my shoulder and raises his foot for me to tie his shoe. I finish and hand him my drink.

"Whatcha reading?" Henry asks Kellen when he stops to take a breath after sucking down half my drink.

Kellen holds up the book.

"The Crooked Staircase," Henry reads, then looks up at Kellen. "What's it about?"

"It is about a woman who is trying to stop some bad people from doing bad things."

"Is it good?"

"Yes. This is the third book in a five-book series, and I can't wait to finish this one so I can read the next one to see what happens."

Henry nods in complete understanding.

"What are you reading?" Kellen asks him.

Henry slides his eyes at me. I look back at him with a raised eyebrow. He reaches into my tote bag and pulls out the book he put in there and holds it up for Kellen to read. He lifts his chin defiantly.

"Harry Potter and the Sorcerer's Stone," Kellen reads.

"Henry! Who got that for you?" I ask. He had been wanting the series for some time now, but I wasn't letting him read it yet because after the first couple of books, it starts to venture into some darker themes that I'm just not sure he's ready for.

"Grandmother and Grandpa got them for me." He looks down at his sneakers. "I mentioned that I'd been wanting them and that you wouldn't get them for me..."

"I will take that up with Grandmother and Grandpa. You can read the first one, but before you read any of the others, you need my permission first. Do you understand?"

"Yes, ma'am," he says, scuffing one sneaker in the dirt.

"It's not that I'm trying to keep you from reading something you want, but the books after this one get kind of scary and I don't want you having nightmares because of what you're reading."

"I'm almost nine!" he protests.

"I know, buddy. I know you can understand what you're reading, but just because you can understand it doesn't mean you can emotionally handle what you're reading."

"Can I sit here and read with Kellen for a while?" Henry asks sullenly. "I don't feel like bouncing again right now."

"I'm going into the house to find Miss Ella. You should probably ask Kellen if he minds sharing his bench."

Henry looks up hopefully. "May I share your bench to read for a while, Mr. Kellen?"

Kellen smiles at Henry and says, "Sure, buddy."

I give up my seat to him. "I'll be right inside if you need me."

"I'll be fine, Mom." He scooches back onto the bench, pulling his feet up to sit cross-legged as he opens his book. Kellen is looking down at him, watching as Henry settles in to read.

I go inside the house, relieved at the blast of cold air that greets me. "Demi!" Ella calls when she sees me.

"Hi!" I reply.

"Where's Henry?" Ella asks.

I hook a thumb at the door. "He's already bounced himself out and decided to join Kellen on the bench and read a while."

A plump woman comes into the room, her arms filled with colorful bags. "Demi," Ella says, "This is Rebecca, matriarch of the Masters family."

"Oh! Hello, dear, it's nice to meet you. Ella's told us so much about you." Rebecca says. She puts the bags on the table where Ella is working, then goes to look out the front window. "So, that's your boy with mine out there?"

"Yes, that's Henry. It seems they're fellow bibliophiles who take books with them wherever they go," I answer.

"He's darling," Rebecca says.

"Thank you," I reply.

"So," Ella says, "feel like working? We're putting together party favor bags for everyone and some items didn't arrive until just a few minutes ago, so we need help stuffing."

"Sure. Can I leave this here?" I ask, motioning to my tote bag.

"Yes," says Ella. "Just put it back here with mine. We can lock it up when we leave to take the favor bags over."

I put my stuff away and get to work.

Both Rebecca and I go to the front window occasionally and peek out at our boys. They seem to be getting along famously, sometimes talking, most often just sitting and reading their respective books. Based on looks alone, they could be father and son.

That thought makes me flinch and my heart squeezes at the fact that Henry will never experience anything like this with his real father. I see Henry look up and back at the house. I duck behind the curtain so he can't see me watching. He says something to Kellen, then gets up and comes toward the house. I go back to working on the bags.

Henry comes in and without ceremony says, "Mom, I've gotta pee."

All of us working on the bags laugh. "Hey buddy, the bathroom is right through there," I tell him, pointing him in the right direction.

He comes out and rubs his hands, placing his book on our worktable. "What are you all doing?"

"Putting things in these bags for the people who came to the party," I tell him.

"Cool," he says, bellying up to the table and peeking in the bags.

"Who do we have here?" Rebecca asks, coming into the room.

"This is my son, Henry. Henry, this is Kellen's mom, Miss Rebecca."

Henry does his pleased to meet you routine, thoroughly charming Rebecca.

"Mom, I'm getting hungry," Henry informs me.

"Okay, we're just about ready to load up these bags to take them over to the big tent. That's where the food is. Do you think you can wait a few minutes until we're ready?"

"Yes, ma'am. Can I help load?"

"Sure!" Rebecca tells him. She puts a few bags in his arms and bids him to follow her to where we have a couple of hand-pulled carts waiting to be filled.

Once the carts are full, we go out front to where Kellen is still sitting. Henry races over to him. "Mr. Kellen, we're finished working and we're gonna take the bags over, then eat. Are you hungry? Do you want to come with us?"

"Sure, buddy, I'll go with you. I could use a bite to eat."

Henry grabs his hand and pulls on it to help him up. Kellen laughs and lets himself be dragged away. Henry stops and holds out his free hand to me. "Come on, Mom."

I take his hand and he bounces along between Kellen and me as we make our way toward the big white tent. Kellen stops and takes the handle of one of the wagons with his free hand from the woman pulling it, and we continue bouncing along.

Gabriella follows with the second wagon and Rebecca follows behind to make sure we don't lose any of our cargo.

Chapter 8

Kellen

I spend my afternoon sitting and reading with an eight, almost nine-year-old and can't remember the last time I had such a pleasant day. Henry is quite intelligent and seems to be very fascinated with astronomy. However, he told me he's about ready to be interested in something else just like he got tired of dinosaurs before focusing his efforts on learning about the stars.

When he comes racing out to me and grabs my hand, it is as if he has wrapped his sweaty little fingers around my heart and given it a tug. I watch him bouncing along between Demi and me. It's a pleasant picture. When I look over at Demi, she grins at me. I can't help but grin back at her.

I help unload the wagons, and Henry is right there helping, too. He can only carry a couple of bags at a time, but he doesn't stop until the job is done. When the last bag is placed, he dusts off his hands and says, "Let's go eat, Mom." It's completely adorable.

She laughs and says, "Okay, buddy, let's go eat."

Then, for the second time today, he grabs my hand. He looks up at me and says, "Come on, Mr. Kellen, come eat with us."

I look to Demi to be sure it's okay with her. She's smiling and nods, so we go get in line for food. Mom and Gabriella come, too, leaving a few people in charge of handing out the bags to the attendees.

I honestly don't know what has happened, but this boy and I have bonded over the past couple of hours of talking about books and stars. He seems intent on keeping me by his side, and I'm not at all bothered by that. Where he is, Demi will be, and it will give me a chance to get to know more about her.

I'm not as slick and suave as my older brothers, so I got used to women being drawn to them and never giving me a second glance. I've taught myself not to want because the minute I do, one of them will step into the room and take it away. Morgan's attached and Demi's not Beckett's type, according to him. Maybe I have enough of a chance to make something happen.

It occurs to me that just because Demi isn't Beckett's type, perhaps he's her type and she'll still overlook me for him. I'll have to take that chance.

It usually takes me a while to warm up to someone, and I'd like to warm up to Demi, at least enough to ask her out. She may say no, but for once I'm going to go after something I want instead of being passive. For whatever reason, I don't want to be passive with her.

I like everything I know about her and want to know more. She's a great mom, from what I can tell. Both she and Henry seem to be incredible people.

Mom and Gabriella go to the family's table and tell Demi to come with them. She does, so I follow her there as well. Henry insists on sitting with me on one side and his mom on the other.

Mom sits across from us. I'm sure she's champing at the bit to interrogate Demi. I know she's noticed me paying attention to Demi so I can imagine she's already planning our wedding and seeing Henry as her first potential grandchild.

Conversations are floating all around the table. I keep half an ear out to hear what everyone's talking about while keeping the other half attuned to Demi and Henry. Mom asks Demi about her psychology practice and seems to take it in stride that Demi focuses on couples having sexual difficulties.

I don't hear Mom's next question. I'm distracted when Henry pats my leg. I look down at him. "What's this?" he asks, pointing at his plate.

"Baked beans," I tell him.

He curls his nose.

"Try them. You never know if you're going to like something unless you try it at least once."

He uses his fingers to roll exactly one bean onto his fork and tastes it, grimacing the whole time until the brown sugar hits his taste buds. Then he perks right up and starts eating more. Mom is watching and laughs at the boy.

I catch movement in my periphery. Someone is coming to the table, and I look up to see Beckett. He crosses the room with his usual swagger, coming to our table with a plate in one hand

and a beer in the other. He sits across from me next to Mom. "What's up family?"

"Who's he?" Henry asks quietly, patting his mom's leg.

Demi, who had been talking to Gabriella in the other direction, turns and says, "What's that buddy?"

Henry looks at Beckett and says a little louder, "Who's he?"

"My name is Beckett," my brother says. "I am younger brother to that ugly old guy over there," he points at Morgan, "and older brother to this bratty kid over here." He points at me.

Henry looks at him stoically and says with all seriousness, "It's not nice to call people names."

Beckett raises an eyebrow at the boy.

Mom says, "That's right Henry, it's not," then turns a scowl on my brother.

Demi turns to her son. She sees barbecue sauce on his chin, takes a napkin and wipes it off as she says, "He was trying to be funny, buddy, but you're right, calling people names, even trying to be funny, is not nice."

"Kid, you're cramping my style," Beckett says.

Henry looks at him for a moment, still serious, and replies, "Maybe you need a new style."

"Ooh...put in your place by an eight-year-old," Morgan says, barking a laugh from the other end of the table.

I could hug this kid.

"Mom," Henry says, oblivious to the byplay, "can we get another one of those snow cone things?"

"Well, would you rather have one of those, or would you rather have ice cream with a brownie for dessert? You can't have both; that would be way too much sugar in one day."

He contemplates his options and decides on the brownie with ice cream.

After he's eaten his fill, Henry goes off to play. Demi watches his movements around the kid's area while still taking part in the conversations around the table. Mothers are fascinating.

I sit back and observe, as usual. It's clear that she's very close with Gabriella, but doesn't seem to have spent much time with Morgan. That's interesting. I wonder how she and Gabriella know each other.

Henry returns and wants Demi to visit the carnival games with him. He grabs my hand and asks me to go, too. How can I deny such a request? We toss rings on bottles and throw darts at balloons. I manage to win a small stuffed red, white, and blue star and give it to Henry.

When the sun starts to set, we move to chairs where we can watch the fireworks. All the kids go to find their parents and get ready for the show while Dad, Morgan, and Beckett disappear to go play with things that go boom. I keep one eye on Mom, but she's next to Gabriella, so I know she's okay. Ella watches out for Mom, too.

The crowd "Ooos" and "Ahhs" throughout the show. After a while, Henry abandons his chair and climbs into his mom's lap. He's almost as big as Demi is, but she gets him settled with practiced ease. Before long, he's dozing off despite the noise of the explosions.

It's full dark, and the show has been going on for a while. People start to filter out, particularly those with smaller children. Demi gets Mom's attention and leans over to say something. Mom nods and hands her keys. I can see Demi's trying to figure out a way to get out of her chair, but the boy has to weigh at least as half as much as she does.

I get up. "Can I help?"

"Yeah, if you don't mind taking him, I just need to go back to the house and get my things," she murmurs.

I nod and with some awkward effort on my part, we shift Henry from her lap to my arms. He turns in my arms and snuggles his head onto my shoulder, and sighs. Asleep, he's dead weight.

I can't imagine Demi carrying him for very long. I take my seat again, waiting for her to return. An unrecognizable emotion surges up in me and I'm not sure what to do with it. I look over and see Mom watching me, a strange look on her face.

Demi hurries off into the darkness. I guess I could have gone to get her things, but I have no idea what's hers, so this is probably better. I look down at the top of Henry's head. His weight is comforting in my arms, and I can feel his little heart beating strong and steady against my chest.

A hand squeezes my shoulder. Demi's back. She circles around me and says quietly, "I can take him back; it's not far to the car."

"I've got him," I tell her and lever myself out of the chair.

Getting a sleeping child into a booster seat is more difficult than it sounds and again, I'm amazed at the mechanics of parenthood. Imagine trying to maneuver a fifty-pound octopus with partial rigor mortis into a tiny seat and then securing it with seatbelts and you might come close.

Between the two of us, we finally get him settled and buckled in. I can't fathom Demi managing it on her own, but it's obvious that she's had a lot of practice.

"Thanks," Demi says quietly.

"You're welcome. I was happy to help."

I want to say more, but I can't manage that yet. I have a feeling anything else I tried to say would end up being like my attempt to keep her from falling. An awkward situation would be made into an abysmal one when I found a way to botch it up.

She opens her car door and lingers for a moment, then says, "Good night, Kellen."

"Good night, Demi," is all I can say.

I watch her get into her car and leave, staring after her until her taillights fade in the distance.

Chapter 9

Demeter

This morning, I'm paying the price for letting Henry have too much sugar and stay up too late last night. He is a bear, and to make matters worse, I missed picking up his book from the table where he'd placed it when I went to get my bag.

Even with my promises to make sure I'd have it back or a new one to replace it by the time he gets back home tomorrow morning, he was grousing about it until he fell asleep in the car. Hopefully, some additional sleep and a good breakfast with his grandparents will settle him down.

To make the morning even more fun, when I show up on their doorstep, I have to stay and talk with them about the books they bought him. Elizabeth, Henry's grandmother, tries to high hand me, saying that she glanced through it and thought Henry could understand it just fine.

I had to explain to her the difference between cognitive processing capabilities and emotional processing capabilities and how the books take a darker turn after the first one. She said she didn't know, and I told her that's precisely why she should have asked me first.

I feel a headache coming on as I start back toward home. There is nothing else on my schedule for today other than getting my car's oil changed, so I plan to spend a lot of time around the pool reading and being a lazy bum. After a stop at a drugstore to get some pain relievers, I'm just getting back into the car when my phone rings.

"Hello," I answer.

"Hi Demi, it's Kellen. I hope you don't mind, but I got your number from Gabriella. I found Henry's book when we were cleaning up last night."

"Oh, thank God! He was so mad at me this morning when he found out I didn't grab it."

"I'm pretty open today and can bring it to you or meet you somewhere to hand it off, if you like."

"Oh," I say, "I'm going to be stuck at the dealership in Norman getting my oil changed for a while."

"That actually works well. I live in north Norman off Indian Hills."

Learning he lives in Norman surprises me. The construction company offices are located toward the north side of the City, so I figured he probably lived closer to that region of the metro.

"You do?"

"Yeah, a friend was building in a subdivision I liked. Anyway, that's a long story. Have you eaten? I can take you to breakfast while you're waiting for your car. It'll be better than sitting in the dealership and you can get the book at the same time."

"That sounds perfect," I tell him.

It really does. After watching the way Henry warmed up to Kellen, I want to know more about him. Even if he and I are friends, if he's going to spend any amount of time around Henry, I need to know him a lot better than I do now.

Beckett had seemed charming when we first met, but he's kind of a dick when he's around his family. I have never appreciated backhanded teasing that bites as much, or often more, as it plays. It appears to be a habit for the most part and Kellen is most often his target, but I don't think he means to be cruel.

Maybe he's oblivious to how it affects Kellen. Although I consider myself to have a practiced eye because of my training, it was obvious to see how Kellen tensed when Beckett joined the table and started making comments.

For all his bluster, this type of behavior often stems from insecurity, and I have no idea why Beckett would be insecure. My psychologist's brain is keen to observe him more so that I can guess at his motivations, however, I will do my best not to indulge it.

It's inappropriate to analyze someone in depth without an invitation. Be that as it may, if he acts the ass around Henry too often, I won't hesitate to call him on it. I will not have Henry exposed to it without counteracting its impact lest he start thinking that behavior is all right.

I had thought Kellen to be the asshole when we first met, but I think Gabriella might be right, I think Kellen's a bit misunderstood. He seems to mean well, but often his intent isn't carried out in his actions and words.

I like the way he's attentive to his mother and saw him behaving the same way with Henry. He and Henry have a bit of a kindred spirit vibe going on.

I make the arrangements to meet Kellen, and I head toward the dealership. My morning is looking up.

I drop my car off early at the shop and get into Kellen's car. I don't know what I thought he would drive but am surprised by the big SUV. He gives me the book as soon as I'm buckled in and I put it in my bag so there's no way I can forget it again.

"Oh, thank you so much! Henry will be thrilled to have it back."

We go to a nearby diner and have a good meal with some pleasant conversation. Kellen is starting to grow on me. I can also see the friction between him and Beckett because it comes through even when Kellen is talking about his brother. I still don't think Beckett means anything bad by his behavior, but he's old enough that he should be self-aware enough to see how it affects his younger brother.

Morgan is the quintessential alpha male. When he walks into a room, it's clear he's in command. Beckett acts like he's on stage every minute, his bright personality easily stealing the spotlight.

Being so much younger than his brothers and seemingly very different from them must have been difficult for Kellen. He's more sensitive and introspective. I keep circling back to the thought that he's a lot like Henry, really.

I think Kellen has the potential to be just as bright and shiny as his brothers, but he appears to have given up trying after a childhood of unsuccessfully competing for attention. He's obviously intelligent, and very handsome, especially when he smiles. His social awkwardness seems to be more from lack of use than lack of ability.

We are just leaving the diner when my phone rings. We hurry to the car, so I can hear better. It's Henry's grandparent's number, which worries me. What could possibly have happened so soon after I dropped him off?

I answer the phone to hear Henry instead of one of his grandparents. He's crying so hard he's practically hysterical. I put him on speaker because he's so loud it's hurting my ear.

"Whoa, slow down buddy. Take a deep breath. That's my guy. Take another one. I need you to calm down a little bit so I can understand you."

A few deep breaths have him able to speak more clearly. He's still sniffling, but he's not sobbing any longer. "Okay," I say, "that's better. Now tell me what's going on."

"She hit me," he says and sniffs.

I go very still. "Who hit you?"

"Grandmother."

"Why did she hit you?"

"She had Gel fix oatmeal for breakfast even though she knows I don't like oatmeal. I didn't eat any, but when breakfast was over, Gel took me to the kitchen and made me toast cuz she knows I don't like oatmeal. Grandmother came in and got mad and said that I should eat what everyone else eats and that if I don't like it, I can go without and that if I get hungry enough, I'll eat what I'm given."

He pauses and takes in another deep, ragged breath. "I got mad and told her I wanted toast. She grabbed my arm and pulled me off the stool and spanked me...hard."

I can picture his little lip quivering as he sniffles.

"I'm so sorry that happened to you, buddy. Mommy's car is getting serviced, but as soon as it's done, I'll come get you. Okay?"

"We can go now," Kellen says low. "Swing by the dealership and get the booster seat and go ahead and go get him."

"Are you sure?"

"Who are you talking to?" Henry asks.

"Mr. Kellen," I tell him. "He found your book and brought it to me. We just had breakfast, and he says we can come get you now once we get your seat from my car."

"Okay," Henry says, sounding every bit like the eight-year-old he is instead of like he's going on teenagerhood like he usually does.

"I'm on my way, buddy. I'll be there soon. I love you Henry Jeremiah Lawson McLean."

"Love you, too. Hurry, please."

"I will, buddy."

I hang up the phone. I am livid. I have discussed corporal punishment with the McLean's at length. I'm not opposed to spanking, but it shouldn't be used for just any infraction and it fucking well shouldn't be used over a goddamn piece of toast.

It is a particularly bad way to deal with Henry. Taking his books away will ensure behavioral correction more quickly than anything.

Kellen lets me be quiet. When we get to the dealership, he takes care of getting Henry's seat, which is a good thing. I don't know if I can speak civilly to anyone right now.

We're passing downtown Oklahoma City when I finally say, "Thank you."

"You're welcome. How often does he see his grandparents?"

"These are his paternal grandparents. He spends every other Saturday with them from early morning until the next morning. He sees my parents practically every day."

I explain to him about our living situation. "That's nice for him," Kellen says.

"It is," I reply. "I don't know what I'd do without my parents. We didn't have much money while I was growing up, but we had plenty of love. I'd take love over money any day, but it's wonderful when you don't have to worry about either."

When we get close, I give Kellen directions. He pulls into their circle drive and I'm out of the car before he puts it in park. He gets out and stands behind me as I pound on the door.

Unsurprisingly, I am met with Robert. Henry pushes past him and runs to me. I want to pick him up, but I need my full faculties right now, so I tuck him in behind me, my stance making it clear that Henry is leaving with me.

I can hear movement behind me and the car door opening. It sounds as if Kellen must be getting Henry into his seat.

"We have discussed punishment, Robert," I say through gritted teeth. "You and your wife are never to hit my son. I don't know how I could have possibly made it any clearer."

He puts his hands up. "It was all a misunderstanding. He's been out of control all morning."

"Did Elizabeth, or did she not, hit my child?"

My fists are clenched at my sides, and I am ready to throw down with him. I am so angry I think my head might explode. I feel Kellen step up behind me again. Henry must be safe in the car, which lets me relax a little.

"Well, yes, but..."

I shake my head and interrupt him, raising a finger at him. "There is no but. Your visitation privileges for today are revoked, Robert."

"But we have plans for the holiday. We were going to take him to the club."

"Take one of your other grandchildren," I bite out before I turn on my heel toward the car.

"Robert," I hear Kellen say.

"Kellen, what are you doing with her?" Robert says it as if he's asking why Kellen has shit smeared all over his shoes.

"She's a friend."

I hear Robert snort in derision, but I don't care. I have my baby and I'm taking him home.

Chapter 10
Demeter

I'm still steaming when Kellen asks, "Is McDonald's okay?"

"Huh?"

"Henry still hasn't had breakfast. I know it might not be ideal, but he's probably starving by now."

"Oh, yes, you're right." I turn in the seat. Henry's absorbed in his book, so I guess Kellen gave it to him when buckling him in. "Hey buddy, do you want a biscuit or chicken for breakfast?"

"Biscuit, please. Can it be a Braum's biscuit?"

"Yes, buddy, it can."

"Got it," Kellen says and pulls into a drive through.

We have a little bit of a tussle over paying for the food, but it's ended quickly since he's the one nearest the window to pay. He pushes my handful of cash away and hands over a card to the waiting attendant.

"Thank you!" Henry tells Kellen, taking the bag then devouring the biscuit like a starving hyena.

"You're welcome, buddy," Kellen tells my son, watching him in the rearview mirror with a small smile on his face.

"You're probably going to want to have it cleaned back there once you're shed of us," I say. "Kids are hard on car upholstery."

"Oh, my upholstery sees plenty of action."

When I chuckle, he says, "Oh...wait...no...I didn't mean that like it sounded." His neck turns pink above the collar of his shirt. "I mean I tend to go camping quite a bit and am always shoving equipment across the seat or sometimes, I'll even put the seat down to put a blow-up mattress in the back to sleep on if the location isn't conducive to a tent."

"Camping, huh?"

That starts an entire conversation about camping. Based upon the number of locations he talks about, it's obvious that he's quite a seasoned outdoorsman. It's also obvious that he loves it.

I notice he keeps an eye on Henry in the backseat. Once the breakfast was sucked down in record time, unsurprisingly, Henry fell back to sleep. He's still catching up after being up so late last night. As soon as he started dozing off, Kellen lowered his voice, but kept the conversation going.

I appreciate his attentiveness to Henry. It's important that anyone who is going to be in my life, whether friend or more, knows that Henry is a part of it. If they can't make room for him, they aren't worth my time.

I am also not blind to the fact that some men target single mothers specifically for their children. Kellen doesn't give me a pedophilic vibe at all, though. However, until I'm completely comfortable with him, I won't leave them alone together unless I can monitor them.

We're passing through Moore when my phone pings with a message. It's the dealership letting me know that one of my tires needs to be replaced and that it will be a while longer than expected because they don't have the size I need and will have to have it sent over from one of their sister dealerships. I glance at Henry in the back seat.

"What's up?" Kellen asks.

I tell him the problem and he volunteers to take us home instead of dropping us at the dealership. That really would be the best option. "Thank you, Kellen. I appreciate it. Henry will probably be out for a little longer, and I'd rather let him get caught up on his sleep."

"Sure. It's not a problem at all. Like I said earlier, my day is wide open."

"Yes, but I would think you have other things to do that are better than carting around me and my kid."

"Nope," he says. "I enjoy spending time with you and Henry."

I'm watching him and notice his hands tighten on the steering wheel. It's unclear if it is because he is not being truthful or if he's nervous about making such an admission to me. Still watching him, I reply, "I enjoy spending time with you as well, and Henry is crazy about you."

I see his hands relax. So it was the nervous admission, then. "My Dad is great with Henry," I continue, "but he can't see the world for the plants and, well, you apparently know Robert McLean."

"Yes, we've done some work for the McLean's, and I went out with their daughter once. Turns out she didn't really like me that much, she only pursued me because her father pushed her to. He was hoping to connect his family to mine. I never knew Jeremiah, though."

"That sounds just like Robert." I look down at my hands in my lap. "Jeremiah was very different from the rest of his family."

"You must miss him terribly," he says quietly.

"I wish he was still here to see his son growing up so fast, but he is not and cannot be. My grief was profound. Honestly, even though it was nine years ago that he died, I feel like I only started to move beyond just making it through each day in the past few years."

I see so much of him in Henry sometimes that it takes my breath away. Now, more than anything, I'm glad my son carries so much of his father in himself so that he can understand something about Jeremiah. He's sensitive and intelligent like his father, but he likes a lot of things that are different from other boys, so he has a hard time fitting in.

We've spent a lot of time with a friend's family and they have several children. But those kids are extremely close with their cousins, and it's difficult for Henry to break into the close-knit group.

That's my biggest worry for him. Beyond me and my parents, he doesn't really have any friends. I work really hard to let him know that there's nothing wrong with being different and that as he grows up, things will change, but it's just not the same when it's your mom telling you that instead of your dad.

I don't know why, but I share all of this with Kellen. Maybe it's because I recognize him as being a different kind of man from his brothers and realize that he must have had similar experiences as Henry. Maybe it's just because I'm tired of feeling like I'm carrying so much of this alone.

Tears start to prickle. It's just an aftereffect of letting go of the adrenaline that was surging through me when I confronted Robert. Yeah, that's all it is. Adrenaline burn off.

My parents think Henry hung the moon and have a hard time seeing how his quirks impact him out in the world, so after a few attempts, I haven't brought it up. They think I'm worried for no reason and brush it off.

I love my parents and love how they love my boy, but I learned a long time ago that they have a hard time seeing beyond their personal experience. I self-parented for most of my life because I had a drive and ambition to which they simply could not relate.

I start to reach for my purse for a tissue when Kellen puts his hand on mine and tucks a handkerchief into my palm. I turn my hand in his and hold it for a moment before using the gift to wipe my damp cheeks.

"Sorry," I say with a humorless laugh, "I don't know what brought all of that on."

"Well, considering it probably wouldn't have been a good thing for Henry to see you kick his grandpa's ass, a few tears to release the anger is a good alternative," Kellen says, looking serious.

My eyes slide to him, completely thrown, until I see the corner of his mouth quirk up. I shove his shoulder playfully and let a little laugh sneak out before I stop it with a glance to the back seat to make sure I haven't wakened Henry.

"He's still asleep," Kellen assures me, smiling fully now.

I watch him for a moment. "You have a great smile," I tell him honestly.

He keeps looking at the road, but I see the tips of his ears turn pink. We're in Norman now, so I give him directions to my house. Once we're parked in the driveway, he looks at it for a few long moments through the windshield while I gather my things.

"This is your house?"

"Yes, wonderful, isn't it? It was bequeathed to me by a dear friend." I get out of the car and start to open the back for Henry, but Kellen's already unbuckling him.

"I've got him," he says. "You'll need to get the door."

He's right, I know, so I open the door between the driveway and the kitchen and hold it for him to pass through. I put my things on the kitchen island and lead him upstairs to Henry's bedroom.

For someone without children or nieces and nephews to gain experience with, he handles Henry easily, setting my boy gently onto the bed without waking him. We back out of the room and pull the door mostly closed before going back downstairs.

Kellen is slow behind me, taking everything in. I can't blame him. Bert's house is beautifully designed and decorated except for the toys that hide in corners and under the sofas and chairs. The artwork has been supplemented by Henry's creations plastered on the refrigerator door and walls in the office, though, and those are priceless.

"I'd give you a tour," I tell him, "but with so much open space and glass, you can pretty well see everything. Do you want something to drink?"

"It's beautiful," Kellen says. "Just some water would be good, thanks."

"Thank you. It's all Bert, though. I can't take any credit." I take down a glass and fill it from the filtered water in the refrigerator, then put it in front of him and do the same for myself.

"Bert?"

I tell him the story of meeting Bert and how I came to be his primary heir. "My Dad has changed some things in the yard and added some of his favorite plants, but other than Henry's paraphernalia that you see pretty much everywhere, it's mostly how Bert left it. The house across the street that has the same exterior look as this one is the guest house, and it's where my parents live."

"That's convenient," he replies.

"It is. I love that they're able to be so close." I sidle up onto one of the stools at the kitchen island. "So, Mr. Kellen Masters, I feel you know quite a lot about me. Tell me about you."

He looks down at his glass. I can almost see the cloak of shyness come over him. He shrugs.

"There's not much to tell, really. I'm the youngest of three brothers and much younger than the other two. Beckett was seven and Morgan was nine when I was born. I guess I was sort of an oops baby. I went to high school at Edmond North, math and chess club, no sports. College at TU for a bachelor's in accounting followed with an MBA. I went to work in the family business after graduation and have been there ever since."

I watch him as he speaks. It's all said without emotion. "You obviously like to read. What else do you like to do for fun besides reading and camping? What are you passionate about?"

His head snaps up at that, as if I've asked him to reveal his darkest secrets. He's very tense for a moment, then he starts to relax.

"Yes, reading and camping. A good hiking trail nearby is a requirement for my campsite choices, but that's about it. I'm just a simple guy."

I hold his eyes for a few long heartbeats, then smirk. "Oh, I think there's a whole lot more to you than that and I would not classify you as simple in any way, shape, or form."

Henry comes down the stairs and shuffles to the kitchen.

"Hey buddy, you feeling better?" I ask.

He nods and rubs his eyes with the heels of his hands as he comes to me and holds out his arms. I pick him up and put his rump on the kitchen counter. He slumps against me and puts his head on my shoulder as I stroke my hands across his back.

I love it when he's all snuggly like this. It won't be long before I won't be able to lift him any longer and I'm going to miss it keenly.

My phone dings, so I lean over to look at it. "Well, that's good timing. My car's ready; do you think you're ready for a car ride or do you still need to wake up a bit, buddy?"

He sits up, flings his arms out wide and stretches, yawning enormously. When he's finished working out the kinks, he sighs and slumps, and nods. "Can we get lunch while we're out? I'm hungry again."

"I'm not surprised. Yes, we can get lunch."

"Can Mr. Kellen come?"

"If he wants to. He needs to take us to get the car first, though, before the dealership closes."

Henry turns to Kellen. "Wanna come to lunch, Mr. Kellen? Nana's gone, so we get to eat out."

I hurry to explain. "Mom usually does all the cooking, but she and my dad are in Tulsa, visiting my sister and her family until Monday. I'm not much of a cook, so I might keep us from starving, but neither of us would be happy about it. Therefore, we tend to eat out when Mom's not here."

Kellen smiles. "I see. I'd love to have lunch with you."

We pick up my car and take it back home, then go to Henry's favorite chicken restaurant. It's his favorite because he gets to go to the playground in the restaurant as soon as he's eaten his food.

Kellen and I sit and talk some more while we watch the kids climbing and crawling all over the place. The conversation is lighter, but I keep drawing information out of him, and he seems to be trying to draw more information out of me, too.

I don't mind. We've got a good flow going on between us, as he gives as much information as he gets. He's starting to relax around me and not censor every word, and the more I get below the surface, the more I like.

Henry comes over and stands next to me and waits for Kellen to finish speaking. I put my arm around him, and he leans against my side. As soon as Kellen stops talking, Henry dives in. "Mom. I'm done. Can we go to PlayDay?"

"I don't think I'm up to that today, buddy. How about we do pizza and a movie tonight instead?"

"Okay. Can I go swimming when we get home?"

"Yes, you may."

"Mr. Kellen, do you want to go swimming in our pool?"

"I don't have any swim trunks with me, Bud, but I would otherwise," Kellen answers.

When we get to the house, I can tell Kellen would like to stay. Without taking any advice from my brain, my mouth says, "I probably have a pair of trunks you could use if you want to swim. I keep some on hand for when my brothers visit." Then my brain catches up and I add, "But you don't have to if you don't want to. You might be kidded out by now."

He smiles. Gosh, he has a really good smile. "Nope, not yet."

I get him a pair of trunks and show him to one of the extra bedrooms to change. I change into my suit, grab towels, and sunscreen, then meet the boys downstairs.

They're already in the water with Henry in 'look at what I can do' overdrive, trying to show Kellen every trick he knows from somersaults to handstands. I get an "Aww, Mom!" when I make him get out of the pool so I can put waterproof sunscreen on him. I slather myself in the goop and leave it out for Kellen to use if he wants.

I circle the perimeter of the pool before choosing my launch point. I yell, "Cannonball!" before I run and jump into the pool, tucking my legs and aiming to land near Henry to splash him as much as possible. When I surface, I hear him giggling and as soon as my head appears, he starts splashing me back.

I alternate between swimming and sitting on one of the lounge chairs in the shade, watching. Kellen is in and out of the pool, too, but seems to have as much energy as Henry does. It's surprising that he never appears to tire of Henry's requests to be thrown in the air or to watch him do something.

I probably spend too much time allowing my eyes to linger on the flex of muscles every time Kellen tosses Henry in the air or swims across the surface in races he almost always lets Henry win. I also look a little too often at the smattering of dark hair on his chest that thins out across his stomach and disappears into the top of his swim trunks.

Kellen laughs with my boy, races him across the length of the pool about a million times, and smiles frequently, allowing his enjoyment of the day to show through easily. When he's not in the pool, he talks with me, the dance of getting to know each other continuing.

It takes longer than I expected for Henry to get tired out, but I can see him starting to slow down, so I tell him it's time to get out. I don't want him to get so tired he needs a nap because if he naps, he'll be up until all hours, and I need to get him back on schedule. Even though it's summer and he doesn't have school, I try to keep him on his normal schedule mostly, so it's not such a big adjustment when school starts.

I send Henry to his room to shower with a reinforcement of using the shower, not the bathtub. He showers alone just fine, but bathing is a bit too much like playtime and he's constantly swirling and bouncing around in the tub. I don't trust the soapy water to keep him from slipping a little too fast and hitting his head, so he isn't allowed to bathe without supervision.

"If you want to shower off the chemicals before you dress, there's stuff in the en suite attached to the bedroom you changed in," I tell Kellen. "You can just leave the trunks in the bathroom."

"That's great, thanks," he says, rubbing his head with a towel as he makes his way down the hall.

I go to my own room and strip out of my suit, my skin feeling sensitive. I'm not sure if it's because of the sun exposure or the thoughts of a handsome naked man in the shower just down the hall.

Chapter 11

Kellen

Focus is eluding me. I stare at my computer and know I need to be working, but my thoughts keep wandering back to the day before. The entire day was spent with Demi and Henry from breakfast to well after dark.

After the swimming pool, Henry asked me if I would stay for pizza and movie night. How could I say no? Not to mention that I had absolutely no fucking desire to say no. The theater room in Demi's house was better than going to a real movie theater.

Of course, Henry zonked out about halfway through, and I had to heft him up the stairs again. I'm going to have to start upping my lifting game if I continue to hang out with them and I fully intend to hang out with them as much as possible. I can't remember another day when I felt so happy and relaxed and able to just be myself.

Demi is incredible. Smart. Amazing. Beautiful. Fantastic. Kind. I can't come up with enough words to say how great I think she is. I am completely, utterly, unequivocally infatuated with her.

And Henry, he's such a good kid. I can't imagine someone like him coming from the lineage of the McLean's. All of my dealings with him have not changed my mind that Robert McLean is an absolute pompous ass. A big part of me wants to help Demi create for Henry what I never had, a safe place for him to just be who he is.

I always felt that from Mom, but it was overshadowed by everyone else in my immediate family. I don't think they intended for it to be that way, but it was. Dad was most bonded with Morgan, and Beckett has never needed anyone's permission to be who he wants.

I didn't get the gregarious, outgoing genes that Beckett did, though. Morgan's take charge alpha dog demeanor wasn't embedded in me, either. Introverted nerd was dumped into my genes in excess, so to the core of our beings we couldn't be more different.

I may only ever be friends with Demi and Henry and if that's all that happens, I'll have to find a way to be okay with that. However, more is what I want, so much more.

I am incredibly attracted to Demi. Last night when I left, I wanted so badly to kiss her. But I could tell that it would have been a bad move.

She lost her fiancé and the father of her child. That had to be so hard on her to lose Jeremiah unexpectedly and then give birth two months later.

I can see why she's still grieving in some ways. An infant is no respecter of grief, nor a toddler. She had to put her own sorrow on hold to focus on caring for her child.

My desire to know her better is driving me to look into what happened to Jeremiah. I also want to see what information I can discover about Demi. I'm not trying to be a stalker; I just want to know more about her, and digging up information is one of my superpowers.

My focus comes online as soon as I pull up a browser window to do some research. Between Demi, Jeremiah, and even Bert, I'm lost to the act of chasing rabbit trails for hours when my phone rings. My heart lurches, thinking it might be Demi.

"Hello," I answer, trying not to sound too eager.

"Hi Kellen; whatcha up to?" It is a woman, but it's not Demi, it's Belinda.

Belinda was a friend. We were friends for a long time, and she was usually my plus one whenever I needed someone to attend an event with me. However, a little over a year ago, she made it clear that she wanted to be more than friends.

I was completely blindsided and had no idea she felt that way, particularly since I did not. Not at all. There wasn't anything I could think of that I'd done to encourage her to think I felt even a little bit that way.

She was persistent, but I kept telling her I didn't want anything more than friendship. Then I fucked up. It was Valentine's Day, and I was feeling low and lonely and had way too much to drink and gave in to her.

We had one night of sex. It was one of the stupidest things I've ever done. I told her the next day that it had been a mistake. She was hurt and angry at first, but then it seemed like everything was fine and we went back to being friends, or so I thought.

She kept pushing and pushing, and finally, I had enough. We went to a charity dinner with my family, and she gave me an ultimatum to either be her boyfriend or we couldn't be friends anymore. I respect her setting boundaries, but things didn't go the way she wanted.

I broke it off, finally and completely, no friendship, no plus one, no nothing. That was back in May and that's the way I've handled it. I do not contact her for anything.

Unfortunately, she keeps contacting me. Every couple of weeks, she'll call me. Just to check up on me, she says, but I know she's trying to keep a foot in the door.

I can't let this go on. It's not fair to her and I need to find some way to make it crystal clear so that she can move on. Letting some frost into my voice, I ask, "Why are you calling Belinda?"

"I was just thinking about you and thought I'd check in."

I shake my head, even though I know she can't see me. "No, Belinda. You've got to stop this. I told you, we're done; there's no friendship or anything else between us anymore. I'm sorry I hurt you. I'm sorry you were misled, but if I hadn't been intoxicated that night, nothing physical would have ever happened between us. You want a boyfriend, and I will never be that because I just don't have those kinds of feelings for you. It's time for you to move on."

"But Kellen..."

"No, Belinda. Just no. I don't want to be mean, but there's no point in continuing this."

"Um...okay. Bye, Kellen."

I don't say goodbye. I just hang up. Having to be so harsh to her makes me feel like crap, but it needed to be done because she just wasn't getting it and I need her to get it. It's been months. It's time.

When she gave me an ultimatum, I'd been proud of her for setting a boundary. Just because it didn't get the outcome she desired, I will respect her boundary. Looking back, I can see it probably wasn't a boundary at all, but an attempt at manipulation. Regardless, she set it. I'm respecting it and she needs to respect my decision.

With the research desire out of my system, maybe I can get some work done. I need to. I'm starting to fall behind and need to catch up. Well, not really behind in any way but my own mindset, but it feels like I'm behind, so it might as well be reality.

I open my document and spreadsheet to see where I left off and what comes next, then settle in, my focus restored.

Chapter 12

Demeter

This entire week feels like I've been running at Mach 2 with my hair on fire and it's only Wednesday. I barely make it to class on time, racing in the door just in time to take my place with the other students. Gabriella gives me a concerned look, but I wave her off to let her know I'm fine.

Mom and Dad got home Monday afternoon. Dad groused about the traffic for a couple of hours before he went to their house to watch television and Mom groused about his grousing. They're almost as bad as Henry is when his routine gets disrupted.

Then my clients yesterday and today have been especially needy with more emotional breakdowns in a two-day time period than I think I've had with them over the past year. Sex is supposed to be fun people!

I'm ready to punch somebody and burn off some of this stress. This class should be just the ticket to get back on track. If I'd been able to get here early to go a round with Victor, it would have been even better, but I'll take what I can get.

I settle my mind and go through the warm-up motions, trying to lose myself in the repetitive movements. When I open my eyes, Ricky is staring at me. He's new to class and although he hasn't done anything overt except stare, he gives me the creeps.

We break up into pairs to spar. I'm with Gabriella as usual and Ricky is paired with the only other woman in our class, Billie. We get in the groove, throwing punches and kicks, practicing dodges and blocks. I'm not paying attention to anything but the dance between Ella and me when I hear Gunnar bark out, "Stop!"

Everyone stops immediately, adopting a version of the military's parade rest stance.

"What was that, Ricky?" Gunnar asks.

"Nothing! It was nothing. She's overreacting."

I see Billie doubled over with a hand on her ribs.

"I don't think so. You're benched," Gunnar barks, signaling at the row of benches on the outer wall. "Billie, let Victor check you out to see if you can continue."

Ricky stomps over to the bench, muttering under his breath. I can just make out what he's saying, and it's not good. He's using words like 'cunt' and 'bitch' and I know he's going to be a problem for the three women in class.

He sees me watching him and must not like the look on my face because when he passes by, he bumps into me hard. My reaction is automatic as my training kicks in, a foot swipes out to throw him off balance. My arms capitalize on his momentum. In the blink of an eye, he's on the floor looking up at me.

I may be the smallest person in the class and a woman, but I've worked hard to gain the skills I need to protect myself and will not let some asshole use me as his punching bag. Never again will I be a victim. Someone might try to victimize me again, but I'll make them regret it when I fight back with everything in me.

Ricky is extremely pissed off. He gets to his feet and growls. I flick a gaze to Gunnar, and he gives me a slight nod, letting me know it's my choice. Either he will stop it, or I can use it to teach Ricky a lesson about targeting women. I nod back.

Ricky comes at me again, and I use the same move, putting him on the floor. The frustration from the week has abated a bit, but it's still there, lurking under the surface. A throw down with Ricky would be a good way to burn it off.

"I heard what you were saying Ricky and women are not cunts," I say firmly.

He pops to his feet and swings a fist wildly at me. I dodge it easily and land a kick to his ribs. We're wearing safety gear, so I make it hard enough that he feels it, but not enough to do any actual damage.

I could, though. Because of my size, my leg strength has been something I've focused on. I could crack, or maybe even break, a rib if I put all my power into it.

"Women are not bitches," I say.

He's got his hands up now, bobbing and weaving like he's a prizefighter in the boxing ring. He jabs, I slide away from it easily and tap him on the back in a taunt. Controlling the mind is a part of Krav Maga. Allowing someone to push you into an emotional space is considered a weakness.

That's exactly what I'm trying to do with Ricky when I say, "You should be careful because one of these days when you hit a woman, she might just hit you back and maybe even kick your ass."

He throws punches. I dodge and block them easily, then sweep his legs. Once he's down, I get him into an armlock and bear down with it until he taps out. In this position, I could dislocate his shoulder with enough pressure.

I let him up, turn my back to him, and am starting to walk away when I hear Gunnar bark, "Ricky!"

I drop and roll and barely miss what would have been a kick to the middle of my back. That's it; I'm pissed. I pop to my feet, my arms in guard position, ready to fight in earnest when Victor steps in front of me. My arms drop to my sides and I stand stock still. Ricky backs off.

It's close to time for class to be over, so Gunnar dismisses everyone but Ricky. I'm sure he's going to be counseled on appropriate behavior in the classroom. He'll either get it, apologize and continue in the class, or he won't, and we'll have an opening in the class again.

"That was crazy," Ella says as we walk out of the building.

"He was crazy," I reply. "I hope he doesn't come back. Guys like that deserve to have their asses kicked."

"So true! Will we see you tomorrow night?"

"I hope so, but my clients have been off the charts this week, so I'm not going to say yes, or I'll jinx myself."

"Okay, we'll hope." She gives me a hug before we say good night.

I get in my car, and my stomach growls its displeasure at not being fed before class. There simply hadn't been time. A deli is between here and home that would be an easy stop and probably not too busy at this time of night, so I head that way.

I get out of the car thinking maybe I should have changed clothes or something, but decide that the deli folks will have to tolerate me being stinky and sweaty from the workout. I'll just get a sandwich to go and eat it in the car on the way home.

After I place my order and turn to sit on the bench they have for folks waiting for carry out orders. My eyes land on Kellen Masters sitting there, totally absorbed in typing something on his phone.

"Typing out War and Peace?" I ask, stopping to stand in front of him.

"Huh?" he asks, looking up at me with owl eyes, oblivious to the world around him until now. "Demi, hi! Just making some notes. What are you doing here?"

"Just got out of class, sorry about the stink...and the sweat. I'm starving, so I thought I'd just pop in and get a sandwich to eat on the way home. What are you doing here?"

"Worked late. Didn't feel like cooking."

"You cook?"

He nods. "Yeah, most of the time. Want to eat in instead of in the car?"

"I can spare about thirty minutes, provided you don't mind the smell. I'll miss getting updated on Henry's story if I'm later than that."

"Thirty minutes, got it."

He looks at his watch, and I smile. Leave it to Kellen to take me so literally. Of course, I was being fairly literal myself, so there's that.

His order comes up first, then mine soon after. We slide into a booth, sitting across from each other. I'm so hungry, I eat quickly and that leaves me free to just talk. It feels nice to have a conversation with an adult where I'm not trying to help them solve their problems.

The more time we spend together, the more relaxed Kellen is. I enjoy seeing this side of him and am glad he feels comfortable enough around me to not have to watch everything he says. He's even kind of funny in a nerdy sort of way.

The old feeling of being watched starts to tingle at the back of my neck, so I sit up straight in my seat. I look around the restaurant but except for us, there's only a very few other people in the place at this hour. No one seems to be paying inordinate attention to us.

Half expecting to see Ricky, I look out the window to the parking lot and don't see anyone there, either, but the angle of the sun makes it difficult to get a clear view of the area. In an effort to settle my heart rate, I take a deep breath to calm myself and gain control before I start to hyperventilate. I notice I've got a death grip on my napkin and relax my hand.

"What's wrong?" Kellen asks, watching me.

I shake my head. "I, uh...I'm not sure there's anything wrong, but I got the feeling I'm being watched. It's probably just the stressful week I've had. When I'm really stressed, the old panic attacks can creep up on me or I'll start getting paranoid feelings of being watched again."

"Old panic attacks?"

"Oh, Gabriella knows, and since I'm working with her on handling the aftermath of her attack, I thought maybe she told more than just Morgan. It's not like I try to hide it. After all, the papers covered the story and trials when it happened, so it's not a secret."

He looks at me blankly, so I go on, but leave out the gorier details. "My first year on campus at OU, I was abducted. Because the cops intervened quickly, I was lucky, but not before I was beaten severely. I had the same kinds of panic attacks and nightmares as Gabriella's experiencing since her attack."

He just looks at me for several moments, his face unreadable. "You said trials."

I nod. "Yes, there were five people involved. Three went to prison, one got a suspended sentence and probation for testifying against the others, and one got off because his family had lots of money and connections."

"Do you worry about him coming back?"

"No, he's dead. I killed him," I say with a shake of my head, then hurry on to clarify. "In self-defense, of course."

He checks his watch. "Oh! Your thirty minutes is up. You'd better get home to Henry."

Well, it looks like I may have squashed any budding interest Kellen might have had in me for friendship. I'm disappointed. He's a good guy; he would have made a good friend. Better that it happened now rather than later because I've been feeling sparks of interest and it's best that those don't get out of hand.

I gather my trash and throw it away, Kellen doing the same. We leave the restaurant together and he walks me to my car. I start to get in, but he hesitates just outside the open door, looking down at me. The sun is behind him, casting a halo around his body.

I'm just about to ask him if there's something he needs when he takes a deep breath and says, "Demi, I was wondering if maybe you'd like to go out sometime."

It comes out in a rush, and I can see his ears pink in embarrassment. He smiles shyly and looks down. "Sorry, I knew if I didn't get it out, I'd lose my nerve."

My automatic reaction is to say no because that's been my reaction to anyone who has shown even a minor interest in me for the past nine years, but I take a beat and smile back at him. "Are you asking me out, or me and Henry?"

He's still not looking at me in the eye. "Well, as much as I think Henry's pretty great, I was thinking maybe it might be nice to go out, just you and me, and if that goes well, we can take Henry next time."

"I think that sounds nice. Yes, I would love to go out on a date with you, Kellen. You have my phone number. Just let me know some potential days that work for you, and we'll plan something."

Now he looks at me, a huge grin spreading across his face. He looks so boyish and pleased. "What? Really?"

I nod, matching his grin. "Yes, really."

"Okay, I'll call you."

"Perfect," I say and get into my car.

"Good night, Demi, tell Henry hi for me."

"I will. Good night, Kellen."

Just like that, I have a date. Slow down and hold your horses, my brain says. You're supposed to just be friends. Then my stomach flutters at the thought of a date, completely ignoring my brain, and those sparks of interest start flaring. It will be the first date I've been on in almost a decade.

Ho-ly shit.

Chapter 13

Demeter

T hursday goes much smoother than the previous part of the week. I find myself in a particularly good mood. My last client for the day canceled so I have time to go home, change, and spend some time with my little guy before I go to have dinner at the Society.

I have pared down my schedule so that I only see clients Tuesday through Thursday. During the summer months, that gives me two extra days to spend with Henry and I wouldn't trade them for the world. He's growing up so fast that soon he won't be so enamored with hanging out with Mom, so I'll enjoy it while I can.

I could cut back even more because I really don't have to work. However, I love what I do, and I'll keep doing it. Someday there may be a reason to stop working, but for now, I don't see one.

As I get closer to my car, I see a piece of paper under the wiper. At first, I think someone must be passing out flyers again. It's posted that it's not allowed, but that doesn't stop people from leaving them from time to time.

When I look around, though, I don't see anything on any of the other cars. I pull the paper off the windshield and turn it over. It is a drawing that looks like a child's handiwork.

Two stick figures are drawn in crayon sitting in what appears to be a diner booth. One has swirls of yellow hair and the other has waves of black hair. The words are not at all something a child would write, despite the handwriting that even includes backward letters.

Deli Girl and Deli Boy, they look so happy and full of joy

But Deli Girl shouldn't trust Deli Boy, cuz he thinks women are just a toy

Deli...as in the deli I was in last night with a man with dark wavy hair? What the hell is this? Does Kellen have a girlfriend or something? If he does have a girlfriend, why is she leaving something like this on my car and why in the hell would he be asking me out? How would she know about me?

The feeling of being watched last night comes back to me. This is just creepy. I get into the car, take a photo of the drawing, and promptly send it to Kellen.

Me: *This was on my car at my office. Care to comment?*

I decide to forego heading home and call Gabriella. I'm hoping she can tell me if Kellen has a girlfriend. Maybe she can; maybe she can't. From everything she's told me, Kellen isn't particularly close with anyone in his family except his mother.

She answers and is at the studio, so I ask her if I can stop by. She agrees, so I head north on the highway. Part of me wants to be angry, but I remind myself that I am jumping to conclusions.

It does make me think that maybe I'm better off going back to not dating yet. Or ever.

I stew in my thoughts all the way to Ella's studio. How could I have been so stupid? I didn't see any sign that might indicate that he was being untruthful. Maybe it's a game he plays.

Stop it. You're jumping to conclusions again. You are a rational adult, so calm the fuck down and be rational. Gather information and use it to guide your decisions.

I turn the radio up to keep my mind from roaming. It doesn't work. Thankfully, traffic is uncharacteristically light, and I make it to Ella's studio in record time.

My phone dings with an incoming message.

Kellen: *What is this? Where are you now? Are you ok?*

I suck in a breath, reminding myself again to be rational. Why is this effecting me so much?

Me: *I have no idea. That's why I was asking you. Ella's studio. I don't know, am I?*

I turn off the sound on my phone and go into the studio. "Hey!" Ella says, looking up from her drafting table with a smile. "What's up?"

I slap the piece of paper onto the cabinet next to where she's working. She picks it up and looks at it, her brows drawn together.

"What's this?" she asks.

"I have no idea; it was on my car when I came out of the office. I think it's supposed to be Kellen and me. We ran into each other last night at the deli over by class. I was just going to get something to go, and he was already there waiting for an order. We stayed in and ate together."

"Ate together, huh?" she asks, grinning.

"Yes, and it's not the first time we've been together. On Saturday, he brought me Henry's book that I missed picking up when I left the party on Friday night. He ended up spending the whole day with Henry and me, from breakfast to dinner and a movie. He asked me out on a date last night. Does he have a girlfriend? Or a recently ex-girlfriend?"

"Wow! He asked you out?"

"Ella! Focus. Girlfriend? Crazy ex-girlfriend? Do either exist?"

"Sorry, yes. I mean, no, not that I'm aware of. I have only seen Kellen with a date once. We went to the homebuilder's charity fundraiser back in early May, and Kellen had a date there. It was the first time I met him. The woman's name was Brenda, or something like that, and they didn't really seem to like each other much. Rebecca kept trying to talk to her, but the woman pretty much ignored her. Kellen's nose was buried in his phone, as usual."

"And that was in May? Two months ago? And you haven't seen her or anyone else since?"

She shakes her head. "Yes, May, two months ago. No one else, but we haven't been to any other events like that one where he'd be expected to bring a date."

I stare at the page. A big part of me wants to be mad. I want to just drop everything related to Kellen and go on as if he was never even a blip on my radar.

I sigh. That's just my fear talking and I know that. The prospect of a new relationship terrifies me as much as it intrigues me. Right now, the fear is jumping all over this as an excuse to shut things down before they go any further.

"I think I need to talk to Kellen," I say.

"Yeah, seems like. So, he asked you out, huh?" I look over to see her grinning at me again.

I can't help but smile back. "Yes, and I said yes. He is a completely different person when you get him off by himself."

"Yeah. I can see how that would be true. At first, I thought he was just a cold fish and kind of an asshole. Now that I've had some time to observe the family's dynamics, I think it's something deeper. It makes my heart hurt for him, but I don't know how to fix it. His mom adores him, but Declan, their dad, only seems to talk to Morgan. Morgan is juggling so many different things that he's oblivious and Beckett, if something doesn't benefit him, he's unlikely to care."

I start to answer when the door to the studio flies open. It's Kellen, breathing hard and looking panicked. He huffs out a breath and focuses on me. "Oh good, you're still here."

"Kellen, my car is parked out front," I answer.

"You could have walked somewhere. I came right over because I had to talk to you."

"Yes, I believe I need to talk to you, too." I hand the paper to him. "Do you know who might have put this on my car?"

He looks at it, frowning. "No."

"No girlfriend? No ex-girlfriend?"

"What?" he asks, confused. "No. I haven't had a girlfriend in a long time. Years."

"What about Brenda?" Ella asks.

"Who?"

"The woman you took to the homebuilder's fundraiser," she supplies.

"Oh, Belinda. No, she was just a friend." He stiffens as he says it, as if something is occurring to him as the words come out of his mouth.

"What was that thought you just had?" I ask.

He deflates. "It could be her."

He tells us about their friendship and her desire for more. He seems embarrassed when he gets to the part about Valentine's Day, when he got drunk, and ended up having sex with her. To my ears, it sounds as if he fell into a trap she laid for him, disguised as a home cooked dinner at her house with liberal amounts of booze applied.

The night when Ella first met him was the night he broke things off with Belinda. He had intended to do it after, but she was reading more into being invited than he intended. Although he had hoped they could still do the friendly plus one thing, once you've stepped over a line, you can't uncross it.

If she was following him last night, she could have easily followed me home and then to work this morning. I thought I was done with being stalked and having to look over my shoulder, but I guess I was wrong.

"Please, don't worry," Kellen says. "I'll take care of this."

"Okay. I believe you will," I say. "However, because I have Henry to think of, it's probably not a good idea for us to see each other until you can resolve the situation. I just can't risk Belinda, or whoever it is, doing something that might impact him."

He's visibly disappointed, but he nods. "You're right. I could never forgive myself if anything happened to Henry."

"Speaking of Henry, I'm sorry Ella, but I think I'm going to skip dinner at the Society tonight and go on home."

"I understand," she says. "Give him a hug from me."

"I will, and I'll tell him you said hello, Kellen."

"Thanks, I appreciate that," he says.

He looks so sad, but I can't focus on that. I have to focus on what's best for Henry.

Chapter 14

Kellen

"Fuck," I say after Demi leaves. "The three of us had such a good day. I can't remember the last time I felt that relaxed and happy. Hell, I don't know if I ever have been. I should have known it was too good to be true."

"It's not over, Kellen."

My eyes go wide. I'd forgotten Gabriella was here. I shake my head. "You don't have to patronize me, Gabriella. Something always happens to ruin things, but it's usually that the woman I was interested in would meet one of my brothers and lose all interest in me."

"Kellen, I'm serious. Demi was excited to go out with you so it's only over if you want it to be over. Deal with Belinda and try again with Demi. She really does like you."

"Are you telling the truth?"

"Do you honestly think I'd encourage you if I didn't know for a fact that she's interested in you?"

I shake my head. "No."

"So, what are we going to do about Belinda?"

"We?"

"Yes, we. Morgan and I might not be married yet, but I consider you to be my family. When trouble comes knocking, family sticks together."

I feel my lips quirk. "I'm glad you and Morgan found each other."

"Me, too," she says. "You'll never know just how much. He saved me." She pauses, her gaze going vacant for a moment before she comes back to herself. "Anyway, that's a story for another day. Back to Belinda."

I talk it over with her. I'm not sure what she might be able to do to help the situation, but it helps to know she's there. It's good to get her input so I can see things from a woman's point of view to help me know how to deal with Belinda.

I had no idea Belinda was apparently following me. It only occurs to me now that her inability to let go might indicate some deeper mental issue. I would have never thought she had those kinds of issues, but I'm no expert.

At first, I thought that maybe the way I talked to her on Sunday might have triggered her. However, I have a feeling that it has probably been going on for a while. Possibly since May, when I first broke things off with her.

I should have completely stopped talking to her then, blocked her number and refused to take her calls. She might have felt encouraged because I would continue to answer when she called. Leave it to me to attract a woman who won't take no for an answer.

First, I need to find out what Belinda is doing without her knowing. I need to know if she's following me or, God forbid, Demi. Gabriella suggests that I should talk to Morgan about hiring a private investigator.

The minute she says I should bring in one of my brothers, I want to drop the whole thing with her. Morgan has never seen me as anything more than a nuisance, and I tell her so. She tries to tell me I'm wrong, but I have a lifetime of experience to go on and she hasn't even been around a year yet.

She tries to get me to come to dinner at their house to talk things over with Morgan. He is, after all, ex-military and might have some unique insights. I can't fault her logic on that part, but I learned a long time ago to keep my expectations low when it comes to my family.

She has a dinner to get to, so I thank her and tell her I'll think about it, but my mind's made up. I'll have to find an investigator on my own and hope I pick a good one. Once I leave to go home, I keep one eye on my rearview mirror the entire way to see if I can tell if I'm being followed.

When I get home, I try to start looking for private detectives, but I'm too wired. I can recognize that I won't be able to focus, so I change clothes to go for a run. It's hotter than hell outside, but I need to burn off some energy or I'll never get to sleep tonight. I probably won't, anyway. Wearing out my body won't help my brain settle down.

After a night of tossing and turning, I give up trying to sleep and go into the office. It's not unusual for me to be the first one in and the last one to leave. As the person in charge of overseeing both finances and human resources for the company, there's always plenty of work for me to do.

I'm in the middle of going over the reconciliation reports from one of our accounting clerks when Morgan sticks his head into my door. "Kel, I need you in my office."

I look up. "What? Why?"

My questions fall flat as I see his back disappearing down the hall headed to his office. My oldest brother is a big man. His tall, broad-shouldered build made him an excellent candidate for the front line of the football team in high school.

I can still remember how pleased I was to be his little brother, sitting in the stands, cheering him on. I was still in grade school when he graduated, then went into the military. When he came home, I was older, but in short order, he was running the company and had no time for his nerdy kid brother.

When I graduated from college, no one asked me what I wanted. I was expected to come into the business and got all of this dumped on me to bring it into some semblance of order.

The company was bleeding money like crazy and on the verge of having to file bankruptcy because no one was tracking anything properly. I'm the one who kept the company from going belly up, but if you ask anyone in the family, or the entire company for that matter, Morgan gets all the credit.

I sigh and get up from my desk. The boss has spoken, so it's up to me to follow. I go down the hall to his office and find both him and Gabriella waiting there.

I stop in the hallway. "I don't have time for this," I tell them, shooting a glare at Gabriella.

"Get your goddamn ass in here, now. Whatever you're doing, it can wait," Morgan says, using his Captain of the Universe voice.

I go into the office and stand in front of his desk. "What do you want, Morgan?"

His voice softens. "Kel, please, sit down. Gabriella told me what's going on and I want to help."

"She shouldn't have told you. Don't worry about it; I'll handle it."

"Yes, she should have. She's worried for you, and I am, too."

"Don't be. I told you, I'm handling it."

"Dammit Kel, I'm your brother. What do you have against letting me help you?"

I can't help it. I should have just walked away and stuffed it all down like I always do, letting nothing show. Spending time with Demi has softened my walls and before I can stop myself, I snort. "Yeah, you're my brother by blood, but other than that, there's nothing brotherly between us. Never has been."

My head is screaming for me to shut up, but I plow on. "It's not your fault. There were too many years between us. I worshipped the ground you walked on when I was a kid. I cheered harder and louder than anyone when you were playing football and was so proud of my big brother, the Marine. You were too caught up with your friends and girlfriends, and your nerdy little brother was just a drag. When you came back from the military, I thought things would be different because I was older, you know. But it wasn't. Instead of friends and football, it was you and Dad and the company. I know he worked his ass off on this company for all of us and I'm thankful for that, but Dad's always only had eyes for the business, Mom, and you. Beckett's always been an asshole to me, but at least I existed to him."

Gabriella sucks in a breath. I know this is getting out of control, so I finally listen to my head and decide it is time to shut up.

I hold up a hand and say, "Listen, it's all water under the bridge now. We're adults and you're getting ready to get married and start a whole new chapter in your life. You've got something new to focus on and I really am happy for you. You've never wanted to know anything about me or my life, so there's no reason to start now. I've gotten used to handling things on my own and I can handle this, too."

Without looking at him, I turn on my heel and go back down the hall to my office and close the door. People are starting to filter into the building. I think if anyone were to come into my office right now, I'd probably take everything I'm feeling out on them.

I leave my door closed, focusing on reviewing the reports. It is an ever-present need to go over everything with a fine-tooth comb. Although I don't have to do all the foundational work, I watch the work of our accounting team like a hawk to ensure that everything lines up exactly like it is supposed to.

I've had to fire employees more than once for attempting to embezzle from the company in some way. With the amount of money flowing through our coffers, it is certainly tempting to some to see if they can get away with redirecting even a little bit of the funds into their own pockets. I finish the last report in my stack and sit back in my chair, rubbing my eyes.

There's a knock at my door. I'm much calmer now than I was this morning, so I say, "Come in."

Beckett sticks his head in the door. "I'm hungry; let's go to lunch."

I look at the time on my computer, surprised that it is, indeed, time for lunch. However, while my mood is better than it was, I'm not ready to deal with Beckett. "Sorry, Beck, I don't have time for one of your leisurely lunches today. I wouldn't be good company, anyway."

"Aww, come on. You know how I hate to eat alone. I won't do leisurely, I promise. We'll go somewhere quick, I swear. You'll be back in a flash."

He's not going to let it go. "Fine," I say.

"Excellent!"

We leave the parking lot in his car. It doesn't take long for me to figure out that I've been duped. He doesn't go to any restaurant; he's headed to our parent's house.

This is not going to be quick. It will probably eat up the rest of the day and be a whole lot of drama. Drama I could have avoided if I'd only kept my fucking mouth shut instead of puking my bullshit all over Morgan's desk.

"Fucking liar," I say under my breath.

"Yep," Beckett replies, unrepentant.

"Just take me back to the office."

"Nope."

We go into our parent's house, and I can smell the lunch that Mom has fixed. My stomach growls in response. I really am hungry, but I'd rather have my meal without the floor show I know is coming.

I go into the kitchen and say hello to Mom, but I can't bring myself to greet Gabriella. She's a nice person and I like her, but I let that kindness and the care I have for her lull me into complacency. I shouldn't have talked things over with her last night.

I know she's friends with Demi, but if I hadn't talked to her about the situation, maybe she would have let me handle it on my own. My lack of foresight that she'd tell Morgan was a mistake on my part. Lesson learned. I won't trust her like that again.

Beckett disappears to the den where I'm sure Dad and Morgan are. I go to the dining room and set the table just like I always do. When I go to the den, I usually end up on my phone typing out notes, but I don't have anything new to focus on right now.

The only conversations I typically keep track of are business related. They usually end in something else I get to take care of. Considering they're taking me away from being able to do all the things I need to take care of already, I don't think I'd be very accepting of something new being laid on me today.

So, I set the table. Slowly. Meticulously. I don't want to be in the den. I don't want to be in the kitchen. I don't even want to be in this house right now.

I go out to the refrigerator in the garage and get a beer, then go sit in my usual seat at the table. Beckett's driving, so maybe getting drunk will help me deal with what I know is coming. Mom raises her eyebrows when she comes into the room, carrying a dish of her lasagna.

She and Gabriella bring in all the food. Normally, I'd help, but well, you know, I'm not in the mood to be helpful. I'm about to get raked over the coals and be told I shouldn't feel the way I feel. So, I'm just going to sit here and fortify my armor with alcohol.

Chapter 15

Kellen

I drink down the beer and am coming back with another when I see the other men coming to the table. Before everyone else gets fully seated, I take my seat, serve myself, and start eating. It's rude, I know, but I can't bring myself to care. Today, my feelings are in the open. I'll apologize to Mom later.

We eat in silence for a few minutes when Morgan says, "I wanted us all to be together for lunch today because some things have been brought to light. It's something Gabriella has talked to me about, but I couldn't really see it for myself until today. I thought we were a big happy family because that was my reality, but I've come to understand that it's not everyone's."

Yep. It's going to be a clusterfuck. I keep eating, and don't look at him, but I am listening. That stupid little kid in me is hopeful, no matter how much I tell him nothing's going to change.

"I haven't been a very good big brother to Beckett and Kellen, but mostly not to Kellen, and I'm sorry for that. It changes today, though. I can't go back and fix the past, but I can certainly do better in the future. Gabriella is happy to kick my ass when I start letting things slide, and it's one of the many things I love about her. I don't know what I'd do without you in the business, Kel. Before you came on board, I was so stressed out I couldn't see straight. I knew we were on the verge of losing everything and I didn't know how to stop it."

Dad starts to speak, but Morgan holds up a hand. "You know it's true, Dad. Things were bad there for a while. Really bad. When Kellen agreed to come on board, he was able to turn it around to where now we're more profitable than we've ever been. Beckett's fantastic at bringing in new business and we're great about following through, but without Kellen, we'd still have no idea how to maximize those efforts."

I look up at him then.

He quirks a smile. "I'm maybe not completely oblivious, just mostly."

I give him an appreciative nod.

"Speaking of kicking asses when getting out of line, Beckett, you're going to stop being a constant asshole. I've always taken it in stride, but you don't constantly belittle me like you do Kel."

"I don't constantly belittle him," Beckett protests.

"If you say more than a single word to him, there's always an insult attached. I love you, but it's out of line. Even Henry noticed it."

"Who's Henry?" Beckett asks.

"Demi's son," Gabriella supplies, "and he's only eight."

"Jeezus," Beckett says, exasperated. "It's just a joke."

"Every once in a while, is a joke," Gabriella says, her voice hard. "Constantly is abuse. As someone who has also lived with this kind of constant negative input, I can tell you it's not funny."

Beckett just looks at her, his face petulant.

"I tell you what, Beck," she says, her eyes sharpening, "you just keep doing what you do and every time you spout off an insult, I'm going to call you on it. Maybe then you'll realize just how often you do it."

"Fine. Whatever," Beckett says, waving his fork in the air.

"We're supposed to be a team," Morgan says, "from now on, I want that to be a reality for us. Things are only going to get more hectic and complicated as the company and family continues to grow, and we need to have each other's back. We need to be able to rely on each other for support when needed. Speaking of need, Kellen has a situation."

He tells me to spill it and gives me the metaphorical floor to lay it all out. I figure that it's now or never. He's trying. I can either jump in and give us the opportunity for a trial run of this new, unified family, or I can keep my mouth shut and keep things the way they are.

I tell my parents and Beckett about everything that's happened over the past week with Demi. Mom's face gets all pleased until I get to the part about her stepping back. Gabriella puts the drawing on the table for everyone to look at, but she's put it in a plastic food storage bag.

"Fingerprints," she says with a shrug by way of explanation.

"No, it's good," I tell her. "From the research I've done, evidence and documentation are of the utmost importance."

I lay out my plan to have a private investigator follow Belinda to see if we can build a case against her for stalking. If we have proof, I can go through the steps to get a protective order issued for me and Demi, if needed.

A piece of paper won't keep anyone safe if it is Belinda, and she's suffering from more than a fit of jealousy. However, if she's just miffed because I didn't want to date her, it might make her back off and finally let go of me for good.

"I have a buddy that has a private security firm," Morgan says. "They aren't private dicks, but they can do surveillance and document it better than anyone. I've talked to the head guy, and he's willing to start right away, if you want."

"Yes," I say, "right away would be good, thank you."

"They'll need her details, address for home, work, and such," Morgan says. "I'll text you his contact information so you can communicate directly."

I nod. "Thanks."

I feel myself start to relax. This didn't turn out to be as bad as I thought it would. For now, I'll remain optimistic. For now.

The conversation starts to get less serious and turn to the normal dinner chatter. Mom, of course, has a lot of questions about Demi and Henry. I let Gabriella answer most of them, but fill in where I can.

Talking about her makes me want to talk to her. I know I should stay clear of her, but maybe we can still talk. She said to stay away so Belinda wouldn't be tempted by Henry or her, but there was nothing about no contact. I'll call her tonight and see how she reacts.

We finish the meal and help Mom clean up. I ride back with Beckett because he's the one I rode with. Also, being around Morgan and Gabriella for any length of time makes me feel like I've been dipped in syrup. They're so gaga for each other. I used to find it a little nauseating, but now that I've met Demi, I think it might not be so bad to feel that way about another person.

We're about halfway to the office when Beckett looks over at me. "I'm sorry, man. Nothing was ever meant by it. I'm just an asshole. Feel free to push back when I get out of line. I really do love ya, bro."

"Thanks. I love you, too."

"What a mush fest, huh?" I look over at him and he's grinning at me.

"Yeah. It was horrible," I reply, grinning back.

When we get back to the office, I check my phone and see the information from Morgan. I contact Jerald Carver at Carver Security and ask him to get started immediately once I supply him with Belinda's home, work, and cell phone information. We set their engagement to cover a week and we'll revisit to review the results.

I now have an excuse to call Demi. Although I probably don't need an excuse, I have one, so I'm going to take advantage of it. I just hope she's not cringing when she sees my name show up on her display.

I dial her number.

"Hi Kellen!"

She doesn't sound like she's disappointed or angry. That's a good sign.

Chapter 16

Demeter

"Hi! How are you?" Kellen asks.

"I'm just peachy. How are you?"

He chuckles at my response. "It's turning out to be a very good day," he replies. "Do you have a minute to talk?

"Sure, just let me go inside where I can hear better."

I gather up my things and go into the house. I was planning to go in shortly anyway, so this is a good excuse. It's hot outside and I need to cool off to regain some of my energy.

"Henry, I'm going in. You have fifteen more minutes."

"Tell him I said hi," Kellen says.

"Kellen says hi."

"Hi Mr. Kellen. When are you coming over again?" Henry calls out.

I step into the cool house. "Hang on a second Kellen." I pull the phone away and tell my mother, "Mom, Henry needs to get out in fifteen minutes. I'm going to be on the phone for a bit, so if I'm not out, please roust him out of the pool."

"Yes, honey."

"Thanks."

I go into my office and close the door. To keep my bare legs from sticking to the leather desk chair, I put my towel down. Once I'm comfortable, I put the phone back to my ear.

"Okay, I'm back. Sorry about that."

"It's fine. I just wanted to give you an update," he says and tells me about his talk with Gabriella and the subsequent goings on today.

I have to smile when he tells me how Ella orchestrated a whole family pow wow and turned everything topsy-turvy in the best kind of way. It's a great outcome, not just for Kellen, but for the whole family. Kellen needs his family, and they need him, and now everyone knows it. I'm even happy Beckett has vowed to be less abrasive.

I like his plan to have Belinda followed and her movements documented. This will let him... us, know the extent of her stalking. Maybe it was just a onetime fit of pique. However, I know first-hand how far people can take things when they feel wronged.

"I'm glad you called," I tell him.

"You are?" He sounds surprised.

"Yes, I am!" I chuckle. "I was just thinking about you and my phone rang."

"What were you thinking about?" he pauses. "Geez, I didn't mean that to come out sounding quite so sleezy."

That makes me laugh. "Yeah, I don't think we're to the sleezy talking stage yet."

"Well, I'm glad to know that it's a possible part of the future," he chuckles.

He has a really great laugh. I'm hearing it more often now and the more it happens, the more natural it sounds.

"I was thinking of you being here last weekend and how good it was to spend some time getting to know you," I say.

"Yeah, I hope we can spend more time together soon."

We talk for a little while longer about nothing in particular. I don't want to hang up, but I can see Henry draping himself over the back of the sofa in imitation of someone fainting. God, I love my boy.

"Well, I'd love to keep talking, but I think my son is trying to signal me that he's about to die of starvation," I say with a laugh.

"You'd better go feed him then," Kellen says, the smile in his voice coming through loud and clear.

"This was nice, Kellen. I enjoy talking with you."

"Me, too. I'll call again soon."

"I'd like that," I say honestly. "Good night."

"Night."

I hang up the phone and hold it for long moments, just enjoying the feelings being stirred up in me. In some ways, my growing feelings toward Kellen concern me. As much as I know Jeremiah wouldn't want me to grieve for him forever, I can't help but think that on some level, I'm betraying him.

I lost myself to the grief for the last two months of my pregnancy. So much so that I am sometimes surprised that Henry is so happy. I know the fetus can be affected by the emotions of the mother, but he was a happy baby and is still a cheerful boy. He has his moments, but even when he's upset, he'll have an outburst to release everything he's feeling and then it's done, blown over like a passing storm.

Once Henry was born, there was no time for grieving. I had a son to care for and babies don't understand that you can't feed them when they're hungry because you can't get yourself out of bed. For years, I focused on just getting through each day before crying myself to sleep to get a little rest before I was needed again.

Was it enough, though? Did I give myself time to truly grieve as much as I should have? I know there's no gauge, no standardized chart to say how long is the acceptable time of mourning, but I still wonder.

There are still times when the grief will sneak up on me. I'll hear a song that we danced to or drive by a place we visited, and the tears will come pouring out of me. Sometimes Henry will do something or say something that is so much like his father that I have to work hard not to break down in front of him.

Am I moving too fast into a relationship with someone new? Should I wait until Henry is older? Or maybe until he's grown? I don't know. I also don't know that there's any right way to answer those questions.

Kellen is just a friend, I tell myself. I'm so conflicted, and it changes from one minute to the next, but the only kind of relationship we have is a friend to a friend. Yes, I've had passing thoughts of infatuation, but I think it's just because a part of me misses being held. Misses having someone to lean on.

I have my parents, but it's different. Oh, so very different from what it's like to have a partner. I miss having someone to confide in who I can trust with my hopes, dreams, fears, and disappointments.

"I miss you," I say out loud to Henry's dead father. It's true; there are moments I find myself missing him every day. Tomorrow will be a particularly tough day because it's the ninth anniversary of the day he walked out the door and never came home again. "I think you'd like Kellen, though."

I close my eyes and take a few minutes to breathe deeply and center myself before I go out to eat supper with our boy.

Chapter 17

Demeter

I take Henry to his Grandparents' house the next morning. I'm glad that he'll be with them instead of with me today. Most of the time, when the anniversary of Jeremiah's death rolls around, I can put on a brave face for Henry's sake. He doesn't even realize it's a day different from any other day.

Today is not a day I can fake it. Maybe it's because I won't have Henry with me, or maybe it's because of the stressful week or all the feelings I've been trying to sort out, but Jeremiah is on my mind. I can feel the grief pressing in, and I know it's going to be a rough day.

After grabbing breakfast, I decide to visit the bookstore again to see if they have any other M.K. Edwards books in stock. I've finished the one I bought last time I stopped in, as well as another two I bought online from the author's back list. I know I should slow down, or I'll be out of books soon and then I'll have to find someone new to read.

However, going home and locking myself into my bedroom to read all day sounds like a good plan. I'll get a pizza, some ice cream, and maybe even some booze. Maybe I should get a hotel room instead of going home.

If I go home, my parents will be close and if Mom picks up on my mood, she'll hover. Yes, a hotel might be the best option. I can run home really quick and pack an overnight bag and I'll be close to pick Henry up in the morning. That's it; that's an even better plan.

"Hi Demi."

Kellen is standing there in the aisle of the bookstore. I was so absorbed in looking at books that I hadn't even realized that anyone was near me. That's not very smart of me.

"Oh, hi." I'm surprised but recover. I clear my throat and manage a smile. "Hi, Kellen, how are you?"

"Good. Um, sorry if I startled you. Book shopping?"

I hold up the two books I have. "Yes, you?"

He has a book in his hand and shows me. It's a thriller. Another book in the series he was reading at the 4th of July celebration.

He looks at me and frowns. "Are you okay?"

I look away, a lie on the tip of my tongue, but I can't school my face to be convincing. I shake my head. "No. Today's a rough day, but I'll be all right."

He just stands there for a minute looking at me then says, "Seven months pregnant..." I see the change in his face as the memory of what I told him starts to fall into place. Jeremiah died when I was seven months pregnant, and Henry's birthday is two months away.

"Is today...?"

I nod, feeling tears well, unable to stop them. Tremors ripple through me. Quickly, I put the books on the closest shelf and turn to leave. "Sorry. Gotta go."

I hurry out of the building, praying I don't run into anyone because I can't really see very well. Holding it together as best I can, I make it to the car and manage to get inside before I breakdown in earnest. I'm digging in the console for a napkin, tissue, something to replace the one I found in the cupholder that's now sodden and falling apart.

The door opens and strong arms turn me, pulling me close. Kellen tucks my head against his chest and wraps his arms around me. He just stands there, rubbing my back and holding me while I soak the front of his shirt with my tears.

A few days or maybe minutes later, the wave of emotion starts to pass, and my tears abate, leaving me breathing raggedly. I relax my hands from their death grip on Kellen's shirt and try to smooth it out, but it's useless.

"Sorry," I say. "I'm usually better at this, but the stressful week has my defenses down and...sorry." I shut up because I'm babbling and it's not helping anything.

"It's just a shirt," he replies. "Do you need me to drive you home?"

I shake my head, but I don't want to let go of him. "No. I can get home. Henry's having a do over weekend with the McLean's, so home is where I intended to go when I left here. Well, there or a hotel. No parents to hover at a hotel."

He's quiet for a few heartbeats, but still hasn't released me. His chin comes to rest on the top of my head, so maybe he's not going to let me go. Maybe we could just stay here like this until morning.

"You could come to my house. No parents there. You can hang out as long as you want and even spend the night. You can hole up in one of the bedrooms and read your books and I'll stay out of the way, or we can watch a movie, whatever you want. I have plenty of room, but if you'd rather be alone, I understand."

I roll his proposal over in my mind. I want to be alone, but I don't want to be alone. What Kellen's offering will give me the option to have both. However, there's a problem with that.

"What about Belinda?" I ask.

"She's being followed. My neighborhood is gated and the ones watching her will notify me if she comes anywhere close to me or the neighborhood."

I let that sink in. It seems like he's got everything covered. I sniffle. "Can we have pizza and ice cream?"

He chuckles. "Yes. What kind of ice cream do you want?"

He stayed there with me in the parking lot for a long time until I felt clear enough to drive. It's approaching lunch by the time I go by my house, pack a bag in case I stay the night at Kellen's, and start toward his home.

I wanted to have my things so that I can go straight from there to pick up Henry in the morning. With a quick call to mom, I tell her I'm going to a friend's house and may be out all night. She doesn't question me because she knows what today is, too.

Kellen gave me the address and gate code to meet him at his house after I packed, and he went to buy ice cream. He assured me that if I changed my mind and decided not to show up, he wouldn't hold it against me.

I pull into his driveway, feeling nervous. And heavy. I feel like I weigh a thousand pounds from the melancholy grinding down on my shoulders today.

Through the windshield, I study his house. It's not what I would have thought of for him, but it suits him. There's a kind of a modern Craftsmanesque vibe with heavy wooden beams holding up the porch eaves and a mix of brick and stone on the bottom third of the façade. The green siding is surprising, though, but since he likes to go camping, maybe it's not so surprising after all.

Maybe this was a mistake, and I should go to a hotel. I'm feeling so raw and undone that there's likely going to be a break-down somewhere in the next few hours. Do I really want him to see me at my worst when everything is so new?

Before I make the decision to run away, Kellen comes out and opens the car door. When he offers me his hand, I take it, sliding out of the car. He opens the door to the back seat and takes my bag out. Once the doors are closed and the car locked up, he takes my hand in his free one and leads me into the house.

We go through the still open front door, through the living room and down a hall to the open door of a bedroom. The light is on, and he sets my bag on the bed.

"This is your room for tonight. If you want to be alone, come in here and I won't bother you. No matter what else is going on, if you need a minute or the entire night, just come in here."

I nod, feeling emotions starting to bubble. "Thanks," I breathe.

"I'm hungry, so I went ahead and ordered pizza and it should be here in about thirty minutes. Ice cream is in the freezer, and I've set out some spoons. There's beer, tea, and water in the fridge. Help yourself to whatever you want."

I nod again, my throat tight. He leaves the room and closes the bedroom door behind him. I sit on the bed for a moment, then look around the room. It's nice and I wonder if Kellen hired a decorator or did it himself.

The mundane thoughts help me get hold of myself again. I continue down the path of mundanity and open my bag. My clothes for the next day are laid out and I move my toiletries into the bathroom.

I'm plugging my cell phone charger into an outlet next to the nightstand when I see the books. Kellen bought the books I'd been planning to buy. I stretch out a finger and touch the cover of the one on top. He's so kind.

I feel my eyes prickle, but the tears don't come. For long moments, I just stand there and stare at the books, mesmerized by the gift. The doorbell ringing snaps me out of my trance.

I pull off my sundress and go into the bathroom to wash my face. The tears made my eyes feel gritty. My face is sticky and

I'm sure my makeup is shot all to hell. I didn't even stop to look while I was at home.

I wash away the soap and study my face in the mirror as I slather on moisturizer. My eyes are red and swollen, the blue irises gone gray.

My stomach growls.

"Okay, okay, I'll feed you," I tell the demanding organ.

I find my way to the kitchen. Kellen is nowhere to be seen. He has set out plates and paper towels along with a fork. I guess he's forgetting the extremely non-dainty way I ate pizza at my house.

I lift the lid of the top box to see that he's already been here and gone. When I look into the other box, I see he's mixed it up with flavors. A slice of each goes onto my plate before I search the fridge for something to drink.

"Fuck it," I say under my breath, and take out a beer.

I was never much of a drinker before Henry but would partake occasionally. As a teenager, I worked all the time to save every penny I could for college, so there wasn't time for the rebellious party life. When I got into college, it was more of the same, working almost full-time hours and taking the maximum load of classes year-round.

Once I had Henry, my opportunity and desire to drink dwindled even more. When I'm with friends, I'll partake occasionally, but I don't get to see them as often as I'd like. Thinking of friends has me making a mental note to set up a get together soon with Lynzee and Sarah.

When I was younger, I thought that someday, when I'd 'made it,' I'd become a sophisticated wine connoisseur. It just seemed like something that successful, prominent people did. Then I tried wine a few times and found everything I tasted to be disgusting so I stopped trying.

The beer isn't bad, so I take it and the plate of pizza and wander around the house. I find Kellen in an office where he's typing away on his computer. He changed into shorts, too, his long, bare legs stretched out in front of him under the desk.

I stop in the doorway and stare at his legs. They're lean and muscled in a way that makes me think he might be a runner. I'm glad he's not one of those super-serious runners that shaves his legs.

Why on earth am I thinking something like that?

"Thank you for the books," I say.

His head snaps up. He hadn't heard me come in. "Huh?"

"Sorry, didn't mean to startle you." My lips curve up on one side. "I said thank you for the books. Thanks for everything else, too."

He grins that beautiful boyish grin. "Oh, you're welcome. Do you like that author? It seems like that's the same one you were getting the last time we ran into each other there."

"Yeah. It's romance, but not your typical barely eighteen tropes where everything is heart-shaped with doves. The characters are more real. More believable."

There's an awkward silence for a moment before I ask, "What were you doing there? At the bookstore, I mean."

"Oh, our offices aren't far from there. I went in early this morning to catch up on some things I didn't get done yesterday. I needed the next book in the series I'm reading, and I like to buy local whenever I can, so I swung by to see if they had it."

I nod, feeling awkward again. I look up to see his MBA diploma on the wall. "Kellen Edward Masters," I read out loud.

I stare at it for a long moment, then shift on my feet, feeling as if my brain is misfiring. I look around, only now realizing that I interrupted him and see him watching me.

My face goes hot. "Sorry, I'll just go." I lift a finger from its home on the beer and point it back over my shoulder.

I go back to the living room and sit cross-legged on the sofa. Once I put my beer bottle onto a coaster on the end table and pull a throw blanket off the back of the sofa, I tuck it around me. It's hot outside, but it's cool inside his home.

I look around for the remote. Kellen walks in, takes the remote off the table by a comfortable-looking chair, and hands it to me. I take it and he goes to the kitchen to get more pizza and another beer for himself.

"Do you want to watch alone?" he asks.

With a shake of my head, I let him know I'm fine with him staying. I want to tell him I'd really like him to stay. What I want to tell him is that I'd really like it if he held me again like he did this morning because I could really use the connection right now. But I don't want to give him the wrong idea, so all he gets is a shake of my head.

I find an old Perry Mason episode and let it play. We've missed half the episode, so I sit through the next one just so I can watch something from beginning to end. I drink all my beer and make it to the end of the program, but only manage to get half a piece of pizza down.

Being on the emotional roller coaster is exhausting, so when I find it hard to keep my eyes open, I put away my remaining pizza and go to the bedroom. I leave the door open and take the top book in hand. The drone of the television carries from the living room, but I don't know if Kellen is still in there watching or if he's gone back to whatever he was doing.

I don't make it through even a chapter before sleep overtakes me.

Chapter 18

Kellen

I watch Demi leave the room. She didn't eat much, but as much as I am concerned for her, I know that grief manifests in the strangest ways sometimes. I also know that there are no shortcuts. When it blindsides you, it needs to be worked through. The best I can do for her is give her the space to get through today.

I leave the television on for the white noise it can provide for both of us and go back to my office. It takes me a moment to re-acclimate, but I can't get back into the flow. It's start and stop because my mind keeps going back to Demi. Part of me wants to go in there, climb into bed with her, and hold her tight until her sadness passes.

I don't want her to get the wrong idea, though. My thought might be that I only want to be there for her, to comfort her, but I don't think that's the message she'd get if she woke up to me in bed with her. I just get the feeling that she's not one to show her vulnerability very often or to many people. It must be exhausting to have to put on a strong face all the time with no one to lean on.

I'm not going to be able to settle down enough to get back to work, so I close out of the document. It's been almost a week since I started having Belinda followed. Other than notifying me whether she comes near my neighborhood or office or Demi's home or office, they don't contact me with every little thing.

In another week, we'll review the data, and I'll make decisions. I had originally wanted to set our touch base at a week, but Jerald with Carver Security suggested two so that we'd have a good baseline of data. Who am I to argue with an expert?

I'm really hoping that if it was Belinda that left the note on Demi's car that it was done in a fit of pique and that now she's moved on and gone back to living her life. Before meeting Demi, I probably would have just ignored it and gone about my usual routines. I can't do that with her, though; Demi is special. She has captured my attention in a way no other woman ever has.

I wonder how Henry's doing with his grandparents today. Surely, they're affected by the anniversary of their son's death, too. Maybe they're cherishing their grandson on this sad day since they'll never be able to cherish their son again except in memory. It must be all right because Henry hasn't called.

I leave the office and go down the hall. Demi's door is open, so I stop and glance in. She's asleep, but her book's on the floor. She must have fallen asleep while reading. I quietly step into the room and pick the book up, placing it on the nightstand.

It doesn't seem like enough, so I go into the kitchen and get a glass of water, taking it back to the room and putting it on the nightstand, too. I hesitate for a moment.

If I leave the water, she'll know that I was in here. I go ahead and set it down; she left the door open, after all. If she wanted complete privacy, surely she would have closed the door.

I watch her for a moment, but don't linger. It would be difficult to explain myself if she were to wake up and find me standing over her, staring, no matter how much I want to.

Her sleep doesn't look restful at all. I go back to the living room with my own book and sit down to read with old crime dramas playing in the background.

I'm not sure what to do with this want or maybe even need that I have for Demi. There have been hundreds of times that I have gone to that shopping center and that bookstore and never run into or noticed her.

Gabriella and Demi have been friends for almost a year and Ella's been with Morgan for months, but we'd never met. Why is it that in just a few short weeks, she seems to be everywhere, including a pervasive presence in my thoughts?

Is this what some people mean by love at first sight? I wouldn't say I'm in love with Demi, though. I have a severe case of like and attraction, for sure, but love?

I'm lost in my thoughts, my book forgotten when Demi shuffles in. She's sleep rumpled and bleary-eyed but also totally adorable.

"Thanks for the water," she mumbles.

"You're welcome," I reply, unable to keep my lips from curling as I watch her shuffle into the kitchen.

She opens the refrigerator and rummages around a bit. She takes out the pizza boxes and another beer, then boosts herself up onto one of the stools at the island. Instead of getting a plate, she eats the pizza right from the box.

A sigh escapes her with her first bite as she closes her eyes and chews. I watch her throat move as she swallows and the way her small hand holds the beer bottle.

"Pizza is my favorite food group," she says, then out of nowhere, she asks, "What are you always writing?"

I focus on her face to see that she's watching me, watching her.

"What do you mean?"

"You always seem to be typing into your phone, and today on your computer. It seems like if you aren't reading, you're typing."

I shrug. "Oh, different things - thoughts, ideas. Often when I'm on the computer, I'm typing emails or other business correspondence."

She raises an eyebrow. "That's a whole lot of correspondence."

"Yes, it is," I agree, "and never ending, it seems."

She keeps eating and continues studying me, managing to get down a couple of pieces this time. After putting the boxes back into the refrigerator, she stares at the oven for a long moment. "Is that clock right?"

"Yes," I confirm.

"I thought it would be later. I thought for sure I had slept a lot longer."

Taking her beer from the counter, she crosses to the sofa where I'm sitting and takes a seat on the other end. Instead of facing forward, she turns to face me and stretches her legs out, dragging the throw blanket over her legs and feet.

"Cold?" I ask.

"Toes are," she says.

I reach under the blanket and wrap my fingers around the toes of one foot, my eyes watching the movement under the blanket. "I can raise the temperature on the thermostat."

She shakes her head. "That's okay. The rest of me is fine, just cold toes. Always cold toes."

She's still watching me, as if she wants to ask me something, but is working her way up to it. My normal tendency would be to get self-conscious, but I don't seem to mind her scrutiny. I want to know everything about her, so I understand the curiosity.

I press her foot against my thigh, covering her toes with my palm. Her other foot moves like a snake under the blanket as she tucks the toes under my palm as well, making me smile. I wonder if she's an overtly affectionate person when she's in a relationship. She is certainly not shy about showing affection to Henry through hugs and touches.

"Thank you for letting me come here," she says after a long silence.

"You're welcome," I tell her again.

"I don't know what it is about you, but I feel very comfortable with you."

"I'm glad. Not a lot of visitors come here, so I thought this might be awkward, but it's not. I'm very comfortable with you as well. When I saw you in the bookstore and realized that you were upset, my first and only thought was to bring you home and help you get through the day."

"I guess it was kismet that we met this morning."

"Seems like."

I glance over at her, but her attention is on the television, watching J.B. Fletcher reveal the killer.

"How old are you?" she asks out of the blue.

"Thirty-five. You?"

"You're not supposed to ask a lady how old she is," she replies, still looking at the television. She's smirking, though, so I know she's not really upset. "I will be thirty-one in October."

Her toes feel warm now, so I pull my hand out from under the blanket. She presses against my thigh. "Don't stop. That felt good," she says.

I chuckle and go back to rubbing her toes. We sit there, watching, but not really watching the television, me playing with her toes and being relaxed in each other's presence.

"You've never been married?" she asks.

"No," I reply, and because I figure the follow-up question is going to be why, I give her that answer, too. "I had a serious girlfriend in college. One weekend, I brought her home and when we went back to school, all she could talk about was Beckett. We broke up soon after."

The next college girlfriend wasn't very serious, but we'd been together for a few months, and she had been asking to meet my family, so I brought her home. She couldn't stand Beckett, but the minute Morgan walked into the room, she only had eyes for him.

"The next one only had eyes for Morgan once they met." I shrug. "Once I graduated and came into the business, I was needed there and didn't have a lot of time for dating. Also, I haven't met anyone since that I liked enough to get serious with."

Until maybe now.

"Tell me about Belinda."

It's not a question, but I give her what she wants.

"A few years ago, we started using one of those services that provides HR functionality like payroll with an app that lets employees manage their own information. Belinda was the account representative that came to work with me on the implementation. We talked a lot and got along. I wasn't attracted to her romantically, but I thought she was funny and easy to talk to. Once the implementation was complete, we kept talking and became friends. I needed a plus one for an event and asked her to go with me."

I pause, a realization hitting me. "Looking back, that may have been my first misstep with her. I didn't have any feelings for her beyond friendship, but she may have gotten the wrong idea with that invitation, even though I told her several times that I appreciated her being a good friend and going with me."

I think about that first time Belinda went to an event with me. She was so excited, but I thought it was just because she had never been to one of those kinds of charity events. She was concerned about having the right kind of dress to wear, so I helped her get something new to wear along with everything to go with it. I can see how she might have read more into it, regardless of what my words were saying.

"Do you think you'd like to get married someday? Maybe have children?" she asks.

I take my time thinking about how I want to answer. Until recently, I honestly thought I'd probably be single forever. My relationships with women had been less than spectacular, and I had my doubts that there was anyone I could be compatible with.

Until now.

"When I was younger, I sought out relationships. Now, my viewpoint is more like Morgan's approach of if it's supposed to happen, it will happen. I can see myself being married and having children, but I don't want to try to force anything."

She's quiet, assimilating what I said.

"I like that answer," she says several minutes later. "I think I have room in my heart to love again and maybe even be married someday. Then a day like today comes around and makes me think I'm insane for even considering it. I miss a lot of things about having a partner, but even so, I'm most concerned about

Henry. He has some good men in his life, but they can have a hard time relating to one another. Even if I were to get involved with someone, if they couldn't care for and relate to Henry, my feelings wouldn't matter; it would be an automatic deal breaker."

"Of course it would."

We sit there for hours, talking and not talking in starts and stops. Topics range broadly from the mundane favorite colors and foods to religion and politics. We eat again, but instead of pizza, I throw together a stir-fry with chicken and plenty of vegetables. Demi helps by chopping vegetables, but swears that if she does much more, it will turn out tasting horrible, which makes me laugh.

She seems to be in better spirits mostly, but I still notice her getting lost in thought from time to time. A few times, I see her standing there with her eyes closed as if she's trying to get herself together. I don't bring attention to it, I just let her work through it because I know that if she needs me, she'll tell me like she did with the simple act of keeping her toes warm.

Sure enough, we're back on the sofa watching a movie and it's getting late. In my periphery, I can see her glancing over at me occasionally, the look of wanting to ask something back on her face. She draws in a deep breath and says quietly, "Kellen."

"Yes, Demi?"

"I want to ask you to do something for me, but I don't want you to get the wrong idea. I also don't want to be unfair to you."

"Just ask, and if I don't want to do it, I'll say so."

"Okay. I just know many people wouldn't say and they'd go along to be accommodating."

I turn and face her. She looks down at her hands, then up at me, and back down at her hands, her face going pink.

I grip her toes, that have been against my thigh since returning to the couch. "What is it, Demi?" I ask gently.

"Do you think...it's really silly so if you don't want to, I understand...but I really miss being held and I was wondering if maybe I could sit close to you and maybe you could put your arm around me or something..."

I knew she'd let me know what she needed, so I open my arms and say, "Come 'ere."

She scoots across the sofa and sits next to me. I put my arm around her, but she doesn't seem comfortable. Taking a chance, I gather her up into my arms and pull her onto my lap. She settles and puts her head on my chest with a sigh.

"Thank you," she says with a sniff.

Something shifts inside me. I won't force anything to happen with Demi, but I don't think I'll have to. In fact, deep down, I know I won't have to. This connection between us is beyond anything I've ever known.

She used the word kismet earlier, and that's exactly what it feels like. Call it fate, destiny, cupid, or whatever. This is the time that I will look back on when we're old and gray and pinpoint it as the exact moment when I knew Demi was the one for me. A great kid like Henry as part of the package is more than I could have ever hoped for.

Now I just have to wait for her to realize it, too.

Chapter 19

Demeter

Henry races out the door to me, the smile on his face driving away the last of the dark clouds from my mind. He always seems happy to see me when I pick him up from his grandparents' house, but today he seems especially pleased.

I think he's going to stop, but he doesn't and I only have a moment to brace before he crashes into me. "Hey buddy!"

"I missed you, Mom."

I laugh into his hair. "You just saw me yesterday."

"I know," he replies, unbothered.

"Say goodbye to Angelica and we'll go."

"Bye, Gel!" He barely turns, but raises his hand in a wave before he scrambles into the back seat of the car and buckles into his booster seat.

Henry isn't the only one feeling light and upbeat this morning. After spending last night with Kellen, I feel the same way. It was an incredibly intimate experience for me. Intimate, but not sexual in any way.

Don't get me wrong, I am intensely sexually attracted to Kellen. However, for him to be able to draw me in to that depth and not take it to a sexual place, as many men would have, showed me a level of integrity and trustworthiness that is very rare in my experience.

Knowing that I was protected and safe let me tap into my emotions and fully experience them. I cried for a long time, sitting there on his lap, quietly at first, then in great heaving sobs. There was no stuffing down or trying to put on a brave face for those around me. Being able to dive that deep was extremely cathartic. I slept more soundly than I have in a long time and when I woke this morning, it was as if a weight had been lifted off my shoulders.

It's the first time since Jeremiah died that I have been able to let the grief take me over like that. In the past, there has always been a need to maintain at least some level of control so that I didn't get lost. I had to keep one eye on the clock to be sure I was able to pull myself together to be there for Henry.

With Kellen there to catch me, I was able to fully embrace the deep emotions that have been stuffed down in the darkest parts of my heart for so long. I took on the cloak of grief and let it wrap me in its heavy, debilitating embrace, giving myself over to it. Because I could let it all out, it feels as if I've turned a corner.

I will always love and miss Jeremiah. He was my first love and I see so much of him in our son, but that recognition feels like a fond reminiscence now instead of carrying the sharp edge of pain and loss. Although I'm sure I'll still have days when it twinges deep inside, the constant weight of it is gone.

Maybe this means I'm ready to move on instead of being anchored in the past and unable to move forward. It feels that way right now, but I'll know more once I begin to test the newfound feeling of being released from the black bars of the cage of sorrow.

"Can we go do something fun instead of going home today?" Henry asks.

"Sure, buddy. Is there something in particular you want to do?"

He shrugs. "I dunno. Just something fun."

"How about the zoo? It's been a while since we've been there."

His little face lights up. "Yeah! Can it just be us? You and me?"

"Absolutely."

I know Henry loves my parents, but when they go to the zoo with us, Dad gets caught up looking at the plants but doesn't like it when we go on without him, so Henry misses half the animals. He also spends time with them almost every day. If he wants it to just be the two of us, that's what it will be.

He's so full of energy today, he wants to see everything. Although I'm feeling energetic, too, I convince him to slow down and take his time. There's no need to rush and we'll stay all day until he's looked all he wants, if that's what it takes.

We're several hours in and his energy is still holding out, so I'm wondering if he'll test my comment about staying all day. Once we stop for lunch in one of the zoo's cafes, the busy morning starts to catch up with him. He gets to see everything, but is ready to go once he's ticked every exhibit off his list.

When we're back in the car, I see I've missed a call from Kellen. For a moment, I think about calling him back once we're home, but I know Henry would love to talk to him. He's mentioned Kellen several times and doesn't understand why they can't see each other.

Once I have the car started and the air conditioning on high, I dial his number.

"Hey there," he says.

Before he can go on, I make sure he knows we have an audience. "Hi! I'm in the car with Henry."

"Hi Mr. Kellen!"

"Henry, how's it going, buddy?"

"Great!" He has to tell Kellen all about the zoo and seemingly every single animal, but honestly, he seems most excited about the gorilla t-shirt we got in the gift shop.

Kellen is patient, letting Henry share his excitement, and it makes my heart warm. Henry relates better to Kellen than he does with any of the other men in our lives. They're such birds of a feather that bonding seems like it's been easy for them.

When Henry finally winds down, I say, "Sorry I missed your call. Did you need me?"

"Always," he replies, which makes my stomach flutter and my cheeks grow warm. "But mostly I was just calling to check on you."

We talk a while longer before hanging up.

"When are we going to see Mr. Kellen again?" Henry asks, his voice laced with drowsiness.

"Soon, baby. Hopefully soon."

Chapter 20

Demeter

I rub my sweaty palms on my skirt. When I was first asked to give a presentation for one of the conference breakout sessions, I thought it would be a great opportunity and a fun experience. I had already agreed to sit on a panel for a topic discussion of unique approaches in psychology when they asked, so I figured since I'd already be here, why not? I must have been temporarily insane.

My phone buzzes, startling me so much I almost drop it. I look down to see a text from Kellen. Just seeing it's from him makes me smile. He had wanted to come hear me speak, but an unexpected issue at work kept him in the City.

Kellen: *You're going to be great. Take a breath. Break a leg.*

I know that breaking a leg is supposed to be good for actors, but I'm not sure about speakers. I start to reply that when another message comes through.

Kellen: *If that doesn't work, picture them in their underwear.*

I barely catch myself, managing to stifle the laugh before it escapes me. After spending the night at Kellen's house last weekend, something has shifted between us. He saw me at my emotional worst and reacted with nothing but patience, support, and tender care.

We have been in contact every day since through texts and phone calls. He's eager to get the investigator's report to see what has been discovered regarding Belinda. I hope it was just a momentary lashing out at a perceived rival, but I appreciate his caution because of the potential impact to Henry.

My introduction begins, so I only have time to send a smiling emoji before I am called up on stage. I pay attention to my footfalls, not wanting last night's dream of tripping and sprawling on the stairs to come to life.

Once I take my place behind the podium, I place my phone with its screensaver of Henry in my view to comfort me. I look out across the session attendees, smiling as I try not to picture anyone in their panties and tighty whities.

There are so many faces. The conference organizers had to change the room they'd designated for me because the one they had originally set aside for me wasn't large enough to accommodate everyone who wanted to attend my session. That was all kinds of surprising and once I realized I'd be addressing twice as many people as I expected, my nervousness ratcheted up too.

I take a breath and use the remote to pull up the first slide, launching into my presentation. Once I'm covering my material, I relax. I've studied this information so much that it's now ingrained in me.

With one eye on the time, I start to wrap up in case there are any questions. I open the floor and am glad I closed a little early because there are several hands that go up.

Fielding questions quickly, I try to take as many as I can before I need to let everyone go to their next session. There's just enough time for one final question, so I choose a woman toward the back of the room. She's tall and very thin with dishwater blond hair and, contrary to most of the attendees, her clothes are extremely professional.

Once she has the microphone, she asks, "What would you advise one of your clients in the case of a boyfriend or husband that has been stolen away?"

I frown. It's completely off-topic. "Well," I say, "I'm not really sure what you mean by stolen away. It's my experience that no one is stolen against their will unless it is a literal situation such as with kidnapping."

She starts to say more, but the moderator has taken the microphone back. The staff member is talking to the woman, probably telling her that the question wasn't relevant to the session. The woman gets visibly upset, gesturing broadly and seemingly at me.

I close by telling everyone that the session is over, thanking them for attending, and releasing them to go on to their next sessions. When I look back to where the woman was, I see the staff member escorting her out.

What on earth was going on there? I wonder what motivated her to ask such a question, but when Henry comes bursting through the door and running down the aisle, I only have eyes for him.

Tilly, my sister, follows him in, grinning. She's carrying her infant daughter as her toddler son races after his cousin. "He couldn't wait another minute. He wanted to come in when we first got here, but I told him it would be a disruption."

The conference is being held in Tulsa, so we're staying with my sister and her family while here. I thought it would be a good time for Henry to spend some time with his cousins and for me to get in plenty of baby snuggles with my niece, six-month-old Amanda. Getting to see my sister and brother-in-law is just icing on the cake.

"Wow! This room is ginormous!" Henry exclaims from the stage as he looks out across the seats. "There were a lot of people in here."

"Yes, there were," I agree with a laugh.

Henry, followed closely by his cousin roams all over the stage, looking out at the audience seats from every angle.

"I am starving," Henry proclaims. "What are we having for lunch?"

"You're always starving," I tell him. "You must be building up for another growth spurt."

"I think I am," he agrees. "A big one."

"Nuggies is close," Tillie offers. "Or Andolini's. Or, since you don't have to be back today, we could go further up the street to Tally's."

"Let's go there. I'm in the mood for some good home cooking. Come on, kiddos, let's go eat."

The next day, I arrive early, eager to sit in on a session about increased collaboration between psychologists and public agencies such as the police department. Today has the lion's share of the sessions, but thankfully, I'm only taking part in the panel discussion. Once that's finished this morning, Henry and I will be free to hang out with our family.

The panel seems to be going well when a man raises his hand to ask a question. He's an older gentleman and I recognize him as one of the attendees from the session I did yesterday. When he is handed the microphone, he introduces himself and emphasizes the Doctor designation before listing off all the letters of every license and professional designation he is due.

Just as I'm thinking I should feel sorry for whomever he's about to address, he says, "Ms. Lawson, after sitting in on your session yesterday, I simply have to ask how you came to the conclusion that utilizing such a perverted practice as, what did you call it?...oh yes, BDSM, would make for an ethical approach to psychology?"

I raise an eyebrow and can't keep myself from adding a smidge of snark when I reply. "Thank you for your question. First of all, it's Dr. Lawson, but I won't bore the audience by listing my various licenses and designations because we'd be here a while." I chuckle along with the crowd.

"What you call perverted, others call an ethical approach to sexual satisfaction. Personally, I don't see what could possibly be considered perverted by the usage of communication, consent, and aftercare. Much less the added practice of safe words and foreplay. If more people used that approach, they might have a lot more satisfying sexual experiences, which would greatly improve their sense of well-being. If you'd like to see research on that, just let me know your email and I'd be happy to forward."

Again, chuckles ripple through the crowd. He looks like he wants to bluster and blow, but the attendant has already taken back the microphone. Take that, you old sourpuss. Don't be a meanie if you don't want people to throw it right back at you.

Yes, that's me, all grown up and everything.

Chapter 21

Demeter

We're on our way home Monday morning when Kellen calls. I answer since I'm on the turnpike and traffic is unusually light.

"Hi Kellen, I'm in the car with Henry on our way home."

"Hi Henry! Long time no see. How are you?"

This leads to a very animated retelling of the weekend with his cousins by Henry. Kellen doesn't seem bothered, so I let it go on for a couple of minutes before I help wind it down. Kellen tells Henry that he wants to hear everything the next time they see each other and secures a promise that it will be soon.

"I'd like to meet with you sometime today, if that's possible," Kellen says.

"Did you receive the report you were looking for?"

He was supposed to talk to the investigators first thing this morning. Based upon him calling me this soon after their likely meeting, I am guessing the news isn't good.

"Yes, and we need to discuss it."

"Okay, I'm about an hour out from home. I can take Henry home, then come to town."

"I have an idea. Why don't you come here? Henry can hang out with Beckett and Gabriella while we talk, and then we can go to lunch so I can hear all about the adventures with the cousins."

"Yeah!" Henry says.

"Okay," I concede. "How can I refuse you getting to hear all about our visit to Tulsa?"

We arrive at the Masters Construction offices more quickly than we would have arrived at home. Henry is so excited to see Kellen again, but upon getting a look at the building, he becomes reserved. When he's in a comfortable environment, Henry can be very outgoing, but in unfamiliar waters, he's significantly more introverted.

We enter the building where the Receptionist looks us over thoroughly as she dials Kellen's office. The lobby is closed off from the rest of the offices. I would like to be able to see Kellen coming, but I can't so I take Henry to the seating area to the side. He sits in a chair, swinging his legs, gawking at the room and taking everything in with owl eyes.

I'm too antsy to sit, so I stand near Henry, keeping an eye on him. Although I tell myself the nerves I'm feeling are because of the unknown of hearing what the investigators found, I know that's a lie. That's part of it, but only a small part.

The bigger part is seeing Kellen again, even though it hasn't been that long since we've seen each other. I've wanted to see him, but now that the moment is nigh, my stomach is full of butterflies.

The front door opens, and Mrs. Masters comes in with her arms full. "Demi!" she says. "What a joy to see you again! Does Kellen know you're here?"

I beam; she's such a sweet woman. "Yes, we're just waiting for him to come get us."

"Oh, nonsense. Come with me," she says, opening the door and waving us through.

"Can I help you carry something?" I ask.

She juggles her load and lets me take an insulated bag she has hanging on one arm. I don't know what's in it, but it's quite heavy.

"Kellen!" Henry calls.

I look up to see him rounding a corner down the hall. As soon as Henry lays eyes on him, he is off like a shot, running toward Kellen, who bends with open arms and catches Henry as he launches himself into the air.

Mrs. Masters is watching the whole thing with a big grin. If I'm not mistaken, she may even be a little misty eyed. "That boy of yours is just precious," she says.

"Yes, he is," I agree, feeling a little emotional myself.

Kellen meets us and puts Henry down so he can take his mother's load. Surprisingly, Henry reaches up and takes Mrs. Masters' hand as we follow Kellen. He likes to have some physical connection when he's unsure, but if anything, I would have thought he'd seek me out.

The older woman talks quietly to my son as we make our way through the maze of offices and cubicle style work areas.

She points things out and answers his questions. Like a life-size whack-a-mole game, heads pop up to see who the unfamiliar voices belong to.

Several of them are greeted by Mrs. Masters by name, so she must visit the offices often. I'm sure the smell of food stokes plenty of curiosity, as well.

We pass an area that looks like a kitchen break room and continue to the back of the building. Kellen puts the food into an empty conference room. "Mom, your surprise food delivery is going to come in handy. We're going to hijack your food for a family lunch so I can relay what the investigators found out."

"Oh, good!" she says. "I woke up this morning with an urge to cook, so it must have been mother's intuition. Go show Demi around and I'll get things ready in here."

Kellen does as he's told, holding Henry's hand as he leads us around. We stop by Morgan's office first, but don't linger any longer than it takes to let him know about their mother's arrival. He introduces us to several people, but there's no way I'll remember them all.

We wind our way around and end up back toward the front of the building. This section of the offices seems more laid back than the rest and when I see Beckett, I know he's the reason. This must be the sales and marketing area, the creative arm of the company. Beckett points me to Gabriella's office, so I go in search of her.

I stick my head in her door. "Am I interrupting?"

She looks up, surprised. "No! Not at all!" She comes over and hugs me. "What are you doing here?"

"Investigator results," I tell her. "It looks like I'm sitting in on your family lunch."

"Oh, that serious, huh?"

"I guess so. Show me what you're working on. That looks beautiful."

I spend several minutes with Gabriella, then we both go to help Mrs. Masters with setting up the food. I raise an eyebrow at Kellen as we start out the door. He gives me a wink and a smile, and I know he's got my boy.

I leave Henry with Kellen because he seems to be in the middle of telling the captive audience of Masters brothers about the skate park near Tilly's in Tulsa. We spent an entire day there and Henry only agreed to leave because he was exhausted from playing so hard.

It doesn't take long for everyone to gather in the conference room. We eat lunch first with the conversation staying light, but once Henry's finished, Beckett volunteers to take him to see some of the heavy equipment. I mouth a *thank you* to him. He just grins in response.

Once they're out of earshot down the hall, Kellen starts to lay out the investigator's report. Belinda has been following both of us on differing days, but not consistently. From the sound of it, she's no longer working, but Kellen says she has a small inheritance from her parents and could go without working for some time without concern.

The most disturbing part comes next. The investigator followed her out of town over the weekend when she went to a seminar. In Tulsa. Belinda was the woman in the audience who asked the off-topic question at the end of my session.

Once it was discovered that she wasn't a registered attendee, the organizers made her leave. She tried to get back in several times and the facility's security was eventually called. Apparently, she had a hard time tracking me once she was banned from the grounds or just gave up and went home soon after.

I breathe a sigh of relief that she didn't discover that Henry was with me. She needs to stay as far away from him as possible. If she doesn't, I'll be tempted to do a lot more than just talk to her.

In light of their report, Kellen is going to file for a restraining order. He wants me to do so as well. I know from experience that a piece of paper won't do much, but getting documentation on the books is a sound foundation to build on should there be further action needed later.

Kellen is also going to contact Belinda's sister in Kansas City and let her know of the obsessive behavior. He isn't sure if it will do anything, but perhaps her sister can intervene or talk some sense into Belinda somehow. It's certainly worth a try.

It's disappointing. I am surprised at how let down I am at the results. It seems I was counting on, hoping for the results to show nothing.

Kellen takes me to find Henry afterward. "I'm sorry," he says quietly as we walk through the building. "I was hoping for better news."

I nod. "Me, too."

"I'll figure something out. There has to be a way to get her to let go."

The food I ate feels like lead in my stomach. I don't want to squash his hope. As much as I want to be able to be hopeful, I know from experience that sometimes, the only way someone obsessed can let go is by dying. Gabriella knows it, too. I just hope that's not the case with Belinda.

We find Henry on Beckett's lap behind the wheel of something enormous and bright yellow. I have no idea what it does, but I'm not sure my son should be the one guiding the steering wheel. He looks adorable in his hard hat emblazoned with Masters Construction, though.

He sees me and waves. I take out my phone and snap several shots before they park the behemoth back where it belongs, and Kellen helps Henry climb down. He's understandably put out when I tell him it's time to go, but at least a little mollified when Kellen tells him he can keep the hard hat.

Chapter 22

Demeter

Kellen and I are maintaining our separation until the protective orders are filed. We talk and text every day, but haven't seen each other since the lunch at the Masters Construction offices. It can take weeks for paperwork to be filed.

With a weekend free, I decided to use the time to connect with some friends I haven't seen for a while.

"I can't believe those babies are getting so big," I tell Lynzee Kearney. "It seems like it was just last year that we met."

"I know," Lynzee replies. "Henry is the same. He'll be what? Nine this year?"

Although it might seem like it was around a year ago, we actually met almost seven years ago when Henry was just two. Lynzee was attending a charity function with Preston Kearney, who had been good friends with Jeremiah when he was alive.

They had gone to school and college together and, both having come from families with money, ran in a lot of the same circles. As adults, they also had business dealings together.

"Yes. He'll be nine in September. He's getting so big that I barely have to bend over to look him in the eye."

"What about you, Sarah?" I ask. "How are things with Mitch? Any signs of marriage and children on the horizon?"

Sarah Cross laughs. "I am married to my business," she replies. "Mitch is fine, but I don't see us taking the leap into marriage, at least not anytime soon, and I'll leave all the baby having to you all. I have plenty of nieces and nephews to spoil rotten, so there's no need for me to be fruitful and multiply."

"You've gotta love a woman who knows her own mind," I say, holding up my margarita glass for a toast.

Lynzee and Sarah both live in Norman, so we gathered at Lynzee's house for Mexican food and margaritas. That saved her from having to find a sitter since Preston was out of town on business. Henry is at the McLean's, so the timing was perfect.

"How are things going with Kellen?" Lynzee asks.

I'd told her about meeting Kellen and our subsequent descent into dating. They don't know about the business with Belinda, so I fill them in.

"Now we're just waiting for the protective orders to be filed and we'll see how we want to proceed from there," I say.

"Wow," says Sarah. "That's creepy. What is it that makes someone hang on like that?"

I shake my head. "There are all kinds of motivations that can trigger someone to become obsessed. Some of them can be broken down easily, but they run the gamut and some are much more serious, requiring medication or even incarceration."

If someone doesn't have intervention with counseling and medication, and the antiquated laws don't take them out of circulation, the results can be deadly. Sometimes the stalker kills the object of their obsession and sometimes, as with me, the stalker is the one killed.

The fact that I killed someone still haunts me, even though it was in self-defense. The taking of another human being's life leaves a scar on your soul that never heals.

"Tell me more about Kellen," Lynzee says. "I've met his brothers, but that was the night that Preston and I broke up when we were first dating and, well, let's just say I didn't spend a lot of time chatting with them. They mentioned Kellen, but I'd never met him."

"When I first met him, I couldn't stand him. Even called him an asshole."

"No way," Sarah says.

I nod in confirmation. "Yeah. But I discovered he was just a little socially awkward, especially when he was around his brothers. He's a bit younger than them and lived his life in their very big shadows."

"I can see that," Lynzee says. "Beckett was very much the spotlight seeker when I met them and Morgan, well, he's got that machismo thing that just clings to him. He doesn't even have to try."

"That's a good way to put it," I reply. "Kellen is more sensitive, more of a deep thinker. When you get him alone or in a comfortable situation, he blossoms. And he's great with Henry. They're very much birds of a feather."

She gives me a knowing smile. "Sounds like there's a lot of potential there."

I simply smile in response. I hope there is potential there. We have to get through this thing with Belinda first, though. If we can get through it.

"Didn't you speak at a conference last weekend?" Sarah asks, and I'm glad for the change of subject.

"I did."

"How was it?"

"It was one of the scariest and most rewarding things I've ever done," I reply honestly.

I tell them about the conference, including being bumped up from panelist to session presenter. When I told them about my session having to be moved to a room twice the original size because of so many enrollments, Sarah gasps.

"Oh my God, that's crazy!" she exclaims.

"It was, but I think that was my favorite part. The panel was fun until some grumpy old man called my work perverted."

"He did not!" Lynzee laughs.

"Yes, he did," I confirm. "Although I really wanted to flip him the bird, I answered like a grownup and the staff took his mic away, so it was all good."

"Good for you," Sarah says, then takes a deep breath. "I've applied to take part in a conference for women entrepreneurs in the spring."

"As a speaker?" Lynzee asks, clearly surprised.

Sarah nods, her cheeks tingeing with pink.

"Wow! That's great!" I say. "I think you'll be a fantastic speaker."

"Really? Do you mean that?" she asks.

"Absolutely! You're smart and the business you've built in such a short period of time is very impressive. When will you find out if you've been selected?"

"They're supposed to confirm everyone by the end of September. I really hope I get it because the potential for growth is fantastic. Attendees will be coming from all over the world."

"All over the world?" Lynzee asks. "Where is this conference supposed to take place?"

Sarah grins. "Hawaii."

"Hawaii?" Lynzee and I both say in unison.

Sarah nods.

"I wonder if Preston can handle the kids for a week alone," Lynzee contemplates. "For a trip like that, surely you need a travel companion."

"Or two," I add with a laugh.

"Let's wait and see if I get it first," Sarah says.

Chapter 23

Kellen

I dial Demi's number. It's not unusual. We've been talking on the phone several times a week since this shitty business with Belinda started, but this is special. I finally have some good news.

"Hey there!" she says when she answers.

"Hi. How's your day going?"

"Well, it was good, but now it's better."

The smile in her voice shines through the phone and puts a smile on my face, too.

"I hope I can make it even better. I am calling to see if you could accompany me to an event on Friday night."

"Um...has something changed?"

"It has. Belinda has agreed to admit herself into a facility for help."

It took a few weeks for them to be issued, but when Belinda was served with the stalking protection orders for Demi and me, she panicked. I had contacted her sister in Kansas City and let her know what was going on when I filed the orders with the court system. When Belinda called home, the sister was able to convince her to seek help.

I had no idea, but one of the reasons why Belinda moved away from Kansas City was because of a similar incident. She became obsessive over a boyfriend who ended their relationship.

Belinda spent some time in a mental health facility there, and when she was discharged, her family thought she was fine. I'm hoping this is the end of it, but I informed the investigator and asked him to add the information to Belinda's file.

"That poor woman," Demi says. "I am glad she's seeking help, though. It could be deeper than just an obsessive tendency. If it's recurring in this manner, it could signify a chemical imbalance, but it can likely be treated with ongoing therapy and probably some medication."

"I'm glad, too. I don't bear her any ill will; I just want her to get the help she needs."

"Sooo...Friday?"

"Yes, it's an event with cocktails, an art auction, that kind of fun stuff. Beckett usually goes, but he has to go to Dallas, so I get to go as the company representative, and I desperately need an escort."

"Desperate, huh?" she asks, her voice doing that playful, sexy thing I am really starting to enjoy. I wonder what she sounds like when the playfulness is over, and she just wants to be sexy.

I chuckle as I shift in my seat. "Incredibly desperate, so please tell me you don't have any plans and can help me out."

She laughs. "I think I can do that. Let me touch base with my mom and make sure she and Dad can watch Henry."

"Perfect," I say. My cell phone signals that I've gotten a text. "Let me know when you find out."

"Will do."

I hope she's able to go. It seems like I've been waiting for this forever. If it hadn't been for Belinda, it would have happened soon after we met. It's three days until Friday and I can hardly wait.

I hang up my office phone and look at my cell. The message is from a number I don't recognize, so I start to delete it, but then the words sink in.

Unknown number: *Does she know?*

I open the text and read the full message.

Unknown number: *Does she know? Have you told her your secret yet? You think no one knows, but I do.*

Panic surges through me. I only have one secret and there's no way anyone could know. Unable to sit still, I stand and pace around my office. What am I going to do?

I'm tempted to call the number but disregard that notion. I don't want to play into their hand. Who's hand? There's no way. Absolutely no way anyone could know.

I return to my work, but my mind keeps being drawn back to the message. Maybe it's Belinda trying to come up with something wild to get my attention. If it's her, she couldn't possibly know, could she?

I think back across the times she was at my house. She wasn't there often and the only way she could know anything is if she somehow got access to my computer. I know for sure that never happened.

My computer has layers of passwords, especially to that section. Belinda is not someone I would have thought clever enough to figure out my passwords. I'm racking my mind, but can't make sense of it.

If it somehow is Belinda, it could mean that she hasn't followed through on checking herself into care. I need to find out more information, so I send the number to the investigator to see if they can trace it somehow. I'll see what they can find out before I decide how I want to respond. If I want to respond.

Once I settle back down at my desk, I have a hard time focusing on my work. The question of does she know keeps rolling around in my mind. By she, the texter can only mean Demi. Maybe I should just tell her.

Secrets lose their power when others know. I just don't know if I can bring myself to admit it after all these years. What would my family think? Mom would be so disappointed in me for not telling her.

And Demi. How would she react? It's all so new with her and if I spill the beans now, who knows how she'll react? Any feelings she might have for me could be squashed before they even have a chance to grow like a flower snatched out of a pot before it fully takes root.

Is that wrong of me? If I keep a secret to draw her deeper into whatever feelings she might have for me, does that make me the asshole? Maybe it does, but I can't risk it.

For now, I'll keep my secret, at least until I find out what the investigators discover. Once I hear from them, I'll decide whether it's time to come clean. Just thinking about it makes me want to throw up or run for an hour or so, something.

I feel incredibly unsettled in body and mind and doubt I get any more work done today.

Chapter 24

Demeter

I can't believe I'm about to have my first date with Kellen. We've spent a lot of time talking and texting, but I wonder if the easy camaraderie we've found in the virtual world will translate when we're face to face again.

I know we haven't really had that problem before, but it's been a few weeks since we last saw each other, and our phone friendship has grown far beyond where we were in person. We've reached a level of intimacy that surprises me. Usually you have to spend a lot of time face to face to reach this place.

I look myself over in the mirror. It's been a long time since I dressed up like this for a social event. I hope I look okay.

Maybe this dress is too short. The last time I went out dressed like this was way before Henry was born. I'm a mom now and maybe moms shouldn't dress like this. The impulse to change is strong.

The doorbell sounds through the house. That settles that; there's no time to change and I have no idea what I would change into, anyway. Time to put up or shut up. I drop my lip gloss into my clutch and head downstairs.

I hear Henry and Mom talking with Kellen as I descend the steps. Henry looks up and sees me and says, "Whoa, Mom! You're all sparkly!"

"Thanks buddy," I tell him, assuming he meant it as a compliment.

Kellen rises from the stool where he is sitting at the kitchen island, turning to look at me. He freezes for a heartbeat. With heat filling his eyes, he says, "You look beautiful."

My face grows warm. "Thank you. You're looking mighty handsome yourself." He does. He has on a dark charcoal suit with a cobalt blue shirt unbuttoned at the collar that makes his blue eyes even brighter. The heat of attraction blooms down low.

"We should probably go," he says, holding out his hand for me. "Mrs. Lawson, it was a pleasure to meet you. We need to go do something fun soon, buddy," he says to Henry while ruffling his hair.

"Yeah! Real soon!"

"Be good for Nana," I tell Henry, kissing him on the cheek. He promptly makes a yuck face and wipes it away. "Thanks Mom, I'll be home late. Love you both!"

Kellen is helping me up into the car and standing so close that I can smell the faint scent of his aftershave. He smells like spice and man. It's heady. Delicious. I look up at him and he's looking down at me, his eyes still heated.

He starts to lean down, and I know he's going to kiss me. He goes slow, giving me plenty of time to say no or stop it if I want.

I don't want to, though. I have been dreaming of kissing him for weeks.

His lips brush mine lightly, butterfly wings on flesh. He's still giving me time to pull back, to refuse his advances, testing me. I want him to know exactly where I stand on the matter, so I tiptoe up the millimeter my heels will allow and press my mouth to his, slipping my tongue against his kiss.

He takes my invitation and deepens the kiss. He tastes my mouth thoroughly and completely before pulling back and resting his forehead against mine. Both of us are breathing a little raggedly.

"We'd better go," he says.

"Or we won't go at all," I agree.

Kellen spins me out and back, pulling me into his arms and twirling us around to the beat of the music. He's a much better dancer than I, so I focus on following his lead. He doesn't let me take a single misstep. Even when my footwork is less than graceful, his guiding arms keep me from stumbling.

I am having such a great time with him! It's better than I could have imagined. We are dancing, and laughing, and having more fun than I've had in a very long time.

I should never have been concerned about the progress we'd made on the phone translating into the real world. It happened so seamlessly that it was almost unnoticeable.

There have been a couple of brief pauses, but only a couple. All our teasing and playful inside jokes have been pulled over into real life and I couldn't be happier. For a long time I thought

I was just fine without a man in my life, but Kellen has me rethinking all of that.

The song ends, and another begins.

I put my hand on his chest and say, "I need some water."

He nods and puts his hand over mine, threading our fingers as he leads me off the dance floor. We get a drink and wander around looking at the art displayed for the silent auction.

I don't see anything that appeals to me, but art has never really been my thing. The pieces that Bert had in the house when he gave it to me are lovely, but if it had been up to me to choose it, I wouldn't have been nearly as successful.

"See anything you like?" I ask.

"Absolutely," he says, squeezing my hand.

I look back over my shoulder and up at him, grinning. "The art, silly."

"Oh, the art...Nah, I'm not much of an art guy. Everything in my house other than family photos was chosen by a decorator."

As we wander through the space, Kellen is stopped often. Although he claims to not be the social butterfly that Beckett is, he does very well at greeting those who stop us. He knows almost everyone's name who says hello to him and introduces me smoothly. I don't know any of them.

I went to a few of these kinds of events with Jeremiah when we were together, including our very first date, when I was only eighteen. He was very comfortable rubbing elbows with socialites and playing the schmoozing game. He could shift gears with ease and go from talking politics with one person to popular culture with the next and world events with yet another.

Sometimes I wonder if I should start trying harder to step into this world, but it has never been my scene. I am all for giving to charity, but I have always preferred to give behind the scenes and don't really need a party or fancy dinner to encourage me to do so. However, I wonder how much of that is my natural inclination and how much is influenced by a lack of acclimation.

My friend Cait from the Society seems to have the same ease in these circles as Jeremiah did and as Kellen does. Maybe it's just because they were born to money. I wasn't, but I have money now, thanks to Bert, and perhaps I need to make more of an effort.

Henry was born to money, both the money I received from Bert, the money left to him by his father's estate, which remains untouched, and that of his grandparents. He needs to be able to function in this world. It will be his choice to embrace it or not, but it's my job as his parent to show him the way so he can make that decision for himself.

I have a feeling that if I am involved with Kellen and the Masters family, there will be a lot more of these types of events in my future. Masters Construction and the Masters family appear to be quite philanthropic. I have a great appreciation for those that make it a priority to give back to their community and to those less fortunate because I know what it's like to grow up living below the poverty line.

My family was rich in love and while we were fortunate enough to have a roof over our heads and food on the table most of the time, I can remember the struggles, too. Once I started working at fourteen, I diverted a good portion of my earnings into helping my parents.

It was part of what drove me to save every penny I could and get good grades so that I could get into college. I want to carry on the love I received from my parents, but I refuse to carry on their mindset of being stuck in poverty.

Kellen leads me to a small seating area, and we sit for a few minutes. "You're an excellent dancer," I say.

"Thanks. Mom made all of us take lessons. Beckett and I took to it, but Morgan says he was so bad the instructor offered to pay our parents to let him stop coming."

That makes me laugh. I can see that about the oldest Masters brother. He's very surefooted, but it is more the sinewy movement of a predator that comes through rather than the graceful movement of a dancer.

"I wanted to take lessons when I was a girl, but we couldn't afford it. Jeremiah used to say that I was an enthusiastic dancer." I make air quotes with my fingers to emphasize the enthusiastic part.

Kellen laughs. "Did he dance?"

I shake my head. "No. He would take me to clubs to let me dance, but he never would."

Is it strange that I'm talking about Jeremiah? After that night I spent at Kellen's on the anniversary of Jeremiah's death, memories of him don't have the same hold over me. He is a fact of my past, but I don't want to give Kellen the impression that he's more present in my mind than he is.

"You've got great natural moves and an excellent sense of rhythm. I think with a strong partner, you'd learn quickly."

"Is that an offer?" I ask with a raised eyebrow.

"Absolutely. I know a great salsa club I'll take you to; you'll love it."

"Ooh...that sounds fun."

Now that I'm sitting down, it's hitting me how tired I am. I think we've been dancing almost non-stop since we arrived. As soon as I saw the dance floor, it drew me like a magnet and Kellen was more than happy to follow me there.

I work out regularly, but dancing uses different muscles and I'm getting the message that I clearly need to work on my dancing stamina. In an effort to stretch my muscles, I lean back on my hands, lengthening my body. Kellen watches me, blatantly looking me up and down.

When his eyes meet mine, I cock my head and give him a questioning look. It's hard to tell in the venue's lighting, but I could swear the tips of his ears turn pink. He covers his embarrassment at getting caught looking by checking his watch.

I don't mind him looking. It pleases me that he finds me desirable. I certainly find him desirable and now that Belinda's out of the picture, if even temporarily, I'm eager to see how this attraction between us progresses.

"It's almost closing time," he says. "I've been having so much fun that I had no idea we'd been here so long."

"You're kidding me!" I say, pulling out my cell phone to verify the time.

He's right. It's almost eleven. I am an adult and don't have a curfew, but with it being this late, Mom will have taken Henry over to their house for the night. Normally it wouldn't be a big deal, but he doesn't sleep well over there and tomorrow he will be going to his grandparents' and when he doesn't get enough rest, Henry can be a bit of a bear. The McLean's don't have much patience with bears or even bear cubs.

Kellen picks up on my momentary concern. "Is everything okay?"

"Yes," I assure him. I can tell he doesn't believe me, so I tell him the thought that flitted through my mind.

"Do we need to go?"

"Not unless you want to. Henry's already asleep and it would be worse to go wake everyone up now to move him to his own bed. Plus, I'd like to get in at least one more dance before we go." I look up at him through my lashes. "Think you can handle that?"He grins. "Yes, I believe I might even have enough gas for at least two more dances left in me."

We dance for more than two songs. Just as we're about to leave, a slow song comes on. Kellen is leading me off the floor, but I stop. When he looks back at me, I don't know what he sees on my face, but he turns and takes me in his arms, pulling me close.

I rest my head against his chest as he sways us to the music. This feels good. And right.

Kellen Masters is sneaking under my radar and I'm not sure I just want to be friends anymore.

Chapter 25

Demeter

I roll over and turn my alarm off, wishing I could sleep another couple of hours. Unfortunately, I can't. I need to get up and shower so I can take Henry to the McLean's house and make it to my usual appointments.

The lack of sleep was definitely worth it, though. The evening with Kellen exceeded all my expectations and even some I didn't realize I had. That last slow dance was memorable enough, but the make-out session when he dropped me off was like the cherry on top of the sundae.

That man really knows how to kiss. We were locking lips like a couple of teenagers right there in the driveway. I was so tempted to invite him in, but when that happens, I want to be able to take my time.

Knowing that I had to be up in a few hours was the main reason I put the brakes on. I am suddenly feeling energetic as I remember that I'll also be spending most of the day with him today. Maybe we'll have an opportunity for round two.

Henry's birthday is in two weeks and Kellen is going to help me shop. I have an idea of what I want to get him, but would still like a man's input. Also, I know Henry will like whatever I get him, but if he knows Kellen helped pick it out, it will certainly up the cool factor.

"Good morning," Kellen says when I let him in later that day. "I like the toes."

I look down and wiggle my newly painted purple toenails. "Thanks."

He leans down and kisses me lightly. "How was Henry this morning?"

"Henry was in an unusually good mood. He's normally quiet in the morning, but today he wanted to know all about our date. What we did, what we ate, everything. When I told him about dancing, he declared it to probably be gross and vowed to never, ever dance a day in his life. He changed his tune a bit when I told him you had dance lessons as a boy and are an excellent dancer. He said dancing may just be partly gross and not completely gross, but he would have to know more to be sure."

Kellen laughs. "So, you told him everything?"

"Everything but the kissing. That would have been akin to a horror movie for him. He still thinks girls are gross except for me and his Nana and that is fine by me. I hope he keeps that attitude until he's in his twenties."

I gather my phone and keys and drop them into my purse as we head out the door. Kellen takes me to what he says is the best skate shop in the metro area. Henry has been fascinated with skateboarding since he saw the huge skate park in Tulsa and is sure he could be the next Tony Hawk, if only given the chance.

I don't know that he'll take to it as well as he thinks he will, but I always encourage him to try new things. Unfortunately, Henry takes after me when it comes to athleticism instead of his father. I'm a decent swimmer and find it easy to work out regularly, but I'm not an athlete.

Jeremiah was good at everything. I hope that someday Henry will find his thing, but until then, I'll let him try whatever he wants, even if it doesn't stick for long. That's one thing that having financial resources affords. We don't have to pick and choose when it comes to Henry's activities.

We're in the shop staring at an array of boards, or decks, as I've been informed they're called. "What do you think?" I ask Kellen. "If you were a nine-year-old boy, would you like the galaxy one, the black and white graphic one, or the one with the green design and the star?"

"I think if you go off his current fascination, the galaxy one would be best, but he has told me he's about done with astronomy stuff. I'd go for the green one. It's got a bit more punch than the other one."

"I agree." I turn to the clerk. "We'll take the green one and I need everything that goes with it for a nine-year-old boy – helmet, pads, everything."

Pretty much whatever the clerk suggests, I get. I know I probably don't really need everything he points out, but he doesn't get too carried away, so I go along.

"You're such an easy mark," Kellen teases as he carries the haul out to the car.

"Only when it comes to my son," I reply with a grin.

"I can certainly understand why."

Kellen loads everything into the back of his SUV and we're off to the next store. When I've just about filled the back of the car with books, toys, wrapping paper and even a robot, we head home.

"Are you going to throw a party?" Kellen asks.

"Just with family." I reply, shaking my head. "I asked him if he wanted to do something with friends, but he said no. As much as I hoped this school would work well for him, I think I'm going to have to change schools after this year. I just have no idea where to. When I asked him about it this year, he wanted to stick with his current school. I had Henry in public school, and he had friends but was frustrated academically, so I moved him to Montessori where he's happier academically but hasn't really made friends. It's very small and the kids in his class have been together since preschool and aren't very welcoming to outsiders."

"That's a shame. You should check out Casady. I've heard it's an excellent school; it's religious, though, and north of Nichols Hills. If you want to go farther north, there's Heritage Hall."

"I'll check them out, thanks. By the way, Henry is going to invite you to his party. It will be my parents and me, plus my sister and her family will come down from Tulsa to spend the night."

"Well, when he asks, I'll say yes."

Chapter 26

Demeter

Once we're back at the house, we have our first awkward moments. When we have something to focus on, like the party, shopping, or even Henry, we can flow together quite nicely. Now that it's just the two of us and we have nowhere to aim our attention, we're at loose ends.

"So, if you were here alone, what would you be doing?" Kellen asks.

"I'm afraid I'm quite boring because I'd probably be reading on the sofa and enjoying the peace and quiet."

"Then let's do that."

I look at him quizzically. "Did you bring a book?"

He chuckles. "Nope, but I seem to remember you having an entire library full of them."

I go upstairs to get my latest tome while Kellen goes to the library. We settle onto the loveseat, my legs draped over Kellen's lap, and settle in to start reading. It feels strange that we're just going to be sitting here reading together.

He looks at my book. "You're still reading that author?"

"Yeah. I'm almost through with her backlist. I don't know what I'll do when that happens. I'll have to find someone new."

"Wow, so you're a genuine fan."

"I've enjoyed this author more than I have any other in a long time."

"Hmm," is all he says before opening the book he selected from the library.

He holds his book in one hand while the other rests on my bare ankle. His thumb strokes over the top of my foot and it's very distracting. Distracting in a good way. I glance down to watch for a moment, but I don't think he even realizes that he's doing it.

I go back to my book, trying to give my full attention to the words on the page. When I've read the same paragraph three times. I close my book and put it aside.

I watch Kellen as he continues to read, seemingly unaware of anything else around him. How can he be so completely absorbed in something and oblivious to everything around him? I figure a little turnabout is fair play.

Although I have no intention of actually reading, I pick my book up again. I keep my eyes on the page, but I pull one leg up, not the one with his hand on it, so that my foot is resting on top of his upper thigh. Slowly, deliberately, I start to move my foot and toes so that I'm stroking lightly back and forth.

His thumb stops stroking my foot, but I don't stop. I turn a page, having not read a single word, and continue the ruse. He shifts in his seat and it's all I can do to keep from grinning and giving myself away.

He closes the book with a snap. I look up, doing my best to radiate innocence. "Is something wrong?"

He's watching me, a smirk on his face.

"What?" I ask, my eyes wide.

"You are rotten," he says.

I can't help it; I laugh. "You started it!"

"I did not!"

He reaches for me, and I laugh, putting up a minimum of resistance before I let him pull me over. I don't know that it's what he intended, but I use the momentum he creates to land on his lap, straddling him. His face goes serious. Mine is soft as I cup his jaw in my hands.

I stroke my thumbs over his smooth cheeks as I look into his eyes. They are such a vibrant blue that at first, I thought they were contacts, but when I saw the same thing in his brothers, I knew it was genetic. His eyes are naturally a blue so deep they make me think I could swim in them forever. He really is a beautiful man.

Not just because he's handsome, but he has such a beautiful mind and heart, too. He doesn't rush me, just lets me take my time, looking my fill. I lean in to kiss him.

He lets me take the lead and I appreciate that. I don't know where I intend to end up, but I will let things unfold organically with no agenda. He seems to be of the same mind, letting me explore with lips and tongue.

He's not rushing, but his body is definitely reacting as he hardens beneath me. My own arousal spikes and my core turns liquid. His hands go to my hips, pulling me snug against him. The zipper of his jeans strokes against my center with every shift and move of my body.

This has gone far beyond mere playful desire. I realize I want more than just another make-out session. I want to do more than kiss.

This has crossed the line into need. More than kisses; I want to taste him. I need more than hands over fabric; I want to touch every inch of him.

I want him.

I. Want. Him.

With my hands on his chest, I push away from him and back off his lap. Once I'm standing before him, I hold out my hand. "I'd like to take you upstairs and make love with you."

He looks at my hand, then raises his eyes to mine. "Are you sure?"

"Yes. But if you don't..."

He doesn't let me finish. He puts his hand in mine and rises from his seat. I lead him upstairs to my bedroom. I'm not shy about sex outside of the bedroom, but Mom often pops over to visit when Henry's with Jeremiah's parents, so it's best if we take things behind closed doors.

When we reach the landing, he sweeps me up into his arms, carrying me like a bride over the threshold of my room. He carries me across the room and, with a knee on the mattress, leans over and lays me in the middle of the bed. He pulls off his shirt and moves to lie with me.

His mouth finds mine as his fingers tangle in my hair. He pushes me back down when I turn and press my body to his.

"I want to take my time with you," he says.

I smile and rub the tip of his nose with mine. He returns to kissing me, pressing himself against my hip, and I can feel that he is still just as aroused as I am. Even so, he takes his time.

He tugs at the hem of my tank, and I lift my arms so he can pull it off over my head. He pulls me to him, reaching around to undo my bra, then pushes me onto my back again. As I lie back, he pulls my bra off.

He just stares at me. I shiver from a chill, my nipples pebbling and watch him as his eyes devour me. He cups my cheek then moves his hand to my hair, twirling a curl around his finger, a small smile flitting across his lips.

His fingers walk down my neck and across my collarbone to the hollow at my throat. He taps his index finger in the divot and moves it down my sternum, between my breasts, and down to my navel.

He rakes his eyes over my torso, this slow examination making my blood simmer. Instead of giving me his warmth, he is stoking a fire from within. I let him hold me and kiss me as I hold him and kiss him.

Then he leans over me, and his warmth seeps into my skin. Into my blood. I want more. The warmth of his skin is full of promise, full of desire.

I want to be closer to him. To feel more of that warmth surrounding me. I shift and lean deeper into him as I slip my arms around his neck, and he wraps me in his. As I sigh against his mouth, the warmth I crave settles around me. Still, I want more. Crave more.

He slips my shorts and panties off and kisses me everywhere, exploring my body from head to toe with eyes and lips and fingers. He touches me reverently with so much tenderness.

With every kiss and every touch, he stokes a fire in my belly. Heat pools and spreads until I am ablaze and drowning in desire for this man.

His hand slips between my legs, cupping my sex. It's so hot there, I am surprised he doesn't burn his fingers as I whimper, pressing back against his palm. He deepens his kiss and slips a finger inside me, stroking it deep. He slips another in with it.

He kisses his way across my jaw, down my neck, lingering when I gasp as he kisses below my ear. His lips graze over my collarbone and finally, I feel his soft lips and warm tongue on the hard peak of flesh that had been begging for attention for some time. A moan oozes out of me as he sucks it into his mouth, his tongue teasing my heaving bosom.

Sheesh! I've been reading too many romance novels!

I giggle as that thought flits through my mind, then his fingers stroke that most sensitive of spots deep inside me and I'm not giggling anymore. My giggles turn back to moans, and I move against his hand. His thumb presses against my clitoris, ratcheting up the heat even more. I feel pressure starting to build as his fingertips hit just the right spot deep inside me again.

"Oh!" pops out.

He stops sucking my breast and buries his face in my shoulder, whispering words too low for me to understand over the pounding of blood in my ears. His focus seems to be intent on hitting that spot again and again as he strokes his fingers hard and fast inside while working his thumb outside, and it is driving me quickly toward an orgasm.

Now that he's found its exact location, he hits it just right again as he kisses below my ear and his thumb flicks my clitoris, kicking me over the precipice. I squeeze him tight as I cry out his name and gasp for breath, every muscle in my body going from hard as obsidian to molten lava in a heartbeat.

"I want you inside of me," I say.

"Hush, I told you, I want to take my time with you."

"You're making me crazy."

"Good." I feel him grin against my mouth.

He kisses me again, deeply, passionately, hungrily. His hand goes to my breast, molding it, caressing it, reshaping it. He tweaks the nipple, making it even harder, then drags his thumb back and forth across the peak.

The relaxed bliss of moments ago begins to morph into tension renewed as he kindles arousal in my body again. He kisses my chin and my throat, working his way down between my breasts, stopping to suck one nipple into his mouth.

He laves it with his tongue, pulling the peak between his lips and nipping it with his teeth. The other breast receives the same attention. I am on fire again, my blood boiling and my body coming alive under his ministrations.

His kisses are agonizingly slow as he continues his pilgrimage southward. He settles his torso between my legs, pushing them wide and kissing the inside of one thigh and then the other. Kissing me everywhere but where I most want his lips to be.

"Please," I whimper.

He blows across my sex, causing me to flinch.

"Kellen," I whine, aching with need.

Raspy chuckles waft up to my ears.

"You are a sadist," I tell him breathlessly. "You're being cru-eloooooh!"

His tongue licks between my lips, turning my protests to cries of pleasure. He explores every fold and crevice with his lips and tongue, driving the pressure higher and higher. I tangle my fingers in his hair, urging him on with words and actions.

He pulls back and flicks that sensitive bundle of nerves with his tongue, causing fireworks to explode. My eyes roll back in my head and my body shakes as sparklers sizzle through my veins. He kisses me on my pubic bone and moves up my body until he settles his hips between my legs and holds me, planting kisses on my collarbone, my neck, my lips.

I taste myself on his lips and kiss him deeper. He groans when I bite his lower lip. The brush of the head of his shaft along my sex taunts me.

With a hiss, I say, "I want you inside of me," as I reach out a hand toward the nightstand. "I got back on the pill, but there are condoms, too."

I can't reach. He kisses me below my ear again, causing me to go limp. "I'm clean," he says. "I got tested a few weeks ago, just to be sure."

I look up at him. "Me, too."

He smiles down at me. "Seems we were both hopeful about where this was going."

I smile, feeling shy. "Yeah."

One of his hands disappears between our bodies, and I lean up to kiss his shoulder. It is so tempting that I can't help myself. I bare my teeth and bite him there. He hisses something and a few heartbeats later, he positions himself at my opening and begins to push inside.

I throw my head back. "Yes!"

He goes slow, knowing exactly how long it has been since I've been with a man. My body stretches around him, the pain a dull ache. Once he's fully seated, he puts his forehead to mine for a moment, giving me time to adjust.

"God, you feel good," he says, his voice brittle.

He begins to move, our bodies undulating together, finding our rhythm. He makes love like he dances, his movements graceful and fluid. I let him lead me in this most intimate of dances.

Without warning, he rolls and puts me on top without breaking our connection. I move on top of him, his eyes watching our bodies where we are connected. My hands pull his up to my breasts and show him how I like to be touched. I let him take over and I throw back my head as I move faster, letting him know how much pleasure he is giving me.

"Oh yes, like that," I tell him as I lose myself in the sensations.

One hand leaves my breast. I miss it keenly, so I look down to see where it has gone. He licks the pad of his thumb and slips it between us. I gasp out unintelligible syllables, the liquid heat of a volcano rising from that bit of contact with my already sensitive flesh.

He growls in response, and I swear I can feel the vibrations of it through his thumb. I can't hold back any longer. The volcano erupts as another orgasm rips through me violently.

He catches me as I crumple forward, my body limp. With a roll, he changes our positions again, and begins to move on top of me, harder and faster, chasing his own release. He growls again and slams his body against mine as he finds it.

He collapses half on top of me, half to the side, but stays connected with me, breathing hard. I sigh with contentment. He takes a few moments to come back to himself, but when he does, he shifts off me, stretching out and pulling me with him to the other side of the bed.

I don't know what I expected, but anything that I might have built up in my mind was no match for the reality. He kisses the top of my head and I shiver. I turn into him, snuggling my body against his.

"Cold?"

"No," I say against his chest. "Just aftershocks."

He chuckles.

We lay there like that for a while, his fingers tracing lazy circles on my back as I just enjoy the feel of him wrapped around me. My stomach growls and breaks the moment. Kellen laughs.

"Let's go downstairs so I can find something to feed you."

I kiss his chest and happily agree. "Okay."

Chapter 27

Demeter

The rest of Saturday into Sunday morning was spent in and out of the bedroom until we had to get dressed to go pick Henry up. The three of us were together all morning, Sunday, until Kellen left to go to lunch with his parents.

I didn't want him to leave, and he asked us to go with him, but I wasn't ready for that. We aren't even officially a couple. I don't think.

On Monday I take Henry shopping for new clothes for school, which starts in a couple of weeks. He's growing like a weed and he's gaining more height than width, so everything is too short from pants legs to sleeves. He hates shopping for clothes but agrees when I tell him we can have lunch with Kellen while we're in the City.

After that, the week falls into my usual routine of seeing clients and going to class. It doesn't feel usual, though. Everything is now overshadowed by thoughts of Kellen. These new feelings make me feel lighter than I have in a very long time.

We talk each night after I get Henry to bed, but it's now Thursday and I haven't seen Kellen since Monday. I miss him. I miss him so much that it worries me a little. How did I become so attached to him in such a short period of time?

I walk into the dining room at the Society to find Cait and Gabriella already there waiting. Arriving earlier than I usually do, I thought I was getting the jump on them. I figured they'd still be in the fitness center.

"Hi!" I say.

"Well, someone looks happy!" Cait says.

Gabriella looks at me knowingly. "Yes, she does. Kellen was awfully giddy at lunch on Sunday, too. I take it you two had a good date on Friday night?"

I school my face and try to keep from smiling. "Friday night and we picked it up again after I dropped Henry at his grandparents' on Saturday morning through to Sunday morning."

Ella looks at me sharply. "Through? He stayed the night?" I can see when the implications of that revelation dawn on her. "Oh. My. God. Did you guys?"

I nod, unable to keep from grinning. I hold up four fingers.

"Four times?" she gasps.

I nod again.

"Oh, my!" Cait says and we all laugh.

"Enough about me," I say. "I missed you in class this week."

"Yeah," Gabriella says, looking down. "I'm going to have to drop out for a while."

"Oh, no! Why?"

She hands me a white card. I frown, looking over at her because I don't understand.

"Turn it over," she says.

I do and see a sonogram showing a tiny fetus. I cover my mouth with a hand. "OMG, Ella!" I look over at her. "Really?"

She nods, her eyes filling with happy tears.

"That's fantastic!" I say.

I know she was concerned that she'd never have children, so it's very exciting that she's pregnant.

"Oh, Ella, that's wonderful!" Cait says. "When are you due?"

"Valentine's Day. How sweet would that be?" she answers.

"Are you still going to get married at Christmas?" I ask.

"That's the plan," she answers. "I never, ever thought I'd be getting married in a maternity wedding dress, but it's either that or put off the wedding and Morgan won't hear of it. He says we either go to Vegas and get married right away or we stick with the current plan. Rebecca would murder him if we ran off to Vegas, so preggo bride it is."

Another of our orientation quint comes in and sits at the table. "Serena!" Cait says, "How nice to see you!"

I'm glad Serena is coming more often. She seems like she is an interesting woman, but I haven't had a chance to get to know her very well. We order our food and are getting caught up when Serena asks me, "Demi, were you around campus corner earlier today? I could have sworn I saw you."

I shake my head. "No, my office is off northwest twenty eighth and Flood. I was there all day."

"Huh," she says. "You must have a twin. She had the same hair, but now that I see you, hers was a little shorter, only about shoulder-length."

"Supposedly, everyone has a twin out there in the world," Cait says.

"I guess so," I reply with a chuckle. "Maybe I should go hang out over there and see if I run into her. It might be fun to meet my twin. How is the remodel of your house going, Cait?"

"Fabulous! Between Ella's designs and Masters Construction team, we're getting close to being done. Ford is very excited to move into his grandparents' house. As soon as it's finished, we're going to have a housewarming and all of you are invited."

"Ford, is that your husband?" Serena asks.

"Partner," Cait answers with a shrug. "We may decide to get married someday, but for now, we're just happy to be together. Ford says he doesn't want anyone thinking he married me for my money."

"If it works for you guys, that's all that matters," Gabriella says.

"What does Ford do?" Serena asks.

"He's a homicide detective with OKCPD," says Cait.

Serena's fork pauses halfway to her mouth. "Really? How did you two meet?"

"We met at the gym," Cait says, then tells Serena their story.

I love hearing her tell it. She and Ford are so cute together and pretty much perfect for each other. To see them together, you'd think they were a couple of teenagers. They can't keep their hands off each other.

It's much the same with Gabriella and Morgan. I've never known two couples who were better matched. That thought brings to mind the fortune teller machine downstairs. Both of them got their wishes.

I wonder if maybe I'm getting my wish, too, even though I didn't make a formal wish. I verbalized my desire to have a man in our lives who could relate to Henry and Kellen certainly fits that bill. He and Henry are very much alike in so very many ways.

It seems that we've been good for Kellen, too. He has really blossomed since we first met. Like Henry has to take his time acclimating to a new situation, he's grown comfortable with us, and it has allowed him to relax and be himself.

The fortune, if that's what it really is, said that a love would be replaced. Does that mean a love in Henry's life alone? Or does it mean that a love in my life will be replaced, too?

I know no one will ever replace Jeremiah, but I won't lie to myself. I'm in serious like with Kellen and although he's not Jeremiah and never could be, his differences are nice. However, I think his differences are actually better matched to Henry.

I know Kellen cares for me, too, but I don't know how much. Stop it, I tell myself. This is crazy. How could a machine possibly predict all of this, much less set it in motion?

I've been to that bookstore more times than I can count, and I have never set eyes on Kellen in there before. He also seems like he goes to that same store fairly regularly.

Had I just not noticed him? Had we somehow avoided crossing each other's path? Maybe we would have run into each other eventually, and that silly fortune is just a coincidence.

I get out of my head and rejoin the conversation with my friends.

Chapter 28

Demeter

"How did I let you talk me into thinking this was a good idea?" I ask.

Kellen laughs. "This is an easy one, barely more than a walking path."

For some reason, I let Kellen convince me that today was a good day for a hike and first thing in the morning, no less. He's right, it's not a strenuous hike, and September is much better than doing this in July, but to me, it might as well be over a hundred degrees because I'm sweating like a sinner in church. My shirt is soaked, my shorts are soaked, even my socks are moist, and I'm sure I stink to high heaven.

He and Henry act like it's a breezy seventy degrees outside and are none the worse for wear. Henry keeps racing ahead but stays within sight of Kellen because I'm lagging too far behind to keep an eye on him myself. He'll invariably find something interesting to look at and wait for us, or rather me, to catch up.

Henry has squatted down to look at something, so Kellen stands sideways in the middle of the path so he can monitor both of us. I finally reach him, and he taps the bill of my fluorescent tie-dyed ball cap. Then he starts walking toward Henry again. I let out a groan and trudge after him.

They're both squatting and looking at whatever has fascinated Henry now. I catch up to them finally. Henry looks up at me with a huge grin and says, "Look Mom! It's a big fat toad!"

Sure enough, there is an enormous amphibian squatting in a puddle of murky water, staring at the two men in my life with indifferent patience. I'm just happy that his lily pad of choice is in the shade.

"He's probably enjoying having a puddle to play in after last night's rain," I comment.

"Yeah," Henry says in agreement.

Kellen curls a hand around my calf and looks up at me. His lips quirk. He stands and pulls my hat off, only to put it on his own head. "Where did you get such an ugly hat?"

"Vacation to Florida," I answer. "We went with my sister and her husband when Henry was five. That's the last time we've been on vacation."

He pulls me into his arms. "Maybe we need to plan something."

I smile up at him. "Maybe we do. Something with air conditioning."

The man is not the least bit damp from the humidity or the heat. It makes me want to smack him. However, he redeems himself when he leans down and kisses me slow and languidly. Henry makes gagging noises, which makes Kellen chuckle against my mouth.

We broke the barrier of being affectionate with each other in front of Henry by accident. We were watching a movie and Kellen had his arm stretched over the seat Henry was sitting in and he was playing with my hair. Then, when Henry took a bathroom break, he returned to find Kellen leaning over and kissing me.

He asked if Kellen was my boyfriend and Kellen told him yes. I was a little surprised by the admission, but I found I liked the sound of it, so I let it stick. Henry just replied, "Good," and restarted the movie.

Kellen still doesn't stay over unless Henry is gone, though. I'm just not ready for that. We've fooled around a few times after Henry has gone to bed, but I've been a nervous wreck the entire time and I can't really relax and get into it like I can when I know there's no chance of him overhearing us or walking in.

"All right, buddy," Kellen says, "I think we need to head to the car before Mom melts completely."

"Okay," Henry agrees, and starts bouncing down the path in the direction of the parking lot.

Kellen keeps pace with me. Considering his legs are about twice as long as mine, he probably feels like he's crawling. He sticks with me, though, holding my sweaty hand in his cool, dry one. I'm back to wanting to smack him, but he's being sweet, so I can't.

He hands me his water bottle and I take it, drinking down the last few ounces of water. "How is it you look fresh as a daisy, and I look like I've been dunked in the lake?" I ask.

He shrugs. "I run all summer, so I guess my body is just acclimated to the higher temps."

I snort. "Masochist."

"Only if you tie me up first," he says low and looks at me with a smirk.

I just raise an eyebrow at him.

The parking lot comes into view, and he takes out his keys to remotely start the SUV so the air conditioner has a chance to run. I hope it's like an iceberg when we get in. Henry is buckled in and waiting for us by the time we get there.

As we're getting situated, he says, "Mom looks like she needs some ice cream to cool off."

Kellen laughs.

"I love you, son," I say with a laugh.

"I know," Henry replies matter-of-factly.

We do get ice cream, but Kellen and Henry go into Braum's for some to take home rather than getting it to eat in the car. Kellen learned that lesson the hard way when he ended up with blue birthday cake ice cream on his leather seats. I warned him, but some things have to be learned the hard way.

Once I flip the A/C up to high, I point all the vents I can reach toward my side of the car. I sit back in my seat and stare outside with heavy-lidded eyes. When they come out of the store, I am struck again by how easily they could pass as father and son.

Kellen is still wearing my hat. It looks ridiculous on him, but that just makes it even more adorable. He takes it off and hands it to me when he gets back into the car.

"I can't believe I forgot I had that thing on."

"But it looks so cute on you," I tease as I put it on the dash.

We're almost to my house when he asks, "Have you thought any more about lunch tomorrow?"

Kellen's mother has invited Henry and me to Sunday lunch at their house with the whole family. I've met the entire family and think they're lovely, but the thought of sitting down to a meal with them in their home...well, it just seems a little daunting. However, I know that's just me.

The few times I went to Jeremiah's family's house for a meal with the family were a disaster. The first time was at Thanksgiving and it seemed they were trying everything they could to run me off. I doubt that the Masters clan would be anything like the McLeans. However, there's no way I can know until I try it, is there?

"Henry," I say, "what do you think about having lunch with Miss Rebecca and the rest of Kellen's family tomorrow?"

"Are they coming to our house?"

"No, we'll be going to Miss Rebecca's house."

He thinks about it for a moment. He really likes Kellen's mother. After a few minutes of pondering while he stares out the side window, he nods and says, "Okay. I really liked that stuff she made before."

Kellen reaches over the console and takes my hand in his. He knows this is another step in our relationship, as do I.

Chapter 29

Kellen

I wake up and look at my phone, surprised by the sun streaming into my bedroom. It's after nine. I never sleep this late.

I roll out of bed and onto my feet but have to stop when a wave of dizziness washes over me. Both my head and my mouth feel like they've been stuffed with cotton. I hope I'm not coming down with something.

Today is an important day and the only way I'd change my plans is if I'm dying. I get up slower this time and make my way to the bathroom. I open a bottle of non-drowsy cold medicine and pop two of the tablets, hoping they'll knock out whatever is going on.

After a light breakfast and a shower, I'm feeling much better, so I figure I must not have the bubonic plague or something worse. Maybe it's just allergies. Not that I've ever had allergies, but there's a first time for everything, I guess.

I have a couple of hours to kill so I think I'll go ahead and get dressed and go over to Demi's. I can't stand being away from her and Henry. I've gotten so used to the added noise and energy a child brings into a home and my house just seems so quiet and empty.

I used to love that quiet, but I have found that's one of the many things that has changed about me over the past few months. My world used to be gray, but now it's full of color and joy and noise and I love it. I wonder if Demi would consider cohabitating.

I know that's a big step, but we're not far away from that now. After work, I go to her house several nights a week and spend most of my weekends with them as well. When Henry's at his paternal grandparents, I stay overnight with Demi. It's just not enough anymore.

Henry opens the door when I ring the bell, and I follow him upstairs. He runs and jumps onto Demi's bed, lying down and opening his book up to read. She's in the bathroom fixing her hair. I put my hands on her hips and lean down to kiss the top of her shoulder.

"Hey you," she says, turning and sliding her hands up around my neck. She tiptoes, stretching up, seeking my lips.

I meet her halfway and kiss her. Henry makes gagging noises in the bedroom. I smile against her mouth.

"You look beautiful," I tell her. "Henry, it won't be long before you'll think kissing is pretty cool."

"Don't say that!" Demi exclaims. "He's already growing up too fast."

"Yeah," Henry replies, not looking up from his book. "I'll be nine in a week."

I go sit on the bed by Henry and leave Demi to finish. "I know. Are you excited to see your cousins next week?"

"Yeah, I guess. They're just little, though. DJ's only two and Amanda's just a baby. They can't really play or anything. Aunt Tilly says that the summer when DJ's five and Amanda is four, she's going to try to talk Mom into going to Disney World. Now that will be fun cuz they'll be old enough to know what's going on."

"That does sound like fun."

Demi comes out of the bathroom. She has on one of those sundresses I like so much, and she has her hair piled up on top of her head, showing off that long stretch of neck where I like to kiss her. I want nothing more than to pull that dress off over her head, throw her on the bed and tangle my fingers in her hair while I fuck her senseless.

"We don't have time for that," she says, clearly reading my thoughts.

"Time for what?" asks Henry.

"Yeah, time for what?" I echo.

She rolls her eyes and leaves the room.

"Come on, buddy, it's about time to go."

"Can I bring my book?"

"Sure. I don't think you'll need it, though."

At my parent's house, Henry undoes his buckle and gets out on my side. As soon as I close the car up, he latches onto my hand, a sure sign that he is nervous. I see he's carrying his book.

I squat down in front of him. "Why don't we leave this in the car? If you need it, I'll come get it for you, okay? It's a little rude to show up at someone's home automatically assuming you're going to be bored."

He absorbs that for a half a minute, then hands the book over. "Okay. I just wanted to be prepared, but if it's in the car, that's good enough."

I smile and put the book away. He takes my hand again and we make our way into my parents' house.

Henry has my mother completely wrapped around his finger. From the first time they met, she has been thoroughly charmed by him. He's quite enamored with her, too. I know a small part of it is that she hopes Demi and Henry will become part of the family, but even if that never happens, they've struck up a friendship that is quite special.

He didn't want to go sit with the men in the den. He wanted to hang out in the kitchen with my mother and Gabriella while they were fixing lunch. Demi fixed the salad, telling my mother the same thing she told me about not being able to cook.

I believe her, but I don't mind. I love to cook and am good at it. It would make me happy to cook all our meals for the rest of our lives.

Henry helps me set the table and is adamant that he wants to sit between me and his mom, so that's where I put his plate. He eats a good amount of everything and tells Mom thank you for fixing the meal, further charming her. When Mom brings out a cake with a candle on it, his eyes go round as saucers.

"A little birdie told me it's your birthday next week, so I wanted to make you a cake," she tells him.

"Oh, Miss Rebecca, thank you," he replies.

He blows out the candle and makes a wish. Once the cake is eaten and the table cleared, Mom gives Henry a wrapped box. "Happy birthday, Henry."

He looks up at Demi. "Mom, may I open it?"

"Of course, buddy."

He tears away the paper and it must be something he wanted because he barely gets the picture on the box uncovered before he says, "No way! This is so cool!" He looks over at Mom and says, "Thank you very much!"

When it's completely denuded of paper, I can see that it's some kind of construction kit that he can put together but it also has parts so he can wire up lights and other stuff. It really is pretty neat. Leave it to my mom to find the best construction related toy for a kid. She's already trying to indoctrinate him into the company.

Without warning, he jumps up out of his chair, runs around the table and hugs Mom. She hugs him back and kisses him on the cheek, patting his back. I swear she has tears in her eyes.

"I'm so happy you like it," she says.

We all move to the living room. Until a few weeks ago, this was my cue to disappear, but I don't feel the need to do that anymore. I hate to say it, but it's thanks to Belinda. If she hadn't started up with her weirdness, I never would have dumped my unhappiness all over Morgan.

I think it may have happened over time because Gabriella had noticed and had apparently already mentioned it to Morgan. However, I went from feeling like an outsider to feeling like I'm really a part of the family in a matter of days. I didn't think it was possible, but somehow, it has all come together.

Between my family and Demi and Henry, I feel more optimistic about the future than I've ever felt in my life. I take one of the armchairs and pull Demi down onto my lap. I've seen Morgan do it just like this with Gabriella and always felt a little jealous, but now I have someone of my own.

Henry climbs onto the sofa next to Mom. They talk low about the toy she bought and when he tells her he likes to read a lot, she has him tell her all about his current book.

I never imagined life could be this good.

Chapter 30

Demeter

"I think I'm going to have to get used to being Henry's second favorite person in the world," I tell Kellen as we clean up after Henry's birthday party with my family.

I sent Mom and Dad home despite her offer to stay and help with the clean-up. She does enough for us. Tilly and Drake went upstairs to put their little ones in bed about the same time I sent Henry upstairs. Even after playing chess all evening on the set that Kellen got Henry for his birthday, Henry insisted that Kellen be the one to tuck him in.

"It's just because I'm new," Kellen says.

He sets down the trash bag he's been stuffing with discarded wrapping paper and party trash. He takes me in his arms and spins me around in a dance move in time to the music that is playing low. We dance, swaying until the end of the song. He gives me a quick kiss and goes back to cleaning.

"We're buddies, but believe me when I tell you that no one can replace his mom in a man's heart."

"Thanks for racing over here after work to help," I say. "I know Mom really appreciated the help with the food. Tilly is almost as useless in the kitchen as I am."

"I was happy to help," he says with a shrug. "Happy to be included."

He takes the bags of trash out to the garage as I put the last of the dishes in the dishwasher and start it. When he comes back in, I'm about to turn the music off when a slow song comes on. "Hang on," he says. "One more before bed."

He loves to dance, and I love that about him. I smooth my palms up his chest and around his neck as his arms go around my waist. He kisses me long and deep. My breasts brush against his chest, causing my nipples to tighten and my arousal begins to rise. When the song is over, he leads me upstairs.

Officially, he's staying over in one of the guest rooms. However, once everyone else is fast asleep, he crawls into bed with me and continues to stoke those beginning sparks of arousal into flame.

We make love slowly and quietly to not broadcast it to the entire house until we're both sated and snuggled together in sleep. It feels so good having him in bed with me and I've found that when he's not there to wrap me up in his arms, I don't sleep as well.

I'm falling for this man. I thought Jeremiah had been my one great love, and that I'd never have another. Somehow, I had convinced myself that I was okay with that, but now I'm starting to imagine a future with Kellen, and it is such a welcome surprise.

He wakes at his usual time of five in the morning. He tries to get out of bed without waking me, but doesn't manage it. When he starts sneaking down the hall like some cat burglar who's trying to evade laser alarms, it starts me giggling, which starts him chuckling. We must be lucky because we aren't exactly quiet but manage not to get caught.

He and I take Henry to the McLean's for their visit, then go back to my house for breakfast with my family. Tilly and Drake leave soon after to go back to Tulsa, leaving Kellen and I to spend the day together. We go to the farmer's market and run some errands together, spending the day hanging out and enjoying each other's company.

We decide to spend the night at his house for a change of pace. He has no problem with staying at mine, but sometimes it's nice to mix it up. He's in his office on the phone with Morgan about something business related, so I decide that it's time for a distraction tactic.

I stand in the doorway to his office for a good sixty seconds before he looks up and sees me. I am wearing only a pair of skimpy black panties, a wide red ribbon wrapped around my torso and tied in a bow to cover my breasts, and one of the silly party hats Tilly brought for Henry's birthday. His jaw drops open.

"Gotta go," he says into the phone and disconnects.

"I thought you might be a little jealous of Henry getting all the presents last night," I say nonchalantly, lifting one of my arms above my head and resting it against the doorframe. I lean into it, stretching my body. "All work and no play makes Kellen a dull boy."

I turn and walk away, untying the bow and letting the ribbon stream out behind me, dragging on the floor as I do. His presence behind me is palpable. I can feel him stalking behind me, tracking my path. Just when I think I'm going to make it to the bedroom, he lunges and grabs me before I leave the living room.

I squeak when he sweeps me up in his arms and tosses me onto the sofa while I laugh like a ninny. He pulls off his shirt and sets it aside, then covers me with his heavy body. He presses his lips to mine and I'm not laughing anymore.

He takes my wrists in one hand and moves them above my head, holding them there. I wrap my legs around him and he growls as he grinds against me, the roughness of his pants pressing into the thin fabric of my panties like some kind of hyper erotic sexual sandpaper. I arch my back, pressing my body against his, needing more contact.

His free hand finds my breast, molding and reshaping it. He pulls his mouth away from mine and says, "Do not move your hands. Do you understand?"

"Yes," I whimper.

He cups both breasts in his firm hands, still grinding his erection against my core. I look up at him to see him looking down on me, watching my reactions. He rolls his hips, creating such a powerful surge of arousal in me I push my head back against the sofa and moan, my eyes rolling back in my head.

His mouth replaces one of his hands, sucking the hard nipple into his mouth, teasing it with his tongue and nipping gently with his teeth. My fingers tangle in his hair. He nips the side of my breast, hard enough to make me yelp.

"Hands," he growls.

"Yes, sir," I say and fling my hands back over my head. I love it when he takes charge.

"Good girl."

He covers both breasts again but moves his mouth down my body, kissing and nipping in turns, driving the pleasure in my body higher and higher. As he shifts, it breaks the contact between our bodies, so I pull with my legs, trying to get it back. He resists me and bites me on the hip.

He pulls my panties aside and slides two fingers into me easily because I am dripping wet. "Is this what you want?" Kellen asks.

"No," I say, breathless as I move in time with his fingers stroking in and out of me. He's really, really great at that. He's pushing me higher, creating the best kind of pressure, and I feel an orgasm racing toward me.

"No? Want me to stop?" His fingers halt their delicious motion.

"No!" I wail.

"You do want it, or you don't want it?"

"I want you!" I gasp.

He grips my panties, and with a hard twist and jerk, he tears them away. He quickly pushes down his pants and positions himself at my opening. With one forceful thrust, he enters me and I cry out.

My legs go back around him and pull him into me with every thrust. He pumps hard against me, our rhythms syncing.

"Is this what you wanted?" he purrs against my ear, his breath a hot caress on my neck.

"Yes! Oh God yes!"

He rises up, his knees on the floor, fucking me with my ass hanging halfway off the couch as he grips my hips to help support me. I'm stretched out before him, completely at his mercy. He watches his body entering mine, reveling in the connection for a moment before his eyes rake up the rest of me.

He growls, "God, you're beautiful."

I have no doubt he means it. My breasts are swaying, and my thought is to cover them, to hold them still. I can feel the ripple of that little pooch on my stomach that doesn't go away no matter how hard I try as he pumps into me. But I can see it in his eyes so full of pleasure and desire that he sees only beauty, and it only adds to my own pleasure and desire.

I want so badly to touch him, but I keep my hands where he wants them. Watching him watching me is incredibly erotic, and I feel the pressure building.

I bite my lip, hoping the distraction will slow it down and I can prolong the pleasure. But he moves his hips, creating even more friction in just the right place and the pressure explodes, setting off sparklers in my bloodstream.

"Open your eyes, Demi," he barks.

My eyes pop open just in time to see him thrust into me and groan as his own orgasm explodes through his body. I watch him close his eyes and ride the wave of his pleasure. When he opens them again, he sees me watching him and his lips tuck up on one side as his ears turn pink.

"Can I move my hands now, Daddy?"

He grins in earnest now. "Yes, Brat."

I raise up on my elbows. "You must have liked the hat because it's the only thing you left on," I tease.

"I love the hat. You should dress just like this every day. Or maybe I should wear it."

He pulls the elastic band holding it on and takes the cone hat off me and puts it on his head, making me laugh. After he strokes himself a few times, he pulls out, then takes his t-shirt and cleans me up then himself.

He stands and pulls his pants back up, then disappears to his bedroom. When he returns, he's gotten rid of the soiled shirt, but has a clean one for me to put on. He pulls it over my head, then kisses me.

"Best present ever, baby, thank you."

Chapter 31

Demeter

I walk into the Masters Construction offices and the reception is much different this time. The woman at the front desk smiles brightly when she sees me come in. "Ms. Lawson, good morning! Mr. Masters is expecting you. Do you remember the way to his office, or should I have him come get you?"

"I remember, thank you."

I make my way to the financial area. Kellen's door is closed, so I pause at the desk of his assistant, Amy. "Hi Amy! Does he have someone in there?"

"No, but I'm not sure if you should go in there. I think he's in a bad mood today."

I frown but go knock on his door anyway.

"Come." I hear him say.

I raise an eyebrow. Come? Does he think a dog is knocking on his door?

I crack open his door and stick my head in. "Come? What's that?"

He looks up, confused. "Huh?" Then he realizes it's me and his whole countenance changes. A smile spreads across his face. "Hey, baby."

I walk in, leaving the door open behind me. "Hey. You look handsome, but then you always do." I peck him on the lips, but before I can step away, he pulls me onto his lap.

"You look beautiful. Very professional." He wraps his arms around me and pulls me in to kiss me.

"Stop!" I say, trying not to laugh. "You're going to wrinkle me, and I won't look professional anymore."

He sighs dramatically and lets me go.

I take his chin in my hand. "It's only until the meeting is done. After that, I'm free until I have to go pick Henry up from school so you can manhandle me as much as your workload will allow."

We are meeting with a publisher who contacted me after the seminar. With Kellen's encouragement, I decided to at least hear them out. I know absolutely nothing about publishing, but thought that with Kellen having a lot more financial acumen than I, he might think of questions I would not. Also, in these types of situations, I tend to leap to conclusions and stop paying attention so he might hear something important that I might tune out.

We're meeting at the Masters Construction offices because they have a conference room we can use. For Kellen to be present, it was much easier for me to come to him than for him to take time out of his day to come to Norman. I know he would have, but he is much busier than I am, so I felt meeting here was best for everyone.

Once I'm back on my feet, I shake my hands out. I'm feeling very nervous because even contemplating writing a book is so far outside my comfort zone that I never even imagined it. I'm no stranger to writing; I can't count all the papers I had to write while going through school, but that's something I knew would only be seen by my professors, not the general public.

"Relax, baby. It's going to be just fine. You don't have to commit to anything today."

I look over at him and realize I've been pacing, lost in thought. "Sorry."

Amy knocks on the doorframe. "Mr. Masters, your appointment has arrived."

"Thank you, Amy. Please bring them to the small conference room by Morgan's office."

"Yes, sir."

She disappears, and he holds out a hand to me. I start to feel nauseated, but I take his hand, his touch helping to ground me.

"Do you want some water?" He asks, opening a small refrigerator that's set into a row of cabinets on one wall.

"No," I reply with a shake of my head. "I'd probably throw it up."

He kisses my temple. "Pick your foxhole," he says, motioning to the chairs, and it makes me giggle, helping to release more of the tension.

There's a knock on the door, so I quickly take a seat on the far side of the table, facing the door so that I can see them come in. Kellen greets the two people who enter, a man and a woman. He shakes their hands and introduces himself.

The man is the same one I met at the seminar, Scott Stimson. He looks a bit like a well-suited owl. He's below average height and solidly built, with thick round glasses that make his eyes look overlarge. He's wearing a tweed suit, much like the one he had on at the seminar. It's positively professorial.

The woman is young. Younger than me, with long dark hair. Taller than me, with a lean, willowy figure. She has big brown eyes that don't stray long from Kellen, even when he introduces me to her.

I immediately dislike Victoria Watts. Not because she is making goo-goo eyes at my boyfriend, but because it's unprofessional.

They sit across from me at the table, and Kellen takes the seat beside me. Scott starts with their pitch covering a lot of the same ground he did when we talked at the seminar.

They think my material is perfect for a book. All I'd need to do is write it and they'd handle everything else from having a cover done to editing to printing to getting it into stores. If things go well, there would likely be a book tour.

It sounds intriguing. I ask about the deadline for writing the book. Ms. Watts answers, but she's not addressing her answer to me, she's addressing it to Kellen. I ask another question and again, Ms. Watts answers, talking over Scott to give the answer, and she addresses Kellen.

I'm not nervous any longer. I sit back in my chair and say with a generous seasoning of Oklahoma twang, "You know, I really hate shopping for a new car."

They both look confused. I look over at Kellen and can see he's trying hard not to let the corner of his mouth tuck up.

"It doesn't matter where I go or what kind of car I shop for, it's always the same. If I'm alone, they ask me if I want to go home and get my husband, which is mystifying because I don't have a husband. If I'm with a man, say a friend, or a boyfriend, or even my daddy, the salesperson seems only able to talk to him. I'll ask the questions since it's my money being spent, but the salesperson always directs their answers to the man." I look Ms. Watts in the eye. "I find it quite irritating and that's usually the last person I buy a car from."

She gets the message and has the grace to blush.

"I apologize, Ms. Lawson..." Ms. Watts begins.

I interrupt her. "That's Dr. Lawson, and it's quite all right. I think I've heard enough. Kellen, do you have any questions?"

"Yes, actually, I do," he says, then launches into a million and two questions about copyright ownership, intellectual property, creative control, revision and buyback rights, royalty splits, and advances.

I'm shocked, but I don't let it show. Leave it to him to do some research ahead of time. I'd been so nervous that I hadn't even thought of it. I wouldn't have known where to begin even if I had thought of it.

Once all his questions are answered, I tell them I'll think about it and get back to them. Scott is very gracious and encourages me to contact him if I have questions. I assure him I will and tell him I still have his card.

Kellen shows them out. I walk with them as far as the accounting department before I let them go on. Instead of hovering by Amy's desk, I go into his office and wait for him to return.

"I kind of like you being jealous over me," he says when he walks back into his office.

With a shark's smile, I say, "I don't blame her for looking, but it pissed me off when she didn't even bother to look at me when responding."

He chuckles. "I'm sticking with the jealous thing. It's better for my ego."

That makes me laugh.

"Come on," he says. "Let's go somewhere I can manhandle you."

Chapter 32

Demeter

I settle into the office at home, determined to start outlining the book that I may or may not decide to write in response to the publishing proposal. If I can get an outline in place, it will give me an idea of how much writing will need to be done and that will help me decide if I really want to take on the task.

If it's too daunting, I'll let it go for now. Maybe when Henry's older, it's something I can pick up again.

The doorbell rings. Mom is out in the backyard with Dad drinking coffee and Henry's at school, so I go to answer it. I open the door to find a tall, thin young man wearing a shirt with the logo for a local courier service on my doorstep.

That's odd. I don't know that I've ever had a courier deliver anything to me here. Normally deliveries go to my office instead of my home.

Oh, well, he's here, so I take a large manilla envelope from him and sign for it. The front of the envelope has a computer printed label on it with just my name and address. There's no return address to tell me who it's from.

Back in my office, I take out a letter opener and slice through the top of the envelope. Inside is a stack of heavy paper with a note on top. I pull it out and turn it around in my hands so I can read the message. It is also clearly typed and printed on a computer, just like the address label.

Demeter,

I'm sorry you're having to find out this way, but he's let you go on longer than any of the others. If it weren't for your precious little boy, I wouldn't have said anything, but he doesn't deserve to be hurt because you were too stupid to listen when I tried to warn you.

He liked your look, though, and now that I can give him that, too, he doesn't need you anymore. Has he told you his secret yet? I imagine not. I think I'm the only other person in the world who knows it.

Like I said, I did try to warn you.

I remove the cover note from the stack to find photographs. Photographs of Kellen and me. When I look closer, I realize it's not me; it's someone who also has blond curly hair, but everything else is different. She's longer and leaner than me and her hair is shorter than mine, but it's clear she's trying to emulate my 'look' as she said in the note.

There are dozens of them. The outfits she wears, when she's wearing anything at all, change. The setting is unmistakably Kellen's bedroom. I stop at one photo and see the ball cap I left at his house after we went hiking a month ago.

It was only there for a couple of days before he gave it back to me. In the next picture, she's wearing it while she's on top of him, facing the camera. The photo shows everything and I do mean everything.

There's another where she has on the silly party hat from Henry's birthday party just two weeks ago. My hands start to shake, and I have to tighten my grip to keep from dropping the photos. Nausea bubbles in my stomach.

As much as I want to stop looking, I can't. Surely there must be some mistake. Maybe he was drugged or something. A lot of these could have been staged to make it look like he was a willing participant, but then there are a couple of shots that remove all doubt.

In one of them, he's behind her, and his hand is wrapped in her hair. He's had his hand wrapped in my hair that same way before. In another, she's performing oral sex on him and again there is a hand tangled in her hair. The shots are focused on her, but it's clear that the hand is fisted and that can't be faked if he was drugged.

Maybe it's all faked, and it's just someone who looks like him. Maybe she broke into his house somehow and took these pictures with another man with dark wavy hair. Then I get to the last picture. She's on the bed, back arched in pleasure as she clutches his hand to her breast while his head is between her legs. The shot clearly shows his upper back, including the scar he got on his shoulder blade from a bicycle wreck when he was a boy.

I am crushed. I drop the last photo onto the desk, unable to stop shaking. How could I have been so blind?

Hurt surfs through my system, riding on a wave of anger. I am so mixed up I don't know what to focus on. He made me believe he was a good man, but I guess I was wrong.

That despair morphs, and the rage takes over, flipping over and over in a cat fight for supremacy. He's good all right. Good at playing whatever this sick game of his is.

I want to track him down and kick his ass. That should be easy enough. I know just where to find him. He should be at work by now.

I wonder if he really went camping this weekend or if he was holed up in his house with her, whomever she is. Maybe he took today off work and is still there. I could go over there and check and if he's there, I can give him a piece of my mind with a few roundhouse kicks for emphasis.

It's bad enough that he's done this to me, but how could he do this to Henry? That thought cuts through all the rage like a white-hot knife. Oh my God, Henry. His little heart is going to be shattered into a million pieces when Kellen just disappears from his life.

The tears come then. Tears for my boy, who is far too young to have something like this happen to him. How on earth am I going to explain this to him?

Kellen is the worst kind of bastard, and I never had a clue.

Chapter 33

Kellen

What is that noise? I look over to my nightstand where my alarm is blaring. I reach up to grab my head because it feels like someone is trying to split it with an axe.

My instinct is to throw the phone against the wall to make it stop. However, I manage to hit the alarm, so I refrain. I look at the time. Why is my alarm going off on a Saturday? My eyes focus and I see that it's not Saturday, it's Monday.

God, what happened last night? I don't remember drinking at all. I try to recall what I did last night, and nothing comes to mind. The last thing I remember is saying goodnight to Demi and Henry on Friday. Where the hell did the weekend go?

I roll out of bed and stand. My ass hits the bed when a wave of dizziness makes my knees buckle. What the fuck is going on?

I make it to the shower but have to step out halfway through shampooing my hair. My guts wretch into the toilet and I dry heave long after I've emptied everything I've eaten or drank in the past week, or maybe the past month. It doesn't stop even after soap runs into my eyes. When I'm fairly sure my stomach is finished trying to turn itself inside out, I finish showering.

I feel like hammered shit. Maybe I'm coming down with something. I look in the cabinet and take out a bottle of pain relievers, popping two into my mouth. Calling in sick sounds like a good idea, but the one thing I do remember is that I have interviews for a potential HR manager today that I'd rather not reschedule.

The company is growing so large that I can't oversee finances and human resources alone any longer. I am willing to relinquish HR to someone else, but I will never be comfortable having someone else take over the financial side of the business. I dress quickly and get ready to leave the house.

It's really bugging me that I can't remember anything after Friday. How does someone lose two days? I check the time. It's still early so I won't call Demi yet.

She's the last person I saw, so maybe she knows what happened between Friday and now. She'll be taking Henry to school soon, so I'll call her when she's likely to be back home. God, my head feels like it's stuffed with steel wool. At least it's not hurting any longer.

Morgan, Beckett and I make it through the interviews. I'm glad they're there because I don't know that I would have made it through by myself. It seems like I'm scowling a lot, so I'm glad that Beckett is there to help keep things light.

When the last person leaves, my brothers turn and look at me. "What's wrong with you?" Morgan asks.

"I'm not sure," I answer. "Maybe I'm coming down with something. I woke up this morning with a splitting headache and I can't remember anything since Friday. The entire weekend is a big empty void."

"Go home," Beckett says. "The company won't collapse without you here for a day and if you're getting sick, I don't want you spreading your germs to me."

"Your concern is touching," I reply sarcastically. "It'll be okay. I'll stay shut up in my office and well away from your area. I'll run background checks and send them your way. Let me know your thoughts on the candidates when you've reviewed all the information."

"Okay," Morgan says, "but if you get any worse, you need to go home and get some rest."

I nod and rap my knuckles on the table in acknowledgement before I leave to go to my office. The time on the computer says it's after eleven, so I pull out my cell phone and call Demi.

"What do you want, Kellen?"

I look at the phone. She sounds so angry.

"Um...Demi...are you okay?"

"No, I'm not."

"I don't understand. What's going on?"

"You are probably the only one who should understand. I can't believe you fooled me so completely. I..." her voice breaks and it sounds like she's about to cry. She clears her throat and takes a breath. "I would have never believed you could be so cruel, Kellen, not just to me, but to Henry..." She does cry now but manages to choke out. "Don't call me again."

The phone disconnects. I pull it away from my ear and stare at it. What the hell is going on?

It seems like I've gone down the rabbit hole and woken up in some alternate dimension. What has happened that Demi believes I'm being cruel? Cruel not only to her, but to Henry. I could never imagine doing anything that could be construed as cruel to either of them.

My intention has been to be the exact opposite. I want to protect them and be a guard against the cruelty of the harsh realities of the world. I need to get to the bottom of this.

When I dial her number, it goes straight to voicemail. I leave her a message telling her about waking up this morning with no memory of anything that has happened since Friday and that I have no idea about what's going on. I beg her to talk to me.

Pride is not something I'll let get in the way of fixing things with her. If only I could figure out what is wrong; that would be a great help.

Her voicemail cuts me off before I finish talking. I can only hope she listens to it, but I won't be holding my breath. What the actual fuck is going on?

I don't hear from Demi all day. I'm tempted to go to her house, but she said I'd done something cruel to Henry and since he'll be home, it's better to confront her somewhere other than the house.

I feel like I'm going insane, so I'll go to her office at the end of the day tomorrow and sit on her until she talks to me. She might kick my ass, but if she tells me what's happening, it will be worth it. Maybe.

I go ahead and leave the office at noon because I still feel like crap and detour to my doctor's office to get checked out. He can't see anything wrong with me but draws a bunch of blood for a battery of tests.

The next day, I'm on pins and needles all day at the office. I leave early to make it to Demi's office before she leaves. I wait until I'm sure she's alone before I go in and ring the bell that signals her that someone is waiting in the outer lobby.

She opens the door and freezes. Her eyes are red and puffy like she's been crying. My heart hurts to see her like this. I hold up my hands, palms out, hoping she doesn't slam and lock the door.

"Demi, please, I don't know what's going on. Won't you please tell me what happened?"

Her face goes hard. The sadness that was in her eyes morphs into hard blue shards of ice. She turns away.

"Demi! Wait!"

I cross the room, ready to pound on the door when it opens. I back up to give her space. She hands me a thick manilla envelope. "I didn't want to leave this at home where Henry might find it, so I brought it here."

I open the envelope and slide the contents out. The note on the front makes me frown. I move the note to the back of the stack and freeze. At first glance, it looks like Demi and me, but when I look closer, I see it's not Demi, it's Belinda with her hair styled like Demi.

So, it's Belinda...and me. But that's not possible. I was only with Belinda once and that was back at Valentine's Day, and I don't remember taking pictures like this. She also didn't look like Demi back then.

I sit down and rub my head. That's it. I must have been drugged. "Demi, I don't remember anything from this weekend. She must have gotten into my house somehow and drugged me to take these pictures."

"So, you didn't go camping this weekend?"

I look up at her, confused. "What? No. Why would you think I'd gone camping?"

She takes her phone out of her pocket and shows me the text message I sent.

Kellen: *Feeling stressed. Going to go camping. Won't be back until late Sunday.* I frown. "I didn't send that. It must have been Belinda. She must have drugged me," I repeat.

"Keep going. Several of those weren't taken this weekend."

I keep going through the photos, feeling a pain start in my chest that gets worse with every photo. "Maybe I was drugged for some and maybe she got into my house and brought someone who looks like me."

Then I get to the last photo. The scar on my shoulder is clearly visible, and it looks like I'm going down on her. My hands are shaking so badly that I almost drop the photos. Oh my God...how did this happen?

"Demi...I...I don't know. I have no memory of this. There's not an explanation I can think of for how this is even possible."

I look up at her. Big, fat tears are rolling down her already wet cheeks. I stand up, wanting to go to her and take her into my arms, but she backs away from me. Pain slices through my heart to know that I'm causing her this heartache.

Her voice is hoarse when she speaks. "I had myself tested for STDs since we never used condoms. Thankfully, it came back clear, but you might want to get yourself tested, too." She takes a breath. "Stay away from me, Kellen, and stay away from my son."

She turns on her heel and goes back into her office. I can hear her sobbing through the door. The sound of her heart breaking tears me apart. I want to break down the door and wrap her up in my arms and tell her everything is going to be okay, but I can't say that with confidence in this moment. I'm too blindsided and can't think straight.

Then another thought comes crashing in. Oh my God, Henry. He's not going to be able to understand why I have suddenly disappeared from his life. I finally found the love of my life and have come to love her son as my own as well. Now the visions I had of love and family are being ripped away from me and I don't know how it happened.

Even worse, I don't know how to make it stop.

Chapter 34

Kellen

I put everything back into order and put it into the envelope. Before I leave, I go to the door to her office, where I can still hear her crying.

"Don't give up on me yet Demi," I say loud enough for her to hear. "I'm going to get to the bottom of this. For what it's worth, I love you and I swear that I did not knowingly do these things."

I hope she can hear the truth in my words. This is not how I wanted to say those three little words that have such enormous meaning for the first time. Not even close.

It's not romantic. It's ugly and dirty and tainted. She might even think it's some form of attempted manipulation, but I have to tell her how I feel. She has to know that she's more than some passing fancy.

I'm not sure how to go about unraveling this knot, but I know someone who might. Making my way out of her office, I call Morgan as soon as I'm in the car. I want to talk to him, but I want to leave Gabriella out of it. She doesn't need to be in the middle of something between her future brother-in-law and her friend.

If this had happened a year ago, I would have been handling it on my own. Thanks to Gabriella's meddling, I feel closer to my brothers than I have in my entire life. I know they'll have my back in this.

Morgan is still at the office and will be for a while, so I head that direction. The offices are empty when I arrive. I let myself in with a key and head to the back of the building. Morgan is sitting behind his desk with Beckett on the sofa as they talk.

"Where's Gabriella?" I ask.

"She was tired, so I sent her home. Beckett will take me home when we're done."

I hold out the envelope to him. "This packet was sent to Demi. It is clearly me in some of them, but I have no memory of these. The woman in them isn't Demi. It's Belinda who has altered her hair to look like Demi's."

Beckett goes to look over Morgan's shoulder as he takes the contents of the packet out.

"What secret?" Beckett asks.

I wave a hand to negate his question. "That doesn't matter. The photos are what matter."

Beckett gives me a long look, but returns his attention to the photos when Morgan moves the cover note out of the way. Beckett whistles. They go through the photos one by one.

I point out Demi's ball cap. "That was only at my house for a couple of days before I gave it back to Demi. That was over a month ago."

They keep going.

"That party hat is from Henry's birthday party a couple of weeks ago."

"So, these were taken over time," Beckett says.

"Yes," I confirm.

They get to the last photo.

"I remember when you got that scar," Morgan says.

"Some of them are obviously me, but they could have been staged when I was unconscious. Others are in my house, but it's not clear that it's me. I can't say it enough. I have no memory of any of this."

They go back through the photos, slowly leafing through them. Beckett picks one up from time to time, holding it under the light on Morgan's desk to study the finer details.

"Like I told you yesterday, I woke up with a splitting headache and no memory of the entire weekend after saying good night to Demi on Friday. She showed me a text I supposedly sent saying I was going camping for the weekend. I didn't send that text. When I left at lunch, I went to the doctor. They drew blood, so I called back on the way here and asked them to check for STDs and drugs that might cause amnesia. He said it might have been too late to discover any drugs, but he would check anyway. Some of the common date rape drugs metabolize out of your system pretty quickly, depending upon what it is and how much I was given. I probably won't hear from him for a couple of days."

Morgan goes back through the photos a third time. I know he's not looking at them for the porn factor; he's looking for clues, so I sit in a chair facing his desk, my face in my hands. Beckett points out that in the ones where it's clear the man is awake and participating, he's mostly cut out of the picture. But in the ones where I'm clearly visible and it's undeniably me, all of them could have been staged while I was unconscious.

"When did you cut the investigators loose?" Morgan asks without looking up.

"When Belinda's sister told me she was going to admit herself to care." I sigh and rub my forehead. "That was apparently a mistake because she didn't follow through, but gave herself a makeover instead."

"I'd say it's time to get them back on the job. If she has found a way into your house, you need to know," Morgan says.

I nod, but I feel so numb. "I may have lost Demi over this," I say to no one. "The package was sent to her. She told me to stay away from her and Henry."

"Hey," Beckett says sharply. I look up at him. "We're going to figure this out. Nail Belinda to the wall, and you're going to get Demi and Henry back."

He looks so fierce.

"Thanks," I say. A small spark of hope ignites in the empty hole that used to be my heart.

Morgan presses a button on his phone and a dial tone fills the air. He punches in a number, and it rings until it's answered by a gruff voice. I recognize the voice of the man who owns the security firm.

Morgan explains the situation to him in concise terms. We talk about options and develop a plan to move forward. It's going to be very costly, but I would trade everything I have to get Demi and Henry back.

It's also going to take time. The longer it takes, the more time Demi has to close her heart to me. However, I have to deal with the threat of Belinda once and for all to keep Demi and Henry safe. She is a threat and can't be thought of as anything else. If she is mentally unstable enough to do something like this, if she's pushed, what might she do to Demi and Henry?

I'll just have to trust that whatever power brought us together will help me repair this rift once the danger is over.

Chapter 35

Kellen

It has been four days since Demi received the photos. It has been three days since I put the security company back on the case. We've installed hidden cameras at my house that are constantly monitored in the hope that she'll come back. I've had someone tailing me to and from work and everywhere I go all day, every day.

They've also been keeping an eye on Demi and Henry. Not monitoring them closely, but just making sure Belinda isn't following them or bothering them in any way. If anything ever happened to them, I would never be able to forgive myself.

They haven't been tailing Belinda because they can't find her. After the investigators were called off because she had said she was going to admit herself voluntarily to care, she moved and left no forwarding address. She also bought a new car, and it has not been registered with the DMV yet. She sold her old car for cash to an individual buyer, which created yet another dead end.

Dead ends. Nothing but dead ends. Every time a lead ends up nowhere, I want to scream. It's only been three days and I don't know how much longer I can take it.

I've called Belinda's sister, but she claims to have no knowledge of her sister's whereabouts and says she didn't know that Belinda hadn't followed through with the hospital admission. She also says she has no idea about Belinda moving or changing vehicles. I'm not sure whether or not to believe her.

I am frustrated and angry and with the absence of Demi and Henry, it's as if every bit of warmth and color has left my world. We talked every day and now, except for words of hurt and anger, I haven't talked to her in a week. The weather outside has turned dreary, cold, and gray, as if Mother Nature has reached inside my heart and cast its sorrowful depths across the sky, but I know it's just the beginning of fall in Oklahoma when she can't seem to make up her mind.

I've been trying to think of ways to draw Belinda out, but so far, nothing I've come up with seems a powerful enough draw. I could tell her she's won, that I realize how much she loves me, but that's too much of an abrupt turnaround and I doubt she'd believe it. Then another idea worms its way into my head.

I feel a spark of excitement because the more I think about it, the more it just might work. I rush down the hall to Morgan's office. Thank God, he's still here. I pull up short when I see Gabriella sitting on the sofa in there.

I've been trying to keep everything as far away from Gabriella as possible so that she's not in the middle. Morgan is laughing. He looks up when he notices the motion in the door.

"What is it, Kel?"

I look over at Gabriella, then back at Morgan.

"She knows," he says. "I don't keep anything from her."

I sigh and shake my head. "I was trying to keep her out of it, so she doesn't feel like she's in the middle. Plus, I didn't want to add to her stress. She's supposed to be keeping her blood pressure down."

"Kellen," Gabriella says, "I'm fine. Please, what's up?"

I vacillate for a few minutes. I'll just have to trust that Morgan and Gabriella know what they're doing. The last thing I want is to expose Gabriella to something that might cause harm to the baby.

"I have an idea. I doubt Belinda would believe that her little scheme worked if I called her and told her I suddenly realized because of it that she's the one for me. However, if I called her and told her it didn't work, that Demi and I are still together, she might come after me to get more pictures."

"Or she might come after you for something much worse," Gabriella says.

"So, what if she does? We've got the cameras at the house, and I'm being followed during the day, so if she comes after me, there will be someone there to catch her."

"You want to put yourself out there as bait?" Morgan asks.

"Yes," I nod. "I want this over with. The longer it goes on, the less likely it is that Demi and Henry will remain safe. I want it done, so there is no more threat to them."

Also, so I can start trying to win her back.

"No plan is foolproof," Morgan says. "There are always unexpected variables."

"I don't care what happens to me as long as Demi and Henry are safe."

It's the truth. Of course, I'd rather stick around long enough to win Demi's heart back, see Henry grow into a man, and grow old and gray with Demi at my side, along with maybe a few brothers and sisters for Henry. However, if the worst happens and Belinda kills me, at least Demi and Henry will be safe from her because she'll be in prison for the rest of her life.

"Kellen, Demi wouldn't want you to take that kind of risk," Gabriella says.

"Right about now, she probably would be totally fine with it," I answer. "She hates me right now."

"She does *not* hate you. She's just hurt."

"I can't blame her," I say. "The evidence she was given is pretty damning. Listen, you need to stay out of this and stay relaxed. I would never forgive myself if something happened to the baby."

"Yeah," Morgan says with a chuckle, "just a clue for your future, telling a hard-headed woman like her to stay out of something is one of the best ways to ensure she won't. I have a feeling that Demi is probably just as hard-headed."

"Damn right she is," Gabriella says, her chin raised in defiance.

"I'll call the security team to let them know my plan and see what they say. Once I talk it over with them, I'll call the number that Belinda used to text me."

"I hope you know what you're doing," Gabriella says.

Chapter 36

Demeter

It has been four days since I received the packet of photos. It has been three days since I cut Kellen out of my life. I'm sitting at the kitchen island with Henry eating supper as Mom hovers.

She knows that something is wrong and can probably guess that it has to do with Kellen since he hasn't been around for the last few days. He had completely infiltrated our lives without me realizing he was doing it.

We talked every day, and he would spend several days a week with us. We were together every weekend. I have laughed and loved with Kellen more than I thought possible.

Had, I remind myself. Had laughed. My heart squeezes. Had loved. That's all over now.

"You should tell Mr. Kellen to come over so you won't be sad anymore," Henry says. "You were never sad when he was with you."

Of course, he doesn't know about the day and night I spent with Kellen wallowing in sadness.

I smile at my sweet boy. "Kellen is busy at work, buddy. He won't be able to come over."

"You should call him, then. Can I call him? I miss him."

I shake my head. "No, buddy, he's too busy to talk on the phone, too."

"You need to eat something," Mom says.

Henry looks at my plate and frowns. "Yeah, Mom, five bites is what you always tell me. You have to eat at least five bites even if you don't feel like it." He holds up his hand, with all his fingers extended, to emphasize the number.

I smile and force down five bites of the food my mother prepared that should be delicious but only tastes like sawdust and lead to my numbed senses. I scrape my plate into the disposal, rinse it, and put it in the dishwasher.

"How about a movie, buddy?"

"Yeah! Do I get to pick it out?"

"Of course."

He races to the theater room.

"Thanks, Mom. Dinner was delicious."

She snorts. "That's why you put most of it in the sink, I'm sure. Why don't you just call him? Whatever it is between you, surely you can work it out."

I shake my head. "No, that's not possible."

"All right," she says. "I won't pry. Let me know if you need anything."

"I will. I'm going to go work in the office after I drop Henry at the McLean's tomorrow, so I probably won't be home most of the day."

"Okay, I'm going home now. There are leftovers in the fridge, and you need to remember to eat. That little boy needs you."

"I know. I appreciate you."

Mom leaves and I head to the theater room to watch a movie with Henry. The next morning, I drop him off to spend the day with his grandparents. For once, I'm glad for them because they'll keep Henry occupied for the next twenty-four hours.

The clock on my computer surprises me. I intended to work on the book outline, but I haven't been any more successful than I was on Monday after getting the packet delivery. It's after one in the morning. Although I arrived at around nine this morning after dropping off Henry, I've spent the whole day staring out the window or at the computer screen and accomplishing absolutely nothing.

I shut down my computer and give up for the day, or night, or morning. Whatever. My stomach cramps when I get into the car. I realize I haven't eaten since dinner last night, or I guess since it's the next morning that was night before last. There's a twenty-four-hour convenience store just down the street, so I stop to buy some pretzels to help settle my stomach.

I'm standing in line when I feel the old familiar itch at the back of my neck. Slowly I turn in a circle but only see a couple of other customers in the store, along with the employees. None of them seem to be inordinately interested in me.

I pay for my purchase and leave the store quickly. When I pull onto the street, I get stopped at the light. Although I'm driving, I open the bag while I'm waiting for the light to turn green, munching on sawdust and lead, hoping to stop the cramping in my stomach.

My headlights wash over a car that looks a lot like mine as it passes through the intersection. That's what draws my attention initially, but when I catch a glimpse of the light blonde curly hair on the woman driving, I'm riveted.

My fingers clench the steering wheel as anger surges through me. The light changes and I race to catch up to the car. She's driving in the direction of Kellen's house.

When I catch up, I get close, but not too close. I don't want her to realize she's being followed. There's the shape of someone in the passenger seat, and I wonder if it's Kellen.

It's certainly tall enough to be based upon the shadow of someone's head above the headrest. Between the reflections of the streetlights and the dark night, I wasn't able to get a good enough look to be sure.

The car turns into the entry to Kellen's neighborhood. It must be the two of them. My hand goes to my mouth as if I can keep the sob from breaking free.

I slow enough to see a thin arm reach out and punch in the code to the gate. It's them. He's with her. I wanted so badly to believe him when he said it wasn't true.

I roll past the turn-in to his neighborhood. I want to go home, crawl into bed and wallow in the sorrow. Then, the anger surges back to the surface and I let it come.

I love you, he said. I don't know how this happened, he said. Yet here he is with that...that...bitch, strolling right into his neighborhood, playing his game and thinking he's getting away with it.

I am beyond mad. Fire spitting, lava puking, pissed off Pele volcano goddess mad is a perfect description. On impulse, I make a U-turn in the middle of the street and turn into his neighborhood, cutting in front of another car coming down the street. Why is there traffic at one in the morning?

I don't care. A liquid hot bubble of magma has replaced all my organs. I'm surprised my fingers don't burn straight through the keypad when I punch in the code.

Instead of driving straight to his house, I go the long way around the neighborhood. That way, they won't see me coming in behind them.

Her car is parked in the driveway. It's the same make and model as mine, but maybe a year newer. Imitation is supposed to be the sincerest form of flattery, but from her, it's just plain creepy.

I park a few houses down the street in the driveway of one that's empty and has been for sale for several weeks and creep down the block to his house. I grip the key in my pocket, ready to use it, but the front door is unlocked.

I slip inside. The living room is dark, but there's enough ambient light that I can see well enough to keep from bumping into the furniture. No sound reaches me, so I pause for a moment.

Whispers from down the hall drift past me, then the voices are louder. I frown, unsure of what that means.

It sounds as if they're in Kellen's bedroom, so I creep closer. Yes, there are two voices, a man and a woman, but the man doesn't sound like Kellen. The voice isn't pitched right.

Now that I'm closer, I can hear them clearly, and the man is definitely not Kellen. I take a chance and quickly pop my head around the doorframe, then away. I close my eyes and try to absorb what I saw.

Kellen is sprawled on the bed, seemingly asleep. The woman is naked and telling the man what to do, how she wants the scene to look when he takes the pictures. I have a decision to make.

I can either go in there, let my outrage fly with metaphorical guns blazing, or I can back off and call the cops. As much as I was primed and ready to do a Vesuvius act like Kellen's house is Pompeii, I think calling the cops is a smarter alternative.

I move back down the hall to the living room, dialing my cell phone. I don't know why I didn't go outside. Maybe I wanted to stay close to Kellen so that if they decided to do something other than the sexual dog and pony show, I might intervene.

I don't know. There's no way I can bring myself to leave him completely alone with them. It looks like I owe Kellen an apology for thinking the worst of him.

The 911 operator answers, and I tell her to send the police and an ambulance to Kellen's address.

"Who are you, and what are you doing here?" a man's voice booms through the quiet.

I spin. It's Belinda's cohort. He's tall, but not as tall as Kellen and has dark hair, but that's where the resemblance ends. The coal dark eyes and pockmarked skin on his cheeks are nothing like Kellen's.

"Who are you, and what are *you* doing here?" I retort, skirting around the furniture to put some space between us.

Belinda comes tromping into the room, tying on a skimpy short robe. "What's going on?" she whines.

"I'm his girlfriend," I say. I can hear the operator on the phone in my hand, but I can't hear what she's saying.

"No, you're not," the henchman says. "She is."

"She is not. She's just some loony tunes stalker who couldn't handle the fact that he didn't want her. The only time he willingly had sex with her, she had to get him drunk. Now she has to drug him."

I know, I know, loony tunes is not an official diagnosis and taunting the crazy woman is probably not a good idea, but Pele and Vesuvius have control of my tongue right now.

Belinda cackles. "You left him. All it took was a few pictures, and you walked away. You didn't believe him when he told you it wasn't real."

"I have a son to protect. That meant removing us from the equation to keep him safe from a nutbag like you. It's what good mothers do." Again, nutbag, not a diagnosis, but still à propos.

Henchman lunges across the back of the sofa at me. He gets a hand on my wrist and claps down, sending pain through my hand, and I drop my phone. I use his own grip to drag him over the back of the sofa, throwing him off balance.

Belinda runs at me with a syringe in her hand. I snap my leg out and kick her in the stomach. She falls backward into the arms of a man who had just come through the front door.

Fuck! I don't know that I can handle three at once.

New guy doesn't help Belinda, though. He wrenches an arm behind her and tells her to drop the syringe onto a nearby table. Henchman is getting up, so I move to where I have some open space.

He lunges at me again, and I use his momentum to put him on the floor. New guy jumps on his back, pins henchman's hands and ties them with zip ties. He's not making any moves toward me, so I back away.

When henchman is secured, new guy stands and barks at Belinda, who is screeching like a scalded cat as she lies on the floor, also secured with zip ties.

"Shut up! Your caterwauling isn't going to help you. The cops are on their way."

He then turns to me. "Ms. Lawson, I'm with Carver Security. Police and an ambulance are on their way."

"Oh my God, Kellen!" I run to his bedroom.

He looks as if he is sleeping peacefully. I check his pulse. It's there, but it's very slow. Dangerously slow. Where is the damn ambulance?

Chapter 37

Kellen

Earlier

I placed the call to Belinda, telling her that her scheme didn't work. She didn't answer, so I just left a message and spent all day Saturday trying to act normal, but it's anything but normal. My normal Saturdays are spent with Demi and with Henry when he's not with his grandparents. I hope this works so I can get my normal back.

I try to work in my home office, but I'm too antsy. The house feels like a cage as I pace from room to room. This waiting for something to happen is maddening.

Remembering that I still have a couple of beers in the refrigerator, I go to the kitchen. Maybe the alcohol will help me relax. I sit on the couch and turn on the television, twisting the cap off the bottle.

At the other end of the sofa, I visualize Demi sitting there with her legs stretched out so she could put her cold toes against my thigh. I swallow to loosen the tightness in my throat. "Hold on, baby, I'm working on fixing everything," I say to her shade.

I drink the beers on automatic pilot while not watching the television, seeing the movement on the screen but not taking it in. The room darkens as the sun sets and I don't bother to turn on any lights. I must have dozed off at some point because I look up a few minutes later to see it's after midnight.

"Well, it looks like nothing's going to happen tonight, so I might as well go to bed," I say to the empty room.

I go take a shower and put on pajama bottoms before going into my room. Although they're not visible to anyone who doesn't know exactly where to look, the bedroom has four cameras to see movement from every angle. The only place in the entire house that does not have cameras is my bathroom. With a wave to whomever is monitoring the camera feeds, I crawl into bed.

I wake up to the sound of beeping. I look over to see Demi dozing in the chair next to the hospital bed. "Demi?"

She startles awake and when she sees me looking over at her, relief washes over her face. "Oh thank God, you're awake." She reaches out and takes my hand.

"What happened?" I croak.

"Belinda broke into your house last night and drugged you."

"So my plan worked. Was she arrested?"

"Yes. Wait. What? Your plan?"

I swallow, but my throat feels like sandpaper. "Is there some water?"

She gets up and hands me a cup of water that has a straw in it. I take a few long drinks; the cold water feels great on my dry throat. She takes the cup away from me.

I look up at her and she's staring down at me with an eyebrow raised. "What plan?" she asks in the same mom voice I've heard her use with Henry.

Uh oh. "I was tired of waiting for something to happen, so I called Belinda and told her that the scheme hadn't worked. I was trying to draw her out."

She punches me in the arm. "You idiot! She could have killed you!"

"Ow!" I grab her hand to keep her from hitting me again. "I missed you."

That got her. I let my head fall back onto the pillow. It feels like it's stuffed with cotton and my mouth feels like I've been chewing on shoe leather. Her face goes soft, and I can see how haggard she looks. The last week has taken a toll on her.

She sighs and gives me the cup of water back. I'm startled by Gabriella and Morgan coming into the room. Gabriella rushes over and hugs me or tries to. It's difficult to get a good grip on a prone man with several months of baby bump in the way. She sets a bag on the bed.

"I'm so glad you're okay!" she exclaims. When she pulls away, she's wiping her eyes. "Sorry, hormones. We brought you a pair of Morgan's sweats and a t-shirt."

Morgan hands a cup to Demi from the tray he carried in. "The coffee is just the beginning of what you get for saving Kellen's life."

"What?" I ask.

"Demi saved your ass," Morgan says.

I look over at Demi, but she has her eyes closed, savoring her coffee. She looks up when the room goes silent. "What? Sorry, I haven't slept."

"How did you know to go to his house?" Gabriella asks.

"Oh. I was leaving my office at about one.""This morning?" Gabriella asks.

She nods. "Yes. I'd been at my office trying to work on the book outline because I didn't want to be in the house all alone. Henry is at his grandparents' house." She tells us about following Belinda and sneaking into the house, calling 911, and the security guy showing up.

Morgan picks up the story. "The cops and the ambulance arrived quickly and arrested Belinda and her friend. They hauled them into one of the precincts and the accomplice spilled everything."

Apparently, Belinda had told him that Kellen was her boyfriend and that it was a game they liked to play. He believed her because, after all, she had a key to his house and knew an awful lot about him. She also paid the guy a boatload of money.

Kellen was drugged with GHB in many of the photos. Apparently last night she only got the initial dose in, but her accomplice said she would dose Kellen several times while they were quote unquote playing and wasn't careful about the amounts. She could have easily overdosed him and probably came close to it the day he woke up feeling like he was sick and went to the doctor.

Once Kellen was out, the guy would help set up the poses and take the pictures. He was also the one who was having sex with Belinda in the pictures where the man was clearly taking part. He said that Belinda told him that what Kellen didn't know wouldn't hurt him.

Morgan isn't sure what all they're going to be charged with, but at the very least, violating the protection order and trespassing. He thinks attempted murder should be added to the list, and I can't disagree with him.

Morgan drops that bomb and lets it settle in the room for a few minutes before he scrubs a hand down his face. "So anyway, that's the entire story. I'm taking my wife and son out to breakfast, then we're going to go home and be lazy bums for the rest of the day. Come on, woman, let's go."

"Can we have pancakes?" Gabriella asks.

"You can have anything you want," Morgan answers.

Gabriella pats my arm before she lets Morgan lead her out. That leaves Demi and me in the room alone.

"It's good to see you," I say, feeling unsure. There is so much more I want to say, but she's been so quiet and withdrawn that I am afraid that if I say too much, she'll bolt. I look up at her and she's crying. "Baby, don't cry," I console. "It's all okay now."

"You could have died."

"But I didn't thanks to you."

I hold out my hand to her. She comes to the bed and takes it but doesn't stop with the hand. She crawls into bed with me and turns her face into my chest as I take her under my arm.

Then she cries, trying to be quiet, but her whole body is shaking. I rub her back in an attempt to console her. "It's all right," I say low. "I'm fine, and we're going to be fine."

She says something, but she's crying and gasping so hard that I can't make out what it is. I kiss the top of her head. "Ssshhh. It's all right now."

We stay there like that for a long time, her releasing the weight of the past week of hurt, fear, and uncertainty while I just rock her and hold her, telling her over and over how much I've missed her and how everything is fine now. It feels so good to have her in my arms and I never want to be separated from her again, so I tell her that, too.

Chapter 38

Demeter

"Go away," I groan and roll over in bed. "I don't have school today."

A man's voice says soothingly, "No baby, no school today, but you need to wake up." Kellen's voice.

Oh my God, Kellen, he almost died. I sit bolt upright in bed. His bed. His hospital bed.

He smooths the hair out of my face. "Shh...it's okay, baby. The doctor just wants to check me out and see if everything's fine to release me."

I look up to see a woman in a white doctor's coat watching us with a bemused look on her face. Trying to be inconspicuous, I wipe the drool from my mouth as heat crawls from my collar bones to the top of my head. I scoot off the bed.

"Sorry," I say.

I go to the bathroom and wash my face while the doctor talks to Kellen. Unsure of how long I slept, I pull out my phone and see that I have about an hour until I need to go get Henry. There's a knock on the door.

"Just a sec."

I blot my face with a paper towel, then open the door to see Kellen standing there in his hospital gown. They've removed his IV so maybe he's going to be released soon. "Hey," I say. "You've lost your tether."

He looks down at his hand. "Yeah, I get to go home. The initial dose Belinda gave me wasn't a large one, and it's just about out of my system. I can't drive for twenty-four hours, but they want me to take it easy for the next day. I guess I have a legit excuse to play hooky from work tomorrow."

My eyes on the floor, I say, "I'm sorry. I didn't believe you."

"I wouldn't have believed me either. To be honest, I didn't believe me. It was undeniably me and I only knew I couldn't remember, but had no idea how to explain it. Demi, please look at me."

I raise my eyes to his. "There you are," he says as his lips tick up on one side. "I love you, Demi. There's no blame in my heart toward you for putting some space between us after seeing those pictures. It was the best thing for you and Henry. It kept you safe and whether or not you meant to, you kept me safe, too. You could have seen Belinda's car and turned the other way, but you didn't. You followed, and you saved my life. We can have a future together because of you, if you want it. I want one with you and with Henry. Do you want one with me?"

A small smile tucks itself into the corners of my mouth and I nod. A big part of me wants just that, but there's a niggling worm of uncertainty in my stomach.

He pulls me hard against his chest, wrapping me in his arms. My arms go around his waist and I lay my hands against his bare back where the gown doesn't cover him.

"I followed her mostly because I got mad. The only reason I went there was to catch you in the act and kick your ass," I say against his chest as I reach down and pat his bare bottom.

He laughs and plants a kiss on the top of my head, letting me go, and says, "I'm glad you did. Let me go empty my bladder before I make a mess on the floor, then we can blow this popsicle stand."

He goes into the bathroom but leaves the door open. I open the bag that Gabriella and Morgan brought and take the clothes to him.

"I have to go pick up Henry from the McLean's. Maybe you'd like to call someone to come get you that can take you home instead."

"Nope. I'd like to go with you to get him, if you don't mind. I've missed both of you so much."

I nod. "Okay. Henry has missed you, too. I told him you have been working, and that's why you haven't been around."

"That's good. I'm glad you didn't tell him I'd never be back."

"I couldn't do that because I wasn't sure it was true."

He comes out, dressed in Morgan's clothes. They're large on him, but he looks like he might have lost a few pounds since I last saw him. I know I have.

"All right," Kellen says. "I'm ready."

"I'm in no condition to do it now, but once we've both eaten and gotten some rest and are back to our usual selves, we need to talk."

He sighs, but concedes. "Yeah, we do."

Henry is ecstatic to see Kellen. They chatter back and forth all the way to Kellen's house. I'm so tired I can't see straight.

We pull up to his house and I tell Henry he needs to wait in the car. A shared look between Kellen and me, and we come to a mutual agreement that Henry doesn't need to see the remains of the police's visit. Henry grouses, but a stern look from me has him grumbling under his breath, but he stays put in his seat.

Inside, it's much worse than I expected. There is fingerprint powder everywhere and they've taken the bedding off his bed. I'm guessing it's stuffed into an evidence bag somewhere. Provided they have jumbo sized evidence bags, that is.

"Let me get some clothes and my wallet and you can take me to a hotel. I'll call my cleaning people and have them come in tomorrow."

I shake my head. "No, you shouldn't be alone after being drugged, in case there are side effects. Get some clothes and your toiletries. You're coming home with Henry and me."

"Are you sure?"

"I wouldn't have offered if I wasn't." Yeah, I am sure.

He shouldn't be alone and now that we're somewhat reconciled, I would rather not be away from him. I know I threw out having someone else come get him, but I'm not exactly firing on all cylinders.

Besides, there's still a cloud between us, namely whatever secret it is that Belinda knew. He's going to have to come clean, whatever it is.

When we get back to the house, Mom is there, fixing breakfast. I hug her, so appreciative of her taking care of us. Exhaustion is swamping me and I'm emotionally strung out, ready to break down into sobs to release the stress of it all, but I manage to hold it together.

I eat until I'm ready to pop, making up for several days of skipped meals. The exhaustion is still dragging on me. Henry has been glued to Kellen's side, so this next part is going to be difficult.

"Buddy, I'm going to ask you to go hang out with Nana and Pops for a few hours. Kellen was hurt last night, and I went to the hospital with him, so I haven't slept at all, and I need to take a nap. Kellen does, too."

"But I can take a nap, too," Henry protests. "With both of you."

"Honey, you slept all night last night. You don't need a nap. I know you've missed Kellen and want to hang out with him, but he needs just a few hours of rest, and you can come back home and hang out the rest of the day with him."

"I'm really tired, though," Henry says, verging on whining. "Please, let me take a nap, too."

"Henry, you do not need to take a nap," I say in a tone I rarely have to use with my son. "You're going to go over to Nana and Pop's house, and we're going to sleep for three or four hours.

I'll come get you when we wake up. I am exhausted, and I don't want to argue with you about this."

"Go to your Nana and Pop's and we'll play a game of chess when you come back," Kellen says.

Henry looks at him with adoration. "Okay!"

I sigh as Mom takes Henry and leaves. Kellen moves up behind me and puts his hands on my shoulders. "Go on, go upstairs and get some sleep."

"Aren't you coming?"

"I...well, I wasn't sure if you'd want me to use one of the spare bedrooms."

"Shut up and come with me." I tell him as I shuffle to the stairs. My emotions are all over the place and I know that at the end of the day we might not be together anymore, but for now, fresh from the hospital, I need him close.

His lips quirk. "Yes, ma'am."

I wake up with Kellen wrapped around me, big spoon to my little. I turn to face him and discover he's not asleep.

"How long have you been awake?" I ask.

"Just a few minutes."

"Fibber," I say without heat.

His mouth quirks. "I got some sleep last night. You didn't."

He kisses my forehead, then smooths the hair out of my face. "I've missed you," he says.

"I've missed you, too. I'm extremely glad you didn't die."

We lay there for a while, just cuddling. Figuring it's better to rip the band aid off, I take a breath and get ready to dive in.

"I guess we should get the talk out of the way before we go get Henry," he says, reading my mind.

Needing to distance myself from him for this conversation, I pull out of his arms and sit up. My head needs to be clear and not under the influence of oxytocin when I hear what he has to say. "Yes, we should. I understand that my reaction to the photos was hasty."

"I don't think so," he says, "and I'm not saying that to speed to a reconciliation."

I start to respond, but he holds up a hand.

"Let me finish. With Henry in the equation, I think you did exactly the right thing. You put aside your personal desire and put him and his safety first. You had no idea how unbalanced Belinda was, so you had to assume the worst. If you hadn't, I can't be sure that she wouldn't have gone after him to scare you off."

I let that sink in for a moment. He's right. If it was just me and him, I probably wouldn't have been so quick to back away.

"You kept Henry safe. You saved my life," Kellen says.

Although I wasn't seeking absolution from him, it feels good that he can see things from my viewpoint. My first instinct will always be to protect my son. I was confident we would be able to come to terms with my reaction to the photos, but this next bit might be the end of us.

"So, that leaves the elephant in the room."

"Elephant?"

"Your secret," I say, looking down at my hands.

"Yeah, it's really not that big of a deal. I don't even know how she found out."

His words are confusing. If it's not that big of a deal, why hide it? Why not tell me?

I get the feeling that he's not going to tell me. It's a feeling I do not like, not even a little bit. When I start to get out of the bed, he pulls me into his arms.

"Relax," he says, reading my mind as he so often does. "I'm going to tell you. You know that author you like so much?"

My brow furrows, confused by the segue. "M.K. Edwards?"

"Yes." He takes a breath and says, "Masters Kellen Edward."

""What?" I say, still confused.

"I'm M.K. Edwards."

"No way."

He nods. "Yes."

Of all the things I expected him to tell me, this was not even close. It was not even in the same stratosphere.

"How?"

"I had dabbled in writing and sold a few sci-fi books to a publisher using a pen name. I wasn't happy with the experience with the publisher and had been thinking of venturing into self-publishing under a different pen name. One day I was in the company breakroom and there were a couple of our female employees talking about a trilogy of books they'd read. Out of curiosity, I bought and read them and was appalled at how horrible they were, yet they were selling like crazy and being touted as porn for housewives. I thought I could do better, so I wrote the first series and learned the ropes of indie publishing. It went well, so I kept going when I learned that readers liked them, too."

Of everything he could have said, this is so unexpected and I'm having a hard time absorbing it. He's talking about it so nonchalantly, like it's no big deal. That is completely at odds with the fact that he seemed to fight so hard to keep it a secret.

"So that's how you knew to ask all the right questions when we met with the publisher. Why did you keep it secret?"

"You know what things were like for me with my family until recently. If my brothers had found out I was writing romance books, I would have never lived it down. I was on the verge of leaving the company because I was so miserable. Writing gave me an outlet and let me know that if I ever reached the breaking point, I could walk away easily. Because I knew I could walk away, it made it easier to stay. However, I also decided that I would never let them, or anyone else, know."

Okay, I can understand why he would keep it a secret from his brothers, because he's right. The way their relationship was previously would have made it difficult to let them know. Beckett would have been merciless in his reaction.

It's also understandable how knowing he had a safety net enabled him to stick it out with his position in the family business. However, it still hurts that he would keep it a secret from me. To know that he didn't feel like he could trust me.

I want to ask him about that, but I can't seem to make the words form because the pain of it is too acute. He knows everything about me. Everything. And yet he didn't feel like he could tell me something that he's now saying is no big deal.

I wonder if there's anything else he's hiding.

Unable to be still any longer, I slide off the bed and he lets me go this time. He's too close. To buy myself some room to think, I go to the bathroom and wash my face.

The alarm sounds in the bedroom, and Kellen shuts it off. He follows me into the bathroom and puts his arms around me from behind as I slather moisturizer on my face. I step out of his arms.

"I should go get Henry. He's probably been watching every minute tick by."

"Demi," he says, but I don't stop. I grab a hoodie out of my closet and put it on, mostly because I don't want to put on a bra rather than because it's cold outside. Once I slide on a pair of sneakers, I walk purposefully out of the room.

Chapter 39

Kellen

Demi's back disappears through the bedroom door. Somehow, I've fucked up, but I'm not sure what I've done. I'm really not very good at this relationship stuff, but that's probably because I've never had one. Not a serious one, anyway.

She seems upset about me telling her everything. I can't imagine that she's upset about me being a published author or writing romance books, but maybe she is. For now, I'll let it rest, but I want to get it all out so we can move forward.

I follow her lead and clean up a little before heading downstairs. Henry comes racing into the house and makes a beeline for me. He's ready to play chess, and he wants to do it now.

"Hang on, buddy. I just woke up. Let me get my brain cells firing," I tell him. "Go ahead and get the board set up and I'll be right there.

I follow Demi into the kitchen and get a glass of water. "You okay?"

"I'm fine," she replies, taking a can of pop out of the fridge and pouring it into a glass.

She doesn't seem fine, though. She seems...brittle. I should let it go, but I can't. Part of me says I should let her chew on whatever is bothering her and come to me when she's ready, but I push on, giving voice to my thought.

"You don't seem fine."

She looks at me with hard eyes and says low enough so that Henry can't hear. "I can understand you not telling your brothers your secret. I can even understand you not telling your mom because there would have been too much of a chance of your brothers finding out. However, I don't understand why you didn't tell *me*. Why you didn't trust *me* after I told you everything about myself, even the things that no one else knows."

She crumples the can and drops it into the recycling, then pads out of the kitchen on bare feet, heading to her office.

There it is. Yep, I fucked up. I should have told her. In particular, I should have told her after Belinda sent that first text about me having a secret.

The minute I knew she enjoyed my books, I should have told her. She all but asked me outright about my writing that day she was at the house on the anniversary of Jeremiah's death.

When she decided to meet with the publishers, that was another prime opportunity to tell her, since it was obvious I knew a thing or two about the publishing industry.

There were a million opportunities and I don't know why I didn't. I thought about it, but defaulted to the safety I perceived in the secret.

Although I am not sure it will make everything okay again, I follow her to the office. Henry has the board set up and is waiting for me. "I'll be right back, buddy."

Without knocking, I walk into Demi's office. She's staring out the back window into the yard. I spin her chair around and go down on my knees in front of her. It puts us at almost eye level, so I take her hands in mine and look her in the eye.

She tenses and I can tell she's tempted to pull away. That stings, but I can't fault her.

"I'm sorry. So, so sorry. I trust you. I trust you with my life, even when I'm an idiot, which happens more than I care to admit. My entire life has been spent *not* sharing. It's not an excuse, just a reflexive habit I've worked hard to build, and it might be difficult to break. I'm probably going to screw up again, even if I don't mean to. I'm sorry I hurt you by making you believe I didn't trust you. Please forgive me and know that I always trust you."

She started out giving me the same hard look she had in the kitchen, but as I apologize, her eyes soften. She doesn't speak, though, so I let her absorb it.

She's heard me out, so I rise off my knees and kiss her forehead before I go back to the living room where Henry is waiting. Now it's up to her to decide whether she can forgive me. I hope and pray she can, but even if she does, I know that won't make everything okay.

If she can't... Well, that's not something I want to think about. I don't know what I'll do if she tells me to leave and never come back. Even worse, what if she tells me she just wants to be friends?

Could I do that? I love her and Henry with everything in me. Could I just be there in the wings, unable to touch her? Unable to make love with her ever again?

I suppose I could live with that in the hope that I could woo her back, but what if that never happened? It would be torture. It's something I might be able to stand for a short time, but how long would I really be able to stand it? A week? A month? A year?

Could I handle it if she met someone else? No. I absolutely could not do that. Whatever it takes, I need to find a way to win her forgiveness. It won't be easy, but whatever it takes is my new mantra.

I love her, and I think she might love me, too. She just needs to realize it and if she'll just crack the door open a little bit and let me in, I'll show her how good we can be together.

Henry and I are on our third game when Demi comes in and sits on the sofa with me. She's not sitting close, but she's in the same room. That's progress and I'll take it.

We're still not back to one hundred percent, but we're getting closer. Inch by inch, I'll do whatever it takes to keep moving us forward. Whatever it takes.

Henry's progressing, too. He's learning chess quickly. The first two games were mostly for teaching, and I could have won easily, but he's doing more playing than asking this time and I have to pay attention.

Chapter 40

Demeter

E ven with a few hours of sleep, my brain feels like it's only firing on half power. For now, I'm not going to make any final decisions about Kellen. He made a mistake. But is it an unforgiveable mistake?

He didn't think he could trust me. From the sound of it, he probably didn't make a conscious decision about it, just acted out of habit. It still hurts, though.

The memory of that day I spent with him on Jeremiah's anniversary sparks. I all but asked him outright if he was a writer and he deflected. That was a decision.

Is there anything else he's hiding? If I ask him, will he tell me? I need to ask him.

Rising from my chair, I join them in the living room where they're playing chess. I take a seat on the sofa with Kellen, but I don't sit close because I don't want to send signals that everything is hunky dory between us. Henry absolutely adores Kellen, and the feeling appears to be mutual. He's so good with my son.

If I can't reconcile myself to move forward because of these feelings that I can't trust him because he won't trust me, what will that mean for Henry? He would be devastated if Kellen was suddenly gone from his life. The past few weeks have provided ample evidence of that.

The only thing I'm certain of is that I can't simply jump back in like nothing has happened. What our relationship, if there is a relationship, will look like going forward remains to be seen. My feelings for him are strong, but sometimes our feelings aren't the only star we should use to guide us.

"Wow, buddy, you're really getting the hang of this," I say when their game ends.

"He's a natural," Kellen says, grinning over at me. "He has a very strategic mind."

His grin is met with a smile, but when my response doesn't match his, the smile becomes tinged with sadness. Yeah, we need to have another conversation and make some decisions. Not today, though. I want to be well rested and clear minded when that happens.

"Yeah, Mom, I'm very stra...smart."

My son draws a grin from me. "Of that, I have no doubt," I tell him.

For a moment, I think of going upstairs to get a book to read while they're playing, but the book on my nightstand is one of Kellen's. I wonder if I'll be able to read any more of the books with the same appreciation. For now, I think it's still too early to test that question.

They play through the rest of the afternoon until it's time for dinner. I send up silent praise for my mom's forethought when

I open the refrigerator to see she's prepped a meal for us and made enough for all three of us.

Henry wants to play some more after we eat, but Kellen begs off, saying his tired brain needs a rest. We watch some television with Henry firmly positioned between us. Kellen puts his arm on the back of the sofa, his hand extended toward me, but I don't react when he twirls a lock of my hair around his fingers.

It doesn't take long for my boy to start dozing. On the weekends when he spends time with his paternal grandparents, he usually goes to bed earlier because of the emotional drain. With the other disruptions to his normal routine, I thought he'd probably have an early bedtime.

Instead of reading, like he usually does, he asks Kellen to hang out with him until bedtime. The two of them talk and I leave them to it, going downstairs to put the chess set up and just generally make sure my house is in order after spending the night in the hospital.

I'm glad I don't have to go into the office tomorrow because I need a day to myself to sort out my thoughts and feelings. Kellen comes downstairs and finds me back in my office.

Rather than my bedroom, this is the place I come to when I need alone time. Henry has the freedom to come into my bedroom at any time, after he knocks, of course, but my office is more sacrosanct. Therefore, it has become the place I retreat to.

"He's out," he says, lingering in the doorway with his hands in the pockets of his sweats, looking unsure.

"I knew it wouldn't take long. He usually goes to bed earlier after being with the McLeans."

"Yeah. I can understand why."

"I know we need to talk some more, but it would probably be best if that happens once we're both better rested."

He looks down at his feet. "Yeah, I agree. I know you're exhausted and I'll go, but I want you to know that I love you and I'm willing to do whatever it takes to work through this."

Emotion clogs my throat, so I nod in response. Although I want to wait to talk in depth, the question I most want to ask needs to be said. With a deep breath, I put it out there.

"Is there anything else you haven't told me?"

I hate that my voice sounds so weak, so uncertain. So vulnerable. My entire life, I've worked hard to stand on my own feet. It was sometimes by necessity instead of choice, but I did it.

After Jeremiah died, I thought I'd never find someone who I could be vulnerable with again. I thought I had with Kellen and now that I'm on the verge of finding out if I'm still being made a fool of, I can't bring myself to look at him.

"Demi, look at me," he says.

When I lift my eyes to his, the anguish is plain on his face. "No. There is nothing else. You now know everything about me; I swear it. Like I said, I'll do whatever it takes to help you know how much I trust you so you can start to trust me again."

I nod again, so emotional and exhausted that I can't see straight.

When I start to get up, he holds up a hand. "Don't get up. When I first went upstairs with Henry, I called Beckett to come get me and he's here, so I'll see myself out. Get some rest, baby. We'll talk more later."

He turns to go and as I watch him leave, a tear escapes and rolls down my cheek before I can dash it away.

Chapter 41

Kellen

My house is a disaster area, but I can sleep in one of the guest rooms. I'd much rather stay with Demi, but I need to give her some space. She's emotional, and a lot of that is probably because of sitting up all night in the hospital with me.

"You look like shit," Beckett says when I slide into the passenger seat.

"Thanks."

"But I guess that's probably to be expected when you almost die."

"Yeah."

He doesn't push me into conversation, which is unusual for him. It's not far to my house and this late in the evening we make it there in just a few minutes. I'm surprised when he gets out of the car with me to go into the house.

"You might not want to come in," I tell him. "The police left a mess in their wake."

"If that's the case, are you sure you want to stay here? You could come stay with me."

"No, but thank you. Sleeping on an actual bed in one of my spare bedrooms is much preferable to couch surfing at your house."

"You could go to Mom and Dad's."

I just shake my head. When I unlock the door and we step inside, Beckett whistles.

"You weren't kidding about the mess, were you?"

"Nope."

He wanders around the room, looking over the mess.

"Are you sure you want to stay here?"

"Yeah. I appreciate you coming to collect me, but I need to get a good night's rest before work tomorrow."

"Work? You're going to work after you almost died? Morgan will probably...no scratch that, Mom *will* come up there and kick your ass."

I chuckle, but there's no mirth in it. Without Demi, even the tiniest spark of happiness is elusive.

"I can't sit around here stewing."

"Okay, but take it easy and be prepared to spill all the beans to me tomorrow. I'm taking it easy on you now because of the whole almost dying thing, but tomorrow, you will tell me everything. Better yet, I'll tell Mom to bring lunch so we can have a family debriefing."

"Fuck you," I say without heat.

"Love you, too. Go to bed."

With that, he leaves. I hope his threat of bringing the entire family together is only a threat, but knowing him, he'll do it.

There's no way to control Beckett's actions and my brain is too tired to do anything but go to bed, which is exactly what I do.

The next morning, I feel like hammered shit again, but I roll out of bed anyway. A little after three in the morning, I woke up in a panic, sweating. My heart was pounding so hard I thought I was going to have a heart attack.

It took me a minute to acclimate because I wasn't in my bedroom, but even once I did, it took me forever to go back to sleep. I got up and checked the doors and windows to be sure they were locked, and made a mental note to contact a locksmith to re-key everything.

I was being honest with Beckett when I said I didn't want to sit around here and stew all day. Yeah, the day could be spent cleaning, but I really don't want to be here. Even if it means facing the family for lunch, I don't want to be here.

Sure enough, Beckett thought his idea of a family lunch was a brilliant one. Mom shows up before lunch with Dad in tow and commandeers a conference room and expects all her children to gather. Although I'm dreading it, to tell everything to the entire family at once will be preferable to doing it piecemeal and having to overcome miscommunication down the road.

Before the official time to gather, Mom comes into my office and inspects me. "How are you feeling?"

"Not great, but I'll be fine."

"Of that, I have no doubt. I won't ask you to tell me everything. I'll wait to hear it with everyone else, but whatever happens, let's not do this again. My old heart can't handle this kind of scare again. Between you and Gabriella, I've had enough to last me the rest of my life."

That pulls a genuine smile from me, and I wrap her up in a hug.

"Love you, Mom."

"Love you, too, Kellen. Now, let's go have lunch."

She takes me by the hand and I let her lead me to the conference room, even though I know exactly where we're going. The family gathers and mom dishes out the food. I give them an update on what happened with Belinda and how Demi intervened.

Because of Morgan and Gabriella, they mostly knew the story, but Mom wanted me to go through it again to be sure she didn't miss anything. She makes me repeat everything the doctor said twice.

Since we're all here, I know it's time to spill everything. No more secrets. Six months ago I would never have dreamed I'd arrive at this moment, but it's here. Thanks to Gabriella, I know my family will have my back. Thanks to Demi, I'm finally ready to be completely real with everyone.

"Now that we've covered the Belinda situation, there's something else I need to tell you."

"The secret," Gabriella says.

"Yes," I answer.

"What secret?" Mom asks, the worry returning after she'd mostly let it go after hearing that the doctor had given me the all clear.

"When Belinda sent the notes to Demi, she mentioned that I have a secret."

Mom's brow furrows. "Are you gay?" she finally asks. "Because I'm fine with that, if you are, I mean, I wouldn't have thought so based on the way you look at Demi, but still, I'm fine."

I laugh, the nerves evaporating. "No Mom, I'm not gay."

Knowing how Beckett's sexual preferences are, as he says, fluid, I move us away from that topic back to the one at hand. Although it's not really a secret in the family, it's not something he dwells on. He is who he is and none of us care who he sleeps with.

"For the past several years, I have lived a little bit of a double life. Unbeknown to anyone, I've been publishing books under a pen name."

"What?" Mom asks. "Why would you need to keep that secret?"

"Because they're romance novels and the website and all the promotional materials say the author is a woman because I thought that would help them sell better."

The room goes silent and the pressure of all their eyes on me makes me want to squirm, but I give them the time they need to absorb it.

"What's your pen name?" Gabriella asks.

When I tell her, she gasps. "I love those books. Oh my God, Demi loves those books, too. She's the one who got me hooked and is one of your biggest fans."

"Yeah. I know. That leads to the next issue. When she found out I'd been keeping it from her, Demi was hurt because she felt like I didn't trust her."

With the reminder of my transgressions, I can't sit still any longer, so I get up and start gathering up the dishes to take them to the breakroom.

"Well, you'll just have to show her she can," Gabriella says. "Demi cares a lot about you, Kellen, so don't give up on her yet."

"I don't intend to. I love her and there's no way I'm going to just walk away. We were both exhausted when we talked yesterday, so we'll get together to talk again. From there, if she doesn't kick me out the door, it's just a matter of proving myself to her and winning her trust back."

Mom pats my hand, but doesn't say anything.

Suddenly Morgan sits up in his chair. "Wait. Those aren't the books that..."

Gabriella grins at him. "Yes, baby, they are."

He slumps back in his seat and rubs a hand over his face. "Well, that's disturbing."

Gabriella just laughs in response.

"Disturbing?" Beckett asks. "Why disturbing?"

Still chuckling, Gabriella says, "The books are what is known as steamy and sometimes we have story time when I'll read him parts, and one thing leads to another..."

Beckett is the one laughing now. "So you got all hot and bothered by sex scenes written by your little brother, then jumped your girlfriend's bones? Oh my God, that's awesome!"

"Darling," Mom says, "having good sex with your significant other is nothing to be upset about."

"That's for damn sure," Beckett says, earning him a swat on the arm from Mom.

Now that it's done, I'm glad Beckett made this happen. Everyone who matters to me now knows my secret, and it wasn't as shocking as I'd feared it would be. With that out of the way, it's time to focus on wooing Demi back into my life.

Chapter 42

Demeter

Kellen and I still haven't gotten together. He's given me space and I think I'm ready to have a conversation with him, but I need tonight more than I've needed it in a long time. When I arrive, Victor is warmed up and waiting.

He gives me time to warm my muscles, then we meet each other on the mats, ready to do battle. Something shifts inside me, like the flipping of a switch and all the fear, hurt, and anger starts a fire in my belly. I want to hit something and Victor can take it.

Rather than letting my emotions control me, I allow them to take me to the edge, letting them sharpen my awareness, add speed and strength to my blows. As usual, he lets me take the offensive, but when I connect for the third time, he raises an eyebrow and starts taking me seriously.

"Somebody came to spar. Whatcha got, Hobbit?"

"A whole lot of emotional upheaval and I'm sick and tired of it," I grit out before I try to sweep his feet. He's ready for it though and gets his hands on me. I roll forward instead of trying to pull away and it throws him off balance.

We go down in a tangle of limbs, but I was counting on this. I shift to pull his arm into an arm bar. Inches. That's how close I get to locking it in before he overcomes his surprise and counters me and gets out of the hold, simply because he's stronger and more practiced than I am.

"Dang it!" I say when I have to tap out.

"What are you upset about? You almost had me. That's progress, Hobbit."

I grumble, and he laughs at me. When the students start coming in, I don't see Billie and it worries me. She hasn't been back since the incident with Ricky.

Maybe he hurt her worse than was clear that night. Or maybe she's just sick of the Rickys that show up from time to time who get a kick out of hurting a woman. When I ask Victor and Gunnar about her, they tell me that Ricky cracked a rib, so she's having to sit out, but they didn't want to broadcast it to the class.

After class, I feel better, more energized. For a moment, I think about calling Kellen, but I don't. Yeah, just call me Queen Chickenheart.

It's been so long since I let someone in enough for them to hurt me. When I began to lean on him instead of relying only on myself, it felt good, but then I was reminded why I hadn't. Trust is great when everyone does exactly what you want them to, but trusting means you're opening yourself up to have your trust betrayed, and that shit hurts when it happens.

The next night, I go to dinner at the Society. Yeah, still being chickenhearted. This time it's just Cait, Gabriella and me. I was hoping Alicia or Serena would show up as a buffer, but with these two, Kellen is likely to be a primary topic of conversation.

No chickenhearts allowed.

Great.

"Hi!" I say, taking my seat.

"Good evening, Demi," Cait says as she rises to give me a hug.

"Hey stranger," Gabriella says with a grin.

"Hey preggo," I say, grinning back. "How are you feeling?"

"Good mostly. Some mornings are miserable, but most are mild. So, when are you going to talk with Kellen?"

I groan. I knew this was going to happen, but I didn't expect it to happen in such a blunt and unavoidable way.

"What happened with Kellen?" Cait asks.

When Gabriella looks at me, I wave a hand, giving her the green light to spill the whole sordid tale. She does, but also surprises me when she tells me about the meeting with the family on Monday where he informed them of everything, including how he hurt me by not trusting me.

Cait reaches over and pats my hand, but doesn't offer any sage advice. Instead, she asks a question. "Do you love him?"

When he'd said he loved me in my office the day I gave him the photographs, I was too hurt for them to be anything but words. Then he said it again before he left my house last weekend. I heard them that time.

My brain says I'm conflicted, wanting to hold on to the broken trust thing. However, as someone who has been trained to understand how people work, I can see how Kellen was hesitant to set aside the feeling of safety keeping secrets had given him.

Am I going to let that seed of fear dressed in the guise of him not trusting me keep me from loving him? Can I let myself love him even though everything inside of me is afraid that he'll be taken away from me like Jeremiah was? After all, didn't Belinda almost make that happen?

For a moment, I set the fear aside and look inside my heart. Do I love him? The answer to that is a resounding yes. Do I love him enough to face my fear? That, I'm not so sure of.

Looking down at my hands, I answer Cait. "Yes, but it's not that easy. What happened with Belinda made me see how easily he could have been taken away from me, and I don't think I can go through that again."

My eyes are hot and gritty as I admit my own dark secret.

Cait takes my hand while Gabriella comes around the table to sit on the other side of me, taking my free hand. "Everything in life is a risk," Cait says. "Your time with Jeremiah was short, but he gave you Henry. Perhaps that was his purpose all along."

I wouldn't trade Henry for the world and I know Jeremiah would never allow me to trade Henry's life to have him back, even if I could. Jeremiah would have loved our son so much.

Finding Jeremiah had been a miracle and although we separated for a couple of years as he gave into his family's demands, we came back together. I thought he'd been the love of my life. Does someone get two great loves?

Could Cait be right? What if Jeremiah's sole purpose in coming back to me was to give me Henry? And how amazing is it that Kellen found us when I had been thinking that Henry needed a man in his life that could understand him? The fortune teller's card...

Is Kellen Jeremiah's replacement? He certainly relates to Henry like no one else has been able to. In some ways, he's better than me because he's a man and has a lot of Henry's same characteristics. If I can't get over my fear, what would I be stealing from Henry?

"I'm sorry, but can we change the subject?" I ask.

"Yes, of course," Cait answers with a squeeze of my hand.

"I'm sorry," Gabriella says, her voice somber. "I didn't mean to upset you."

Shaking my head, I say, "It's okay. It helped."

Cait waves a server over and we turn to other topics. My mind is distracted, only half heartedly taking part in the conversation. By the time I leave, I know it's time for me to have that talk with Kellen.

He's been patient enough.

Chapter 43

Kellen

When Demi's face flashes on my screen, my heart leaps in my chest. Finally!

"Hi," I answer, trying not to sound too eager.

"Hi. I think I finally have my head on straight and I'm ready to talk."

"Okay. Where are you now? I can come to you."

She chuckles. "I'm on my way home from the City."

"Do you want to come here, or I can meet you somewhere..."

"I'll come to you if you're not busy. I should be there in about ten minutes."

"No, I'm not busy."

The call disconnects, and excitement surges through me. Yeah, I know she could be coming to end things with me forever, but until she speaks those words, I'm going to hope for the best. Hope is all I have at this point.

I'm prowling around the house when she arrives. From the moment she called, I could not sit still. When the doorbell rings, I race to the front door, then stop. "Get a grip, man."

After a few deep breaths to settle myself and put on an air of nonchalance, I open the door.

"Hi," I say. "Come in."

"Hi. Thanks."

She seems shy and tentative, her eyes look tired and sad. Has she been crying? I can't really tell because she doesn't seem to want to look me in the eye.

My heart lurches. Is that a sign? Is she here to tell me we're done so she can walk away? I don't know what I'll do if she does that. The hope I felt a few moments ago has turned to water in my belly and my nerves take over.

"Can I get you something to drink?" I ask to change the direction of my thoughts.

"No, thank you. I'm good."

She moves into the living room and sits on the sofa. It seems I'm not the only one feeling nervous. Instead of sitting next to her, I take a chair beside the couch.

"So, I've come to a realization this evening," she says.

"What's that?"

Her eyes are on her hands in her lap. "I was all set to tell you I didn't think we'd be able to be together."

I lean forward, but she holds up a hand. "Please, let me get it all out."

With a nod, I sit back in my seat.

"I met Jeremiah when I was seventeen. We talked and got to know each other and when I turned eighteen, he asked me out. Soon after that first date was when I was...when the...the attack happened. I wasn't able to get around on my own steam, so

Jeremiah took me to his house to take care of me while I healed. We became very close."

She stops talking, seemingly lost in the memory. With a small shake, she starts talking again.

"Something happened, and we broke up. Two years later, we saw each other again for the first time. We got back together, and I became pregnant soon after. Then, in an instant, he was taken away from me. From us, Henry and me."

I'm not sure why she's telling me all this, but I let her talk. She's not one to just meander aimlessly. There's a point to be made, so I need to let her make it in her own time, no matter how much I want to reach over and shake her to get her to cut to the bottom line.

"When I found out you hadn't trusted me enough to tell me your secret, I was hurt, but once I stepped back and looked at it with a clinical view, it was understandable. However, I let fear latch onto that initial hurt, take it in, tuck it down deep, and twist it. Tonight, I realized that what happened with Belinda reminded me that someone I love can be snatched away in a heartbeat and that's the fear that had melded itself with the hurt and blown it out of proportion."

Oh my God, no wonder she was so upset. It hasn't been that long since the anniversary of Jeremiah's death. It's completely understandable that this whole thing hit her so hard.

"I was afraid," she breathes. "Am afraid."

I'm out of my seat and kneeling before her, taking her hands in mine. They're ice cold, so I wrap them in my fingers to warm them.

"Oh honey. I understand. And I'm kind of new to this, but it seems that everything is a risk. We could lock ourselves up in the house and take a tumble down the stairs. Or we could go out and live our lives to the fullest and grow old together. We can't let fear hold us back because the risk is worth the reward."

"I know. That's what I realized tonight, but I'm still afraid."

"If it hadn't been for you and Jeremiah, there would be no Henry, and that would be a travesty. Who knows what wonderful things we can create together? Sometimes we have to feel the fear and do it anyway."

"I know and I want to, but I wanted you to know."

What she said sinks in.

"You want to?"

She nods.

"And did I hear you right? Did you say you loved me?" I ask with a grin.

Finally, she smiles. It's tentative, but it's there and her cheeks turn pink as she nods. I brush my thumb over the color.

"That's all we need, baby."

I pull her into my arms, thankful when she lets me. Her arms go around me, squeezing tight and nuzzling against my neck as she lets out a ragged breath. She's shaking and for a moment, I think she must be crying, but her voice is steady, albeit quiet, when she says, "I've missed you."

"I've missed you, too. It's been hell without you."

"So where do we go from here?" she asks.

"Forward," I reply. "We can take it slow, if that's what you want. As long as we're moving forward together, that's all that matters to me."

Chapter 44

Demeter

It's the weekend before my birthday and somehow my son and my boyfriend tag teamed and hornswoggled me into going camping. However, I refused to sleep on the ground in a tent, so when Kellen showed me the travel trailer he rented to appease...or really, bribe, me, how could I say no?

We're on our way to God knows where to spend the weekend in the woods. He's told me where we're going, but for some reason, it doesn't seem to stick in my mind. Selective memory, I guess. Henry, on the other hand, knows exactly where we're going and he is beyond excited.

As soon as Kellen proposed the adventure, Henry was all in. He looked the location up on his tablet and could probably tell me the exact GPS coordinates, as well as the entire history of the area.

It's going to be fun, and that's all I care about. They'll do all the camping stuff while I'll have a weekend of lazing around doing a whole lot of nothing.

Henry bends Kellen's ear the entire way and I'm once again struck by the way Kellen interacts with Henry. He never gets tired or frustrated with him. Never tells him to be quiet or to stop asking so many questions.

We left Norman right after I was finished with work and we arrive at the campsite about three hours later, just as the setting sun is casting colors across the sky. Kellen gets the trailer in place and set up like he's an old pro, Henry a shadow following him everywhere and asking questions about everything.

Once that's finished, there's not time for anything else, so we go inside and get ready for bed. The buzz of Henry's excitement has used up all his energy, so once he gets his sleeping bunk set up the way he wants it, he settles on the couch slash bench for the dining table next to Kellen to read.

With a smile on my face, I go to the tiny bathroom to wash my face and change clothes. Once I put my things away, I go join my guys on the sofa and snuggle next to Henry. He moans and complains with a few "Aww, Mom's," but doesn't resist me when I put my arms around him and pull him close.

As is our usual nightly ritual, he starts telling me about what he's read. When he yawns for the third time, I say, "All right, buddy, it's time for bed."

He starts to give me another protest, but it's cut off by another yawn. I kiss him on the forehead and let him go, watching as he scrambles up into the bunk. Kellen changes in the bathroom, then pulls down the Murphy bed where we'll be sleeping.

I'm not really tired, but if we stay up, Henry will fight going to sleep and they're supposed to get up early to go fishing. We snuggle up in bed and talk in low voices and I guess I'm more tired than I realized, because the cool breeze and quiet noises of nature floating through the open windows have me drifting off to sleep wrapped up in Kellen's arms.

"Shh, buddy, we don't want to wake up your mom," Kellen tells Henry for the umpteenth time. He's so excited about going fishing for the first time. Once Kellen reminds him to be quiet, he goes back to whispering, but after a few seconds he forgets and starts talking normally again.

Finally, they're dressed and ready to go into the still-dark morning in search of a bounty of fish for their lures. As Henry tromps out the door, Kellen leans over and kisses my smiling lips. "Faker," he says against my mouth, his own curved in a smile, too.

"Have fun," I say.

Henry's chattering carries back to me for quite a while. I hope he's not disrupting the other campers too much. However, based on the smell of campfires and cooking food, I have a feeling I may be the only one still nestled in their covers.

I don't care, though, I'm going to enjoy it. Although I didn't intend to go back to sleep, I must have because when I look up again, sunshine is filtering through the windows. Sitting up, I stretch and yawn and look around at our little camper.

It's tiny, but perfect for the three of us. If we have any more children, we'll need something larger.

What the crap? Where did that come from?

It only took us a few days to fall back into step with each other after the big talk. In a lot of ways, anyway. We still haven't had sex again, but I'm getting closer to being willing to move into that level of intimacy again.

The fear still lingers in the darkest recesses of my mind, but it's gone from a blazing bonfire to an occasional flicker. If I pay too much attention, it grows, so I try not to turn my gaze that way too often.

I roll out of bed and, on my way to the bathroom, start the battery operated coffee pot Kellen prepped last night before we went to bed. When I come out dressed and ready for the day, the sweet bean nectar is ready for me. Between drinks, I make our bed and put it back into its cabinet so it's not taking up the entire room.

With that, I find my current read, and head outside to sit in a comfy chair and enjoy the morning. I'm not sure how long they'll be gone, but if they don't come back soon, I might be tempted to cook and that could be dangerous for everyone.

There's a lot of activity around the campground. People are cooking around campfires, taking it easy and talking in low voices. Some are headed off with packs on their back like they're going hiking or something. Oh God, is Kellen going to want to go hiking?

I'm so not an outdoorsy kind of woman. Maybe it should just be the boys that go camping from now on. They're probably going to hate me being a drag the entire time.

After a few chapters, my stomach starts growling and I'm just about to go back into the camper to find something to eat when familiar voices reach me. When he sees me, Henry comes racing to me, his fishing pole swinging wildly in his grip.

"Mom! We had so much fun and I caught a fish but Kellen says it wasn't big enough to eat and not the right kind anyway so he threw it back but it was really gross when he was trying to get the hook out for a minute I thought he was going to pull the eyeball out and that about made me barf..."

"Whoa, buddy, take a breath," I say, laughing.

He stops and dramatically sucks in a breath, expanding his little chest as far as it will go and raising his shoulders, then lets it out in a whoosh. This makes me laugh more.

"So you had fun?"

He nods and bends down to scratch his shin. "What's for breakfast? I'm hungry."

"Well, Kellen took my pop-tarts off the shopping list so you'll have to ask him."

Kellen, who has been standing by watching the interplay with an amused smile, finally speaks up. "How about some eggs and sausage?"

"Good," Henry replies.

The rest of our first day of camping is relaxed and after a very messy foray into the world of s'mores making, we get cleaned up and crawl into bed. Kellen pulls me close and starts nibbling at my neck. "Stop that," I whisper.

He chuckles. "Unh uh."

I turn in his arms and we end up making out until Henry's voice carries down to us, "Stop kissing, I'm trying to sleep."

It's all I can do to keep from laughing out loud.

"Sorry, buddy," Kellen says, in a choked voice, trying to hold back his own laughter.

Fishing is on the agenda again for the next morning and this time, they come back with something to show for their efforts. Kellen said it was because they finally got the right bait, but when Henry's attention was elsewhere, he told me Henry finally settled down enough to stop talking and scaring the fish away.

After lunch, my fears come to life as Henry announces we're going to go on a hike. When I tell them it should be a guy's hike, Henry insists I have to go with them. So, I slide out of my flip-flops to put on some real shoes and ready myself to face the wilderness.

We meander down a trail with Kellen in the lead, Henry between us, and me lagging at the rear. It really is pretty terrain, but I'd be fine seeing it in photograph form. Kellen keeps looking back to check on me and I keep smiling and waving. They're loving it and I don't want to be the party pooper. It's not horrible; it's just not my thing.

We finally reach the destination Kellen wanted to show us. Of course, the boys are fascinated.

"Mom, look! This cave is what the whole place is named after."

"Is that so?"

Henry launches into the story of how wild west outlaws would hide out here to keep from getting caught by the authorities. He mentions names like Jesse James, Belle Starr, and the

Dalton brothers. I wonder if he researched who those people are or just learned their names in association with the park.

Once we've crawled all over the inside and outside, we start to head back. Kellen hangs back with me while Henry races ahead while staying in sight of us.

"You okay?"

"I am," I reply.

"You're not really digging this, are you?"

I shrug. "I enjoy you and Henry enjoying it."

"But you still rather be back at the camper reading a book."

It's not a question, but I reply anyway. "I didn't have a lot of opportunity to be athletic or engage in a lot of activities when I was a kid, so I never experienced camping or anything like that. Maybe if I had, I'd enjoy it more now. However, I also know that unless we're willing to venture out and try new things, we might miss out on something we'll like."

"Does that mean you'll go fishing in the morning?"

He's teasing me, but I don't mind. I take his hand in mine, then bump into him and say, "Nope."

He laughs.

The rest of our time is spent in much the same way with good food, messy desserts, and just hanging out being together. When we're putting everything away after breakfast the next morning in preparation for going back home, I have to admit I'll miss being in our little outdoorsy cocoon of peace.

Chapter 45

Demeter

"Are you ready?" Kellen asks me as he opens my car door.

Last weekend was all about doing something special with Henry. Kellen made it seem like it was for my birthday, but I think he really just wanted to spend some time with us after being separated during the whole Belinda thing.

The night of my actual birthday, he came over for dinner and cake. Tonight it's just the two of us since Henry is at the McLean's. He asked me what I wanted for my birthday and I said I wanted to go dancing so he's taking me to the salsa club he told me about months ago.

"I am," I reply as I put my hand in his.

As soon as the music reaches me, I want to move. And move, I do, for the next hour or so. Kellen finds us a table so we can take a break when I tell him I'm thirsty.

"I thought that was you!" someone says.

I turn to see Lynzee dragging her husband Preston along behind her.

"Hi there!" I say and give her a quick hug. "What are you guys doing here?"

"Same as you, I reckon. Date night."

Kellen and Preston shake hands and murmur greetings. Apparently. they know each other. I never knew my world was so small.

The men leave Lynzee and me at the table while they go after drinks for us. "Do you come here often?" Lynzee asks.

"First time. Kellen used to come here sometimes, but it's the first time we've come together."

"Same. Preston had been here before, but this was our first time coming together. I've been telling him I wanted to go dancing so finally, we left all the kids at his parent's house for the night and here we are!"

"Gotta love grandparents," I say with a grin. "That's where Henry is, too."

"So it looks like things are going well with you two," she observes.

Looking over toward the bar where Kellen stands talking to Preston while they wait for our drinks, a warm feeling rolls through me. "It is," I answer. "It's going very well."

She puts a hand over mine. "I'm overjoyed to hear that."

When the guys return, we sit and talk for a while about business and art and children before going back out on the floor. Throughout the night, we dance and visit with our friends, then it seems we all run out of steam about the same time and make our way outside.

The temperatures have dropped, and the air is chilly. I rub my upper arms against the cold. "It feels like a cold front is coming through."

"Yeah," Lynzee says and pulls me in for a quick hug. "We should do this again. Have a double dance date."

"That's a great idea," I agree.

"Enough chitchat, woman," Preston teases. "I'm freezing."

"Yeah, yeah," Lynzee says with a grin as he pulls her away. "Bye, y'all." She waves over her shoulder. I grin back and wave.

"Let's get you to the car," Kellen says. "It's downright cold."

We hurry across the lot. Well, as much as I can hurry in heels and a dress that is cute but tight and not very warm. In the car, he turns up the heat and I'm clicking on my seat warmer.

"Thank you for tonight," I say. "That was really fun."

"You're welcome, baby. It was fun."

He asks me how I know Lynzee, and I tell him about knowing Preston because of his friendship with Jeremiah and that I met Lynzee through him. I ran into them at a charity event when they were first dating.

It's the same event Jeremiah took me to on our very first date many years before. That was my first time rubbing elbows with some of the most wealthy members of Oklahoma society. Jeremiah had dressed me up, and I truly felt like a fairytale princess.

I was so happy that night. Now, I hate going to that event because of all the memories it stirs up. Foolishly, I allowed the

McLeans to pressure me into going a few years ago to 'represent the family' and that's when I ran into Preston and Lynzee.

It was so hard being there. I didn't take a date, so it was just me and the McLeans and considering I'm not their favorite person, really, I'm one of their least favorite people, it was just a horrible evening all the way around except for meeting Lynzee. The next year, I went over to their house for dinner instead and that helped me say no to ever going again.

I reach over and put my hand on Kellen's leg and he covers it with his. We've made so much progress over the past few weeks, and I can't believe I was ready to walk away from him. He's become a constant in our lives.

"I love you," I say into the dark.

He pulls my hand to his lips and kisses it. "I love you, too, baby."

When we get to my house, he parks in the garage, then we make our way through the dark house. There is enough ambient light coming from the dim spotlights Dad has set up in the backyard that we don't need to turn any lights on inside.

Since getting back together, we haven't been intimate. Usually, he walks me into the house, then leaves to go home. This time, I hold his hand and lead him upstairs with me.

In my bedroom, he comes behind me and unzips my dress, smoothing it off my shoulders as his fingers trace along the top of my shoulder, followed by light kisses. Tiny spiders of anticipation tickle down my spine, causing me to shiver. The dress falls to the floor and kisses are trailed up my neck to a particularly sensitive spot under my ear.

"You are so beautiful," he says.

I lean back against him, eager to return to our former intimacy. Kellen has been infinitely patient with me and we've waited long enough. My hands go to his face when I turn in his arms, tracing the lines that weren't there when we met.

The weeks of fear and worry have left their marks. "So are you," I say, and I mean it. He is more beautiful to me than I could ever tell him with words.

He's quick to discount his looks, always comparing himself to his brothers. Morgan is larger, broader, and more masculine, but his brutal attractiveness doesn't appeal to me. Beckett is certainly pretty in a Zac Efron kind of way, but he knows it and uses his beauty as a weapon to get what he wants.

Kellen has their same coloring with dark hair and vivid blue eyes, but his handsomeness is unassuming, if that's possible. It's easy to overlook which is what I did when we first met.

His build is slighter than Morgan's, more delicate, but not without strength. He's not as perfectly put together and in your face as Beckett, but his attractiveness is there in spades. When you take the time to look, it's breathtaking. Kellen is who he is and who he is, is mine.

Leaning up on tiptoe, I pull his head down, our lips meeting in the middle. Strong arms go around my waist as my hands cradle his head for a moment before my fingers fork through his hair. I press my body against his, loving the way he feels, especially the erection I can feel straining against his trousers and pressing into my stomach.

My hands move to enable nimble fingers to undo the buttons of his shirt. When I reach the bottom, I press my palms against his firm abs and smooth them up his torso, pushing his shirt off over his shoulders before moving my hands back down. My fingers unfasten his pants as our mouths continue to kiss and explore each other.

Once he's worked his way out of his shirt and his pants have hit the floor, he hooks his hands under my thighs and picks me up. My legs going around his waist as he carries me to bed.

He lays me down, moving his mouth from mine and kissing down my neck. I take his face in my hands again and turn his face to mine.

"I need you."

He starts to say something, but I put my fingers over his lips to silence him.

"I know you probably want to take your time, but right now, I'm telling you, I need you."

His lips quirk, and he hooks his fingers in my panties while I pull off my bra. In a matter of seconds, I'm naked. He pushes off his boxer briefs and settles his hips between my thighs.

One powerful thrust and he's buried deep inside me. This is exactly what I wanted. He can take his time next time, but right now, I want him to fuck me.

Take me.

Make me completely his.

Again.

When I put my hands over my head and grab hold of the headboard, he understands and begins to move. His pace is punishing, just as I want it to be. Hips pistoning against me, his hands reach up to fondle my breasts. When he tweaks a nipple, I rasp, "Harder."

He obliges and pinches hard, drawing a cry of pleasure from me as I throw my head back into the pillow. My hips undulate in time with his thrusts, and a powerful explosion begins to boil in my blood. Kellen puts his hands under my hips and grips me tight, holding me still as his cock continues to punish my sopping cunt.

The orgasm begins to rise, and I look up to see Kellen watching me. Our eyes lock and my lips part, panting. I hold his gaze, letting him see what he's doing to me.

His eyes are dark and hot, but when the orgasm slams into me, I can't stop my eyes from closing and losing his gaze. Kellen follows me over the edge as my pussy grips his cock like a vise. He holds me there, his cock pulsing deep inside me as his body finds release.

After long moments, he pulls out and moves to my side, pulling me close. With a kiss to the side of my head, he utters a sigh. I snuggle close, luxuriating in the last vestiges of post-orgasmic bliss.

My fingers trace paths through his chest hair as we both lie there quietly. It is difficult to believe that four months ago we didn't know each other, and when I met him that first time, I called him an asshole. A giggle burbles in my throat.

"What's funny?" Kellen asks.

"I was just thinking of the day we met and how I called you an asshole."

"Did you?"

I kiss him on his sternum and he rolls to pull me on top of him, then his fingers begin working through my curls. "Yeah. It was under my breath as I was walking away, but I did."

"Well, I didn't make a very good first impression," he says, a chuckle making me bounce on his stomach.

I turn my head and rest my cheek on his chest. "I'm glad I gave you the chance to make a second impression."

"Me, too."

I must doze off because when I look up, it's dark in the room and Kellen is snoring softly. Trying not to wake him, I shift to move to his side but his arms tighten around me and he stirs. We make love again and this time, I don't intervene when it seems as if he wants to touch and taste me everywhere.

Kellen was right when he said the risk is worth the reward, and I intend to make the most of this second chance of ours. Whatever comes, we'll face it together and do our best to make a life and a home for us and for Henry.

I couldn't have asked for a better man to step into the role of Henry's mentor and father figure. They're so much alike that it's almost as if he's Henry's biological father. He's not, but in some ways, I think he'll be a better role model for my son than Jeremiah would have been.

Everything came easily to Jeremiah. He was outgoing and gregarious, and people just naturally gravitated to him. I know I did. But that's not Henry. Henry can be reserved and introverted and a bit awkward when interacting with others, much like Kellen was when I first met him.

A part of me will always love Jeremiah. He was my first love, and he gave me our beautiful boy, but he is in the past and I don't want to live there anymore. The future is ahead.

A future with Kellen.

That day at the Society comes to mind when I received the fortune. Without realizing it, I made a wish that day for me and for my son that has come true, just like the card said it would. As sleep pulls me under, that last thought echoes in my mind.

Maybe there's something to that machine after all...

The End

Get a **FREE** copy of a bonus scene that gives a peek into the lives of Demi and Kellen a few months later.
https://dl.bookfunnel.com/2oi1515be9

If you enjoyed A Secret Revealed, do me a solid and leave a review! It's not a book report; it's okay to keep it short. Have fun! Be honest!
https://mybook.to/RevealedKitMcKenna
Thank you loves!

XOXO

Kit

About the Author

Kit McKenna writes romance books that are dreamy, dirty, and sometimes have a splash of darkness and danger set against the backdrop of Oklahoma.

Kit is a born and raised Oklahoma gal who has lived here her whole life except for a brief detour to hang out in the mountains for four years. She is an artist and free spirit who loves roaming around in the woods and finds great joy in the unusually and sometimes darkly beautiful. Kit has worn a lot of hats in her life, a server, a factory worker, nightclub manager, office administrator, state drone, and business owner.

A bit of a dichotomy, she loves all things positivity and light, but still loves to play in the dark. Her favorite book offerings range from authors like Eckhart Tolle to Stephen King. Her favorite movies are horror and holiday is Samhain (Halloween) but she still loves a good romance. She's a huge sucker for a story where the underdog comes out on top.

If the bar doesn't have a good cider, she'll opt for a fine whisky.

She comes to writing later in life after tiring of reading books that seem to only focus on perfect, perky, barely legal heroines.

Her stories are about real people who have their own demons, drama, and challenges to overcome.

You can find her on online at:

Website – www.kitmckenna.com

Facebook – @authorkitmckenna

Instagram - @kitmckennaauthor

TikTok – @kitmckennaauthor

www.ingramcontent.com/pod-product-compliance
Lightning Source LLC
Chambersburg PA
CBHW050920030726
47503CB00007BB/2387

"So do I," I reply before I turn to go back to my office.